THE BOOKSELLER OF MOGGA

ANAND SUSPI
Author of `Half Pants Full Pants'

Chennai • Bangalore

CLEVER FOX PUBLISHING
Chennai, India

Published by CLEVER FOX PUBLISHING 2024
Copyright © Anand Suspi 2024

All Rights Reserved.
ISBN: 978-93-56487-75-8

This book has been published with all reasonable efforts taken to make the material error-free after the consent of the author. No part of this book shall be used, reproduced in any manner whatsoever without written permission from the author, except in the case of brief quotations embodied in critical articles and reviews.

The Author of this book is solely responsible and liable for its content including but not limited to the views, representations, descriptions, statements, information, opinions and references ["Content"]. The Content of this book shall not constitute or be construed or deemed to reflect the opinion or expression of the Publisher or Editor. Neither the Publisher nor Editor endorse or approve the Content of this book or guarantee the reliability, accuracy or completeness of the Content published herein and do not make any representations or warranties of any kind, express or implied, including but not limited to the implied warranties of merchantability, fitness for a particular purpose. The Publisher and Editor shall not be liable whatsoever for any errors, omissions, whether such errors or omissions result from negligence, accident, or any other cause or claims for loss or damages of any kind, including without limitation, indirect or consequential loss or damage arising out of use, inability to use, or about the reliability, accuracy or sufficiency of the information contained in this book.

There is nothing to writing.
All you do is sit at a typewriter and bleed.

- Ernest Hemingway

There is nothing to reading.
All you do is sit with a book and blossom.

- Anand Suspi

CONTENTS

Mogga, Circa 1970   1

(I) THE FARM

1.	Original, Big, And Begur	5
2.	The Lord Of The Rings: Part 1	10
3.	The Lord Of The Rings: Part 2	15
4.	13 New Days	21
5.	A For Athatha	25
6.	A Ray Of Hope	30

(II) THE SCHOOL

7.	Chennamma Begur Primary School	37
8.	Cylinder	42
9.	Books Vs. Books	46
10.	Fat Books	50
11.	The Sweeper	55
12.	Old Jungle Saying	60
13.	Original Writing	64
14.	Tick. Tick. Tick.	69
15.	School To Signal	72
16.	The Three-Parts Case: Part 1	78
17.	The Three-Parts Case: Part 2	82

(III) THE SIGNAL

18.	Twenty Rupees	89
19.	A Waste Of Time	94
20.	Higginbothams	99
21.	The Legend Of Tempo Tony	103

22.	The First Sale	109
23.	Percentage Ravi	115
24.	Woe Is Me!	121
25.	Science Of The Signs	129
26.	Robot	134
27.	Jackie	138
28.	The Big Monsoon Sale	142
29.	The Writer Who Wasn't	148
30.	Artificial Intelligence	152
31.	Cosmos	157
32.	Writer's Block	161
33.	New News Nagaraj	169
34.	Herculees Pirate	175
35.	A.K.A.	179

(IV) THE NEW BEGUR

36.	The Man With No Name	189
37.	Only Chips, No Trips	193
38.	The Man Who Saw Tomorrow	198
39.	Y.B. Vs. Parents	203
40.	Y.B. Vs. Cylinder	208
41.	Y.B. Vs. Begur	215
42.	Farewell To The Master	222

(VI) THE STATUE

43.	The Last Walk	231
44.	Statue of Cylinder	234
45.	Cylinder Circle	239

(VII) THE BEGINNING

46.	Mobile Circle	245

MOGGA, CIRCA 1970

It held no significance for anybody in the larger world, yet it carried weight for most people within a 20-kilometre radius. To the innumerable villages around it, in a small part of southern India, Mogga was the big brother.

Life in the town of Mogga was idyllic. The earth was extra fertile, and the seasons never missed their beats. It was neither prone to floods nor famine. Summers were steady, monsoons were generous, and winters so pleasant that during those months, it actually took effort to think negative. As a matter of fact, as per the records maintained at the Mogga Police Station, during winter every year, cases of burglaries, pickpocketing and moped thefts actually came down. For as long as one could recollect, none of the seasons had misbehaved. Unerringly, they stuck to their schedules and let the residents stick to their syllabus of life. With the top and the bottom taken care of, the people of Mogga had lived their middle-class existence for years. It was a peaceful living devoid of groans. Of course, people from the wealthy to the beggary and everyone in between had their own issues and everyday concerns but none so troublesome to make anyone hate one's life or that of others. Sufficient and self-contained, it threw up few distortions and fewer ambitions.

The people of the town often remarked to outsiders, "And we also have the Tunga river."

The `and' and `also' added emphasis to the natural treasures of this little town just in case someone thought that it wasn't blessed enough.

Only one man, Begur, had often thought, upon hearing this statement, `Does Mogga have Tunga or does Tunga have Mogga?'

To him, the river owned the town, not vice versa. He always imagined the Tunga river in conversation with another, remarking with a certain pride, "And I also have the Mogga town."

Begur was a highly unusual mind, a mind fed on books all its life. An extreme oddball, he read voraciously, thought deeply and spoke sparingly. If not for him, the town of Mogga would not have had its bookseller, Cylinder.

(I)
THE FARM

(1)

ORIGINAL, BIG, AND BEGUR

At forty-six years, why was he unmarried? Why would someone who owned acres of farmland teach in a primary school? Why did he have a collection of over thirty thousand books but only four shirts?

These, along with subsidiary questions had been pondered over and posed in conversations by the people of Mogga for years. Over a period, the town had moved beyond. Now, if someone happened to pose a `Why?' or a `How come?' regarding him, they replied with nonchalance, "Begur Sir is like that only."

He left most people speechless and clueless including his own parents. He was sparse with conversation and spent all his time reading. Once, years earlier, when his mother had questioned him over his collection of books Vs. clothes, he had responded without a moment's hesitation.

"Mom, it doesn't take much to cover one's body but a lot to uncover one's mind."

Shaking her head, she had muttered, "Now, you are talking like Ramana Maharshi."

He was the only child of rooted, hardworking and liberal-minded parents. One could say that the Begur family was an aberration. Usually, the rich had oddities straying towards the negatives of life but not so in their case.

His grandfather, who was commonly referred to as Original Sir by the people of the town, had been a wealthy, well-read and well-travelled man. He belonged to an ancestry of landed gentry which had over generations assiduously worked and increased their wealth and land holdings. While agriculture was his profession, literature was his passion. Along with his wife Chennamma, he lived a happy and prosperous life. Prosperity was a given, and happiness is what he created in things, small and big.

She wasn't as educated or well-read as him. But as time went by, she got into the habit and particularly loved reading Enid Blyton, one of the recent and popular authors. These books took her back to her own childhood, one that was good and balanced but surely not adventurous. They made her re-live her growing-up years vicariously. Needless to add, he had been a big influence and inspiration. He made her laugh with observations, comments and acts, both silly and sublime.

Every day, at breakfast, lunch and dinner, she had the habit of asking him if the chutney or the curry or the sabzi carried `balance' — the right mix of salt, spice, tang and a hint of sweetness wherever required. `Balance' was one of her go-to words. After the first few months of marriage, when he had been consistently asked about it, he had said, "Two ens and two ems. There's balance."
She had no idea what he had meant till he had written down her name on a piece of paper and made her look at the alphabets.
"There's balance in your name, your nature and everything you do."
After this, on some days, when her cooking erred and he would comment (never complain) about extra spice or tang or salt, she would say with glee, "Two ens and two ems."

In 1948, they had completed the construction of the large, 10-roomed estate house on the sprawling 21-acre farm. It had a living and dining room, two bedrooms, two bathrooms, a kitchen, a storeroom, a covered utility room (on the ground floor), and a bathroom upstairs. Needless to add, every room irrespective of its hierarchy was spacious. The centrepiece of the house was a massive room on the first floor, bigger than both the bedrooms. This was the room for books (the 'Books Room' or the 'Book Room' or perhaps 'Something Else' room) for it deserved a name as imaginative as what it would hold. During the planning stage itself, after much deliberation, he had coined a term for it: The Airport.

When Chennamma had raised her eyebrows with befuddlement, he had replied that this is where they would take off from, on flights of glorious discoveries of far-off lands, cultures and minds. She had laughed with delight and desire for The Airport.

The Airport housed a divan, two easy chairs, a study table and hundreds of books. Beyond work, this is where they spent most of their time. Unfortunately, they didn't have much time on their side. Within a year, he died abruptly of a heart attack. He was fifty-three. Less than a year later, Chennamma suffered a cardiac arrest while reading. Both had taken off from The Airport never to land again. It was a strange occurrence. They had been physically active all their lives, were vegetarians, consumed nutritious farm produce, never had disagreements or stress of any kind, between them or with anybody.

They had one son, whom people referred to as Big Sir. He and his wife were dutiful and managed the running of the farm as efficiently as his parents had. The only thing they lacked was an affinity for books. The Airport was dusted every day but hardly used. They had one son and the current populace of Mogga addressed him as Begur Sir. To them, the family details before Original Sir didn't matter and the matter of the family lineage after Begur Sir didn't exist. He was the end of the line.

Begur Sir was fortunate to have been born into a rich fold. It was a blessed beginning but depending on how one looks at it, it could also be a claustrophobic curse. Most people born into an alignment of stars such as his didn't get the freedom to explore their own identities. They were naturally expected to walk their pre-destined path.

Such lives usually unfolded in one of two ways:
Some would tread carefully and build on it. To them, legacy always came with a clause in bold letters called `responsibility'. Others would dance and destroy what would have been carefully compiled for decades.

But Begur had decided to sidestep the path altogether. He had chosen literature over land. Money and material possessions held no charm. From a young age, books had been his bedmates. The Airport was his bedroom, playroom, living room and study. If he had his way, it would have become his dining room as well but that was the one thing his parents had insisted against. So, every day, whenever it was time to feed the body, he would bring it down, eat in silence, and immediately go back upstairs with his hungry mind. It was no surprise that he could quote obscure writers and writings but not the mandi prices of copra or the factory prices for sugarcane. His grandfather's genes had made a comeback after skipping a generation but with an extreme twist.

After completing high school in Mogga, he had enrolled himself in the prestigious Maharaja College in Mysore. Being the throne of the erstwhile Mysore State, it was a learner's destination. It boasted of several reputed colleges, each of which boasted of several luminaries of the time. Truth be told, this was factually correct but characteristically untrue. It was a part of southern India; there was something in the air, soil and water here that produced brains but not braggadocio. Everything (the people, the flora and the fauna, monuments and machines, bridges and dams, forests and hills) went about their duties without bragging. They understated and overdelivered.

After pre-university, he left for England for his graduation in English Literature from Reading. During his time there, he travelled around quite extensively whenever he could make time from his academic pursuits. He went to Stratford-upon-Avon. He toured East Sussex to feast on the grand house of Rudyard Kipling and Virginia Woolf's cottage. Over a long weekend, he went all the way down to Devon to visit Agatha Christie's summer house. He travelled to Hampshire to see Chawton's Cottage where Jane Austen had composed a lot of her work. He walked around Guildford in Surrey laughing and cackling by himself, remembering stories and lines by P. G. Wodehouse.

One year, during the long Christmas break, rather than come home to Mogga, he had decided to tour Scotland. He knew the cold could kill him but he had much fire in his belly for this particular trip. It was a hallowed land that had produced unforgettable names, of writers and their creations — Alistair MacLean, Dr. Jekyll and Mr. Hyde, Peter Pan, Arthur Conan Doyle. In Edinburgh, he walked up and down Nicolson Street, remembering random facts across subjects. The Britannica Encyclopedia had been his bible while growing up and he was finally walking the street where it had been first published. Clad in layers and sipping tea in a café, he ticked off everything from his list except the last item. While all the places on the list were close to his heart, this destination was lodged in his heart. Going to the Isle of Jura meant travelling 200 miles, and into a territory where the windchill could get quite unendurable but he had to do this at any cost.

The next morning, he headed to a remote part of the northern Inner Hebrides, to a place called Ardlussa, from where he had to travel a few more miles deeper. When he finally got there, he stood staring at a Scottish countryside stone cottage. Shrivelled and shivering, he looked at Barnhill House with a smile so wide that it could warm the hearts and hearths of this entire village. From the big box of trivia tucked inside his head, he pulled out the significance of what he was staring at. Barnhill House belonged to David Astor, the editor of the Observer. This is where a severely unwell George Orwell had spent his last few years, writing 1984.

"Big Brother! I am not referring to the tyrant in your book."

He smiled and paused. He had rehearsed this imaginary conversation on his long journey.

"I have to tell you this. In the same year that you sat here and completed 1984, my grandparents finished building The Airport. And that is where I have read your masterpiece, many times over. I salute you, Sir!"

He stood staring at Barnhill House for a long time.

(2)

THE LORD OF THE RINGS: PART 1

On Begur Farms, everything was in accordance with what happened every evening. Begur's mother was in the kitchen preparing dinner. Sharda, the domestic help, after chopping vegetables, had just left for her small outhouse so that she could start to cook dinner for herself and her husband. Begur's father as usual was downstairs sitting with the ledger of the farm's accounts. Begur as usual was upstairs inside The Airport immersed in a book.

Before turning a page, he cast a downward glance and saw the 3-month-old infant lying peacefully, tucked in a tiny bed on the floor. The child was looking at him with curiosity. Of course, any infant's eyes hold nothing except drowsiness, or curiosity about what it sees, but to Begur it seemed that the child was curious about what he was reading. He smiled, held up the book and started his one-way conversation.

"I am reading Lando. It's a western, child. When you grow up, I'll make you read it."

He saw a gleam in the child's eyes and continued.

"It's by Louis L'Amour. A great writer, and a fighter; rejected nearly two hundred times before his initial work was picked up. Two hundred times! That's a lot of rejection. Do you know where he got his fighting spirit from? He was a boxer before he was a writer, a prizefighter who won most of his fights."

Upon hearing this, the child's eyes grew wider with astonishment and admiration for Louis L'Amour, or so it seemed to Begur.

The child was a recent phenomenon in Begur's life. After years, this was the first time Begur had regular human company and miraculously, that hadn't bothered him. Begur had always been inept around people, uninterested in them—his interactions with his parents, servants and anyone else had always been functional. Since the time he was a kid, books had kidnapped him from reality. And yet, he was happily sharing his space, time and thoughts with this yet-to-be-named infant. It had surprised everyone on the farm, and his parents the most.

The child was the son of Sharda and Adarsh, the two retainers who had been with the Begur family for a long time.

Several years earlier, when Begur was still in elementary school, these two had strayed onto the farm. Sharda was a 16-year-old orphan when she had come in search of work. Adarsh, a year older than her, had arrived three months later. Coincidentally, he was an orphan too. Initially, they worked as apprentices to the more experienced farmhands helping out in a variety of chores. Both were sincere, industrious and always happy. With nothing behind them and knowing nothing about what lay ahead of them, they lived in the present, every single moment. They possessed no thought or action which was about themselves. It was always about what eased the lives of others. They did whatever was asked of them, ate whatever was given to them, laughed at whatever was said about them, and never felt or expressed any consternation or conflict. They were truly an aberration. They lived so effortlessly that though they were at the bottom end of Maslow's pyramid of human motivations, it seemed that they were on top.

As time passed, they developed a liking for each other even as everyone on the farm including Begur's parents developed extreme fondness for the two. Gradually, they started helping out with chores inside the house. From dusting to sweeping to washing utensils and clothes, chopping vegetables, helping Begur's mother rearrange the contents of her almirahs every now and then, sitting with Begur's dad with a calculator while he went about his accounts, they were seen about the house for most part of each day. At the time, Begur had just entered his teens and had already become what he would be for the rest of his life—a shunner of people and a devourer of books. The only ones he interacted with regularly were Sharda and Adarsh. They were in their late teens and were the youngest on the farm.

One day, Begur's mother had tasked them with also dusting The Airport every day. This was done after consultation with Begur, and his acceptance. Begur had led the two upstairs, their first-ever entry into the upper storey of the house. Inside The Airport, Begur had explained the order of books, the do's and don'ts, the absolute must-nots and had ended with a gentle but firm remark.

"Handle every book with as much care as a devout priest cares for his idols."

While they had nodded, he had added, "Books and idols! They are much the same. Both carry imagination. Both carry stories. Both carry hope for mankind. But between the two, I'd rather worship books."

Since that day, Sharda and Adarsh spent time inside The Airport every day. They knew the little master's love for books and displayed equal love and reverence for them despite never having read anything.

Years rolled. One day, when they were in their mid-twenties, Sharda and Adarsh decided to get married. To everyone on the farm including Begur's parents, this was a natural progression. As a wedding present, they offered the newly-weds something highly unusual and extremely benevolent. They constructed a small outhouse, twenty metres from the main house and asked them to live on the farm.

Meanwhile, Begur finished his schooling and left for Mysore, and to England thereafter. Life on the farm continued steadily and smoothly for everyone. There was only contentment, and no complaints in any quarter of the farm or the calendar. The only issue if at all, was that Sharda and Adarsh despite their keenness, could not have an issue.

Begur returned from England and settled back inside The Airport. He continued to add to his collection of books, buying newer titles from newer authors across genres. Life carried on, on the farm.

Towards the second half of 1971, nineteen years after marriage, when Sharda and Adarsh had crossed their forties, when they had given up not just hope but also the rare wistfulness, when it had seemed that destiny had made its decision long ago and moved on, Sharda conceived. A wave of excitement and happiness flowed through Begur Farms.

When Begur (sitting inside The Airport devouring yet another book) heard the news, the first thought that struck him was: The Lord Of The Rings.

He had been quite overwhelmed when he had discovered the fact that it had taken J.R.R. Tolkien nearly seventeen years to finish his magnum opus. Among all the renowned literary works, this was perhaps the longest time that a writer had spent in conjuring and creating it.

He thought to himself:

`More than a decade and a half, and some! In that length of time, rather much lesser, mankind could, would, and has cut up terrifying mountains and built roads, constructed dams over unheeding water bodies, erected skyscrapers, designed and sent rockets into space, changed constitutions and currencies and whatnot! Indeed, this is an unusually long timeframe, to produce a book, or a baby.'

His swirl of thoughts continued.

`Millions of people do either within a year or two but then, books and babies ... hmmm ... both are not totally in one's control. One can try as much but if it's not to be, it won't be. Till it ought to be.'

He stared out of the window, scratched his forehead subconsciously and continued with his overloaded musings.

'Like Tolkien, will Sharda and Adarsh also produce something extraordinary? Only time will tell.'
He smiled and went back to his book.

On May 5th, 1972, Sharda gave birth to a baby boy. Happiness flowed through Begur Farms, along with the platitudes.
"He's a cheerful child."
"He'll make you proud. Mark my words!"
"I can see that he'll grow up and become someone important."
"His eyes are so inquisitive."
"God has taken His time to make him. He's special."
"He'll make a name for himself."
"It's written on his palm that he will not work on the farm."
Begur participated in the happiness by smiling to himself and muttering, "The Lord Of The Rings."

(3)

THE LORD OF THE RINGS: PART 2

Despite being branded a `happy child' by the people on the farm, he was, like any other infant, cryful too. Whimpers and wails were the only ways with which he could communicate with the world; rather, the quick and easy ways to get attention.

A few weeks into his birth, Sharda was back to her routine on the farm. The couple handled all their daily chores without much hassle. They would carry him and his tiny bed to the main house, twenty metres afar, lay him down on the floor, and go about their work. True to their nature, Begur's parents were very accommodative. Not for once did they feel that their servants' frequently wailing child inside their home was an intrusion. Instead, they behaved like surrogate parents ... well, grandparents. It hardly bothered Begur since he was mostly upstairs and lost in some book or the other. When it came to dusting The Airport, Adarsh would go up while Sharda would take care of other chores downstairs, within the vicinity of her child.

One day, sometime in the 8th week, egged on by Begur's parents,

Sharda and Adarsh took him upstairs for the first time. It was early evening. Begur was at his desk reading a book. As soon as he heard the wailing and the footsteps, he got up and turned around. While Sharda and Adarsh looked apologetic, he smiled and said, "The Lord Of The Rings. Welcome to Heaven from Middle Earth."

They didn't understand what he said. In fact, they had never understood most of what he said or meant in all the years on the farm. But to them, Begur Sir had always been different, never difficult.

Seeing his smile, they smiled with comfort even as Adarsh, carrying his child, stretched his hands towards Begur. Everyone on the farm had lifted the child at least once except him. Sharda and Adarsh felt sheepish that it had been almost two months and that they had not proffered this privilege to the little master, the one they had grown up alongside, since the time they all were young.

Begur smiled back sheepishly and held out his arms displaying the book that he was reading. Without a word being said, he made it clear. `I am holding a book and therefore cannot hold the baby.'

There was awkward silence. Begur was unsure about what he could or should say to a wailing infant. Moments later, he cleared his throat.

"Child! This is The Airport. From here, you can go anywhere in the world. Even to outer space. You can roam any land, the skies, the seas, even the depths of the ocean."

He stopped as abruptly as he had begun, lost in thought.

`What had he just uttered? Why did it sound familiar? Where had he heard these exact words before?'

A strong sense of déjà vu enveloped him.

"Begur Sir, he stopped crying as soon as he heard your voice." Sharda broke his thoughts.

He looked at the child and saw the child looking inquisitively at him.

"Let's take him around The Airport."

He began to walk slowly around the perimeter of the large room lined with bookshelves. Sharda and Adarsh followed. He stopped suddenly, pulled out a book, turned around and addressed the child.

"I told you about the depths of the ocean, right? See! 20,000 Leagues Under The Sea by Jules Verne. A remarkable read."

The child's eyes were at full stretch gazing at the book cover. Begur placed the book back and continued his journey along with his commentary.

"The Airport can transport you to places you know of, and places that you've never heard of, or even imagined. Sit here and go anywhere!"

The child maintained pin-drop silence even as Begur spoke with fervour.

"Go beyond Mogga. Go around the earth. Go above it or underneath it. Go ahead of time. Go back in time. Even sidestep time. Now, that would make for stupendous sci-fi material. Go into facts, fiction or fantasy. Go into romance, action, adventure, philosophy, horror, drama, crime, mystery, tragedy and comedy. Go into the netherworld of spirits, demons and zombies. Go into prose, poetry or plays. Sit here and go anywhere!"

He stopped, turned around and saw three sets of big eyes, out of which two sets looked big but blank. The third set looked curious and captivated. He stared into them and got lost again momentarily, in his déjà vu. Shaking his head, he turned ahead and shuffled forward. The slow trudge continued. The gang of four turned the corner of the second wall, walked three steps alongside the third wall when Begur stopped again, abruptly. This portion of the wall carried a full-length mirror ensconced between the bookshelves.

He held out the book he was carrying. Sharda took it. He stretched his arms towards Adarsh and with awkwardness took possession of the infant. He held the baby in front of the mirror and addressed its reflection.

"Child, do you see yourself? You look good. You look curious. You look self-assured."

The child stared at the mirror and all the things it reflected.

"Mankind has invented extraordinary things, but I think that these two are the simplest and yet the most important inventions. One, is the mirror. It reflects how we look."

He stood still, holding the child. The child didn't twitch. His parents, standing behind, didn't twitch. After what seemed like a minute, Begur spoke again.

"The second one, significantly simpler and more important than the mirror, is the blank page. It reflects how we think."

He turned around, handed over the child to Adarsh, took his book back from Sharda and sat down in his chair. Sharda and Adarsh stood looking at him, unsure if he had anything more to say. Rubbing his chin, Begur looked at the infant.

"A blank page! The most submissive thing ever! It just sits in front of you — passive, patient and pliant. You can do anything you want with it. It beckons you to write glorious things. Yet, it is that one thing that challenges mankind the most. A blank page can blank your mind. It can muddle it to the point where your thoughts become incoherent. Sometimes, it cajoles or coerces you to put down something and then makes you feel inferior, inept ..."

The child listened in rapt attention.

"Imagine! The Airport carries millions of pages all of which were blank at some point in time. They have been brought to life by dreamers who dared to put pen to paper, page by page. Now, if sitting amidst this isn't joy, then what is?"

He kept staring at the child as if he expected a response.

Sharda piped in. "Begur Sir, he hasn't made a sound in the last twenty minutes."

"Leave him here while the two of you go about your work. I think he likes it here."

"But Begur Sir, he wails frequently. He will disturb you." Adarsh said meekly.

"Every time he wails, I will read to him. A different story or a different part of a story. Don't be surprised if he forgets even his hunger pangs."

Sharda and Adarsh, both looking like blank pages, looked at each other to be sure if they were on the same page as Begur Sir. At a slight nod from Adarsh, Sharda hurried downstairs and came running up with the tiny bed. She placed it on the floor next to Begur's chair and Adarsh tucked the child into it.

"Thanks, Begur Sir."

"Begur Sir, whenever you feel he's disturbing you, let us know. We'll take him away immediately." Sharda added.

Begur nodded dismissively and reopened the book that he was reading.

Sharda and Adarsh walked backwards slowly, looking alternatively at

Begur and their child. The child kept looking up, craning its neck towards the bookshelves.

"Sharda! Adarsh! Aiyo!"

They halted and stared at him.

"This déjà vu! Where had I heard all these words before? It was bothering me. I finally got it. Grandfather!"

He broke into a gigantic grin.

Sharda and Adarsh only understood the reference to his grandfather. They smiled equally big, and with love and reverence, uttered in unison, "Oh! Original Sir."

Since that day, for most part of each day, the child became a part of The Airport. Sharda would bring him to the main house around 9:00 AM when the Begur family sat down for breakfast. While the parents usually discussed things about the farm, news around Mogga, and happenings in the larger world, Begur always sat in silence picking on his breakfast and feeding on the local English newspaper, Malnad News. Depending on the news and how it was reported, he would make faces and sounds — grin, grunt or groan. Then, while his parents would round off their breakfast with filter coffee, he would slurp on tea. His time in England had switched his preference.

Begur's parents would then head out to work, out of the house, onto the farm. Begur would head up to his den. Adarsh would follow him carrying his child and place him comfortably next to Begur's chair. Then, the couple would go about their work. Every now and then, when it was time to feed him, or clean him, one of them would gingerly step into The Airport, pick him up, do the needful and place him back again.

After finishing the morning chores, Sharda would head to her outhouse around noon to prepare lunch. An hour later, Adarsh would carry his child and join her. After resting for a while, around 4:00 PM, they would come back to the main house. Begur, after his afternoon siesta, would have his tea and get back to his books. They would leave the infant next to him and get down to their chores. Around 7:00 PM, after helping out Begur's mother in the kitchen, Sharda would head back to her outhouse to prepare her dinner. She and Adarsh would eat by 8:00 PM and one of them would clean up while the other would come to The Airport to pick up the child. This routine had been going on smoothly for nearly a month.

On this day, at around 7:45 PM, Sharda and Adarsh were back in the outhouse preparing dinner. Begur was having an excited conversation with the child about Leo Tolstoy. Suddenly, he heard a loud explosion. He looked out of the window and saw a big ball of fire inside the outhouse. There was panic and pandemonium. He ran down. Begur's parents were already out of the house running towards the outhouse. A few labourers who were still on the farm came running from a few odd directions. There were shrieks emanating from inside. The fire raged mercilessly. While the people frantically ran helter-skelter to fetch pails of water, Sharda and Adarsh stumbled and staggered around, aflame. The fiery dance was so quick that it allowed no time for the others to be of any use. Within fifteen minutes, the outhouse and its occupants were history. People shrieked and sobbed as they stood helplessly, robbed of their Sharda and Adarsh. The gluttonous fire, after snacking impulsively, calmed down and crackled lazily.

Inside The Airport, the child waited for ten minutes. Begur's trips to the toilet never lasted more than that. It then rolled its eyes upwards, craned its neck as much as it could, to catch sight of him. When it didn't, it lay down still, shut its eyes and tried to feel Begur's presence. Then, for the first time in nearly a month, the child wailed inside The Airport, even as the wail of a fire engine was heard in the distance.

(4)

13 NEW DAYS

After an extremely long and painful night, a new day dawned. But it failed miserably in diminishing the trauma and misery on the farm. Everyone, including Begur's parents, wept copiously time and again as they carried out the formalities and rites. They also spoke copiously about Sharda and Adarsh, fate and fickleness of life, and questioned God with vehemence. Their humility towards Him got replaced with harshness. It was an extremely long and painful day. As the day gave way to night, the sentiments remained the same. The only thing that changed was the fact that dinner was cooked for two people less.

Then, a new day dawned. The `new day' had its own existential issues and challenges that it dealt with, every single day. To begin with, it wasn't sure whether it was manmade or God-made. All it knew was that it was the intermediary between the Creator and His or Her creations. Every morning, it was either sent out by the One & Only or called upon by billions. Irrespective, it woke up every day with a long and challenging to-do list:

It had to bring forth the first breath for some, take away the last breath from some, provide glorious hope for some, open up amazing opportunities and possibilities for some, throw up unseen disasters for some, shake up some, mollycoddle some, make new relationships and break old 'n' weary ones, make new millionaires and minions, urge new writers to pick up their pens for the first time, enthuse new readers to pick up a book for the first time, create new diseases and vaccines, aggravate or pacify winds, tides and volcanoes, create history (good, bad and ugly, albeit on hindsight) and all of this, merely a fraction of what all it had to do – across people, places, other living beings, elements of nature ... an endless and complex list every day.

As regards people, depending on what it doled out to whom, millions praised it, and millions cursed it. And then, there were the millions in between who it didn't affect one way or the other and they would say, "It was just another day."

The `new day', at the end of each day, could never figure out whether it had had a good day or a bad one. Every day, it would be a hero, a villain, and a good-for-nothing. It had been damned to be perpetually confused. Over a vast period, probably early on from the beginning of time, it had become impervious and just went about itself, impassively.

The damned `new day' kept dawning. As days and nights rolled over, the minds and hearts of the people on the farm started to simmer down. Bitterness ebbed away, and the pain grew smaller and smaller in the rear-view mirror. They addressed Him with humility again, beseeching Him not to create such mishap and misfortune in anyone's life. They also beseeched Him with hope, asking that the child be given a long, happy and promising life. Begur was equally saddened and had his own bouts of thoughts about life, and the lack of it, but the only coherent line that his mind came up with, to sum up the misfortune was: *An orphan plus an orphan left behind an orphan.*

Oblivious to all of this, the yet-to-be-named infant went about his days. Begur's parents, aided by some of the farmhands, took care of him. They would coo happy nothings, sing folk songs and bhajans while they cleaned, fed, massaged, changed clothes, and whatever else was required. But for the most part of the days and nights, he was tucked inside The Airport next to Begur's chair. The child couldn't move, and the adult hardly moved. Every time he was plucked from here and taken out, even when it was to feed him mild sunshine, breeze and the chirpings of birds, he usually became crabby. The Airport was his no-wail zone. Consequently, Begur, the man-child, became the man to the child.

For the first time, after being unable to read for a lengthy period of a week, Begur went back to his routine but with a slight alteration. He would pick his book, usually a new one, but at times an old one as well, one that he hadn't read. In addition, he would pick up several other books off the shelves and place them on his table. This lot of books would be those that he had already read while growing up, or while grown up. He would read his book for a while, shut it, pick up a book from the lot, read out excerpts from it to the infant lying on the floor and go back to his book again, and repeat the sequence. For the first time, he now read for himself and someone else. He loved it. He had never had the chance and therefore had never even considered this concept but circumstances had put him in this joyful epicentre. It got him to revisit his favorite books, re-live paragraphs and rejoice at the mastery of literary giants.

"As we grow older and realise more clearly the limitations of human happiness, we come to see that the only real and abiding pleasure in life is to give pleasure to other people." Begur said and smiled at the child.

Before the child could mistakenly admire him for his words of wisdom, he clarified.

"That is from Something Fresh by P.G. Wodehouse. You'll hear a lot about him from me."

He opened another book and read out slowly so that the child could register, while he could savour each word.

"My mind rebels at stagnation. Give me problems, give me work, give me the most abstruse cryptogram or the most intricate analysis, and I am in my own proper atmosphere. I can dispense then with artificial stimulants. But I abhor the dull routine of existence. I crave for mental exaltation. That is why I have chosen my own profession, or rather created it, for I am the only one in the world."

"Child, that is Sherlock Holmes in The Sign of Four."

After reading out a few more excerpts from a few more books, Begur went back to his book. One could say that he did this for his own delight but it kept the child happy and let the others on the farm go about their regular work. It worked for all—the one on the floor, the one in the chair, and the several on their feet.

On the thirteenth day, as he sat at his desk reading, he looked out of the window and saw his parents and the labourers at the remains of the outhouse. Since the night of the catastrophe, no one had gone near it. The mere sight of the site filled everyone with so much anguish that they had simply stayed away from it. Now finally, they began clearing the debris. Some started picking up charred items while some began to sweep the outer edges. His mother started to sing a devotional song. The others joined her. They cleared and swept as they sang at the top of their voices. No one wept anymore, visibly or audibly. Begur kept staring at the broomsticks and thought about the concept of time.

"Tonight, the `new day' will perhaps sleep a little less troubled." He said to himself.

(5)

A FOR ATHATHA

Life on the farm regained its cadence. Attended to by a lot of people, the child grew up comfortably, mostly inside the Airport in the company of Begur. He grew up hearing stories none of which he understood yet seemed to enjoy. He heard stories of romance, revenge, murders, mysteries, childhood adventures, travel, espionage, courtroom dramas, wars, mythology, science fiction etc. Begur did have the discernment of what could and should be read out to infants but had decided to discard it. The child would enjoy what he enjoyed.

Days grew into weeks, weeks into months, and he began to move. This was the crawl-and-bawl stage and Begur was initially troubled that his reading routine would be greatly impeded. Initially, he kept a somewhat careful watch to make sure that the child didn't try and crawl down the staircase or crawl up to things and tug at them. Surprisingly, it turned out to be smooth. Every now and then, the child crawled around the large room, staring at the books on the shelves, touching the ones on the lowest rungs, gurgling, making incoherent sounds as if he was having conversations with them, and at times even smelling them. When he got bored, he would make a louder noise, loud enough for Begur to get out of the pages of his book and focus on him. Begur would turn around, and depending on which fraction of the room the child was at, tell him trivia about the authors and books that lay in front of him.

"What happened? Why are you making a noise? Do you know which book is in front of you? Doctor Zhivago. And do you know that Boris Pasternak was the first author in history to refuse the Nobel Prize for Literature? Tch, tch, tch, tch, tch ..."

Only recently, Begur had figured out a ruse that mostly worked with children. He would begin or end his sentences with sounds. At this age, sounds conveyed a lot more than words. The trivia and the sounds usually did the trick, and the child would go back to its preoccupations whatever they would be, and Begur would go back to his book. In case the child still felt neglected and cranked up its crankiness, Begur would hold up his book.

"See! I am shutting my book now. And picking up another to read to you. Now, this story is so amazing. You've not lived your life if you haven't heard this. Come here, quickly!"

The child would always crawl back and sit at his feet and Begur would read out passages to it.

As the months added up to a year and a little more, he uttered his first word; rather a sound on the brink of being a word. As Begur walked back to his desk from the toilet, he saw the kid sitting at the foot of his chair, looking up and excitedly saying, "Boo. Boooo. Booo."

For a moment, Begur stood confused trying to decipher what he was trying to utter.

"Oh! Book, you mean? Yes, of course. Get your K soon."

He held up what he was reading.

"This is The Diaries of Adam and Eve by the master humorist, Twain. Didn't you hear me laughing even inside the toilet?"

The child reached up for the book. Begur uncharacteristically let him have it, keeping a close watch in case the child characteristically handled it sloppily. Strangely, the child held the book, turned it this way and that way, turned it around, turned it over, opened it, smelled it, and handed it back to Begur.

He sat down in his chair and spoke to the child.

"Did you know that Mark Twain visited India? In 1896. He spent quite a few weeks travelling around. 1896! My grandfather would have been a little older than you. If he had been sufficiently older, I am sure he would have travelled anywhere in India to catch a glimpse of Twain; perhaps even shook hands with the hand that penned such classics. Anyway, do you know what Twain had to say about India?"

He saw an expectant look on the child's face and quoted Twain's words from memory.

"India is the cradle of the human race, the birthplace of human speech, the mother of history, the grandmother of legend and the great grandmother of tradition."

The child's eyes went big as if assimilating but Begur didn't spare him any time.

"While that's wonderful, do you know what my favourite quote of Twain is, about India? Ha ha ha ha ha ha ha!"

The child refocussed on Begur either shaken by his booming laughter or eager to hear.

"Millions of people trying to break boulders with dhotis. Ha ha ha ha ha ha ha!"

The window pane shook mildly. Over the years, it was used to these reverberations every now and then. Finally, Begur contained his paroxysm and explained.

"Child, you see, Mark Twain travelled around India by train. And what did he see? Mostly, people by the riversides and water bodies in interior India, washing clothes by banging them down on boulders. What a visual impression! What a verbal description! He was an absolute genius."

The child smiled, perhaps tickled by Begur's effervescence. Crawling back into his bed, he lay down making unintelligible, happy noises. Begur smiled and went back to his laugh riot, The Diaries of Adam and Eve.

 Suchlike was the child's early upbringing that long before he could utter `Ma' or `Pa', he became familiar with exotic sounds such as Dickens, Wilde, Twain, Dostoyevsky, Carrol, Verne, Hugo, Spark,

Maupassant, Morrison, Pushkin, Hemingway, Kipling, Faulkner, Rand, Golding, Nabokov, Fitzgerald, Huxley, Marquez, Kafka, Tolstoy, Orwell, Salinger, Gorky, Bellow, Forster, Asimov, Dahl, Greene, Borges, Burgess, Wells, Christie, Blyton, Wodehouse, Doyle, Kawabata … to name a few.

One day, for the first time, the child touched the second rung of the bookshelves. He hauled himself up briefly, felt a few books, wobbled, and sat down hard. This was a new discovery, one that excited him very much. Was it the excitement of being able to stand on his feet or was it that he could now reach out to more authors and titles? Only he could tell. Nonetheless, he began to crawl with confidence to different parts of The Airport, touch the books on the second rung and make twisted sounds of discovery and joy. By now, Begur, who wouldn't trust most grown-ups with his books trusted this child. He wouldn't maim any book, neither a cover nor a page.

One morning, the Begurs were at the breakfast table and Begur's mother had the child on her lap, feeding him. Begur was eating in silence immersed in Malnad News, the local daily. His father picked up an apple and asked the child, "A for?"

The child didn't seem interested.

He repeated the question a couple of times. The child didn't respond.

"A for apple!" He said with extra stress on the last word.

As the child looked at him, he smiled and asked, "A for?"

The child thought. It was trying to recollect. Begur's parents waited with hope.

Slowly, the child uttered, not clearly but confidently, "A for Athatha."

Begur's father looked mildly disappointed.

"It's apple … aa … pa … pa … la … apple."

The child looked confused. It thought for a few moments before saying, "A for Athatha".

This time, it said it in a way that seemed like it was trying to correct Begur's father.

Placing the apple back on the table, he commented to his wife, "Poor baby, he'll get it soon."

"He's already got it.", piped in Begur without looking up from the newspaper.

The senior Begur turned towards his son.

"What is Athatha?"

"Dad, he's saying A for Agatha, meaning Agatha Christie, one of the greatest mystery writers of all time."

The parents looked at their son, looked at the child, looked at each other and shook their heads. Begur smiled at both of them.

[There wasn't a semblance of distance and discord between the parents and the son. Neither party had, at any point in time, felt remorse or rancour towards the other for being markedly different. They understood each other deeply and loved each other dearly. It was quite fascinating, this absolute contrast and yet the affection that marked this relationship. Begur was so well-read that his mind could assimilate any inconsistency and make sense of it. On the other hand, his parents, never having read books, looked at life with so much simplicity that to them, everything was destiny.]

"Dad! Apple, ball, cat ... zebra. The child will learn all of that. That's not a big deal. But if he can, at this age, learn about the great thinkers and writers, he might grow up to become one of the greats. Who knows?"

The three of them looked at the child. It smiled, ignorantly one would suppose.

Begur's parents got up and started clearing the table.

As Begur held the child's hand and led him upstairs, he asked, "M for?"

(6)

A RAY OF HOPE

"B for beetroot and I don't like it."
The child said matter-of-factly as the Begur family sat for dinner. He was now inching towards his fifth birthday and could read, write, doodle, sing rhymes and parts of the national anthem, understand a joke and crack one too, and speak his mind as good as most children of his age.
"Beetroot is good for blood pressure. You should have it." Begur's mother countered with firmness.
"B for books. I can have them at dinner, breakfast and lunch." The child countered back mischievously and grinned, looking towards Begur for appreciation.
"Son, we need to talk.", said Begur's father as his wife served everyone.
Begur didn't register his father's statement and continued to be immersed in his reading. For once, it wasn't the newspaper but an inland letter. He had received it that afternoon and was now reading it

for a third time. It was from Amritendu Roy, a Bengali classmate from his Reading University days. Long after they had graduated and gone their own ways, Roy continued to write to him occasionally. He knew of Begur's manic obsession with books and whenever he came across a new, promising writer, made it a point to shoot off a letter to Begur. This was Begur's rare connection with the outside world.

Begur was re-reading the letter because it surprised him, in a fundamental way. Roy spoke of a fresh voice in Bengali literature, one that had begun to entertain and enthral readers. Roy stated that this was the kind of writing that everyone should savour but unfortunately, Begur and every non-Bengali could not even nibble on it, forget feasting on it. Given how the paragraph ended, Begur found it tantalising.

In the next paragraph, Roy spoke of Badshahi Angti (The Emperor's Ring), Gangtokey Gondogol (Trouble in Gangtok), Sonar Kella (The Golden Fortress), Kailashey Kelenkari (A Killer in Kailash), and about a Bengali detective called Feluda. He added that while Feluda was loosely or largely inspired by Sherlock Holmes, it was the sort of writing that everyone had to read. After ambling about in the expanse of the inland letter, Roy had, in the final paragraph, named the writer. The initial paragraphs had gripped Begur's mind, and the final one had twisted it.

`Satyajit Ray, the auteur?

Also an author?'

Begur knew of Ray's reputation as a filmmaker, one so big that the biggest of names in world cinema loved and worshipped his craft. But movies were not Begur's medium. He vaguely remembered watching a few regional movies as a kid when he had been whisked along by his grandparents, along with his parents. Later on, when he went abroad and met a mélange of people from various parts of the world with varied interests, most of whom were passionate about literature and cinema equally, he had continued to be a bookworm. It was a bit odd. If one could cherish great writing, it was quite natural to appreciate great writing overlaid with great acting, cinematography, sound, editing, and watching it on a screen manifold bigger and bolder than a book page. It was a breathtaking experience for most people including those who understood nothing about good writing. For Begur, somehow the written word moved him more than motion pictures. In the light of this, he was amazed that Satyajit Ray whom the world revered as a filmmaker could also write so beautifully. How many people could manage these two mediums, the big screen and the small page, with so much artistry and aplomb?

The only other name that came to his mind was Woody Allen. He knew about his movies and had read his first book, Getting Even. His zany, comic fiction wasn't for the straight-minded. He suddenly broke into a laugh remembering one of the lines from the book.
`I do not believe in an afterlife, although I am bringing a change of underwear.'
His writing was hysterically haphazard and Begur couldn't wait for more of Woody Allen's words. Now, Roy's letter made him yearn to read Ray's writing and he eagerly hoped that someday, the great man would write his stories in English.

"Son, you need to eat, and we need to talk.", said Begur's father between mouthfuls.
Begur put down the letter, looked around the table, saw the child picking on his beetroot lazily, started mixing his food and made eye contact with his father.
"Sorry, tell me."
His father turned to look at his wife and turned back towards Begur.
"Your mother and I have been thinking and discussing. This is the 25th year since your grandmother passed away. She was special. This is the 5th year since Sharda and Adarsh passed away. They were also special. This child will soon be five. He's also special."
Begur squinted trying to connect the dots. His father chewed on his food, forming his sentences.
"There are so many people in Mogga and around who are not as fortunate as us, or even this child for that matter. They have the intent but not the income to educate their children."
Begur stopped chewing and looked at his father.
"We have that parcel of land in the centre of Mogga. In the memory of your grandmother, and in the service of unfortunate, underprivileged children, why don't we start a school?"

Begur's look turned into a stare. It was a large, generous thought. It took him time to digest.

All his life, he had been so caught up with books that anything outside of them didn't even get an entry into his mind. He finally nodded.

"Son, we know that you prefer not to step out of your room. But if we need to do this, you'll need to help us out. Of course, I'll enlist the contractor and get the building up. You'll need to enrol the staff, the kids, and oversee the functioning of the school."

Begur thought lovingly of his grandparents, smiled at his parents who smiled back and went back to the remainder of their dinner.

"And this A-for-Athatha, B-for-Books child will also attend proper school and learn from books that are meant for his age." His mother added.

"I like all the books that are upstairs." The child said and grinned.

(II)

THE SCHOOL

(7)

CHENNAMMA BEGUR PRIMARY SCHOOL

Chennamma Begur Primary School was a single-storeyed building on a one-acre plot. The campus held varieties of flowers and fruits, mostly along the perimeter of the compound wall—hibiscus, rose, marigold, gooseberries, sapota, pomegranate, mango and jamun trees. The trees had been on the site since the time Begur's grandfather had purchased the plot. The entry to the school was a sloping bund with two large metal gates adjoining which was a small gate through which the kids walked in and ran out. The school taught underprivileged kids, providing free food and uniform.

It was 8:00 AM on a Monday and Rangappa, the 48-year-old school administrator-cum-gardener-cum-peon limped up to the main gate. Before unlocking and pushing it open, he stood with his forehead against it and thanked the Lord, and the Begurs. Then, humming prayers and looking around the campus, he limped down the sloping bund and made his way to the school building. As usual, he was the first one on the premises other than a variety of birds that chirped happily from all directions. The school was just a month old and so was his routine. He had an hour before the three teachers would arrive. Classes began at 9:00 AM, and the thirty-three kids would walk in noisily five minutes earlier. He got down to work.

He swept the Staff Room and dusted the four wooden tables, three of which were equal in size while the fourth was bigger. This was reserved for Begur Sir, or Big Sir. It was bigger not to cater to the trustees' egos but to accommodate the extra paperwork. He then swept the corridors and the classrooms, and proceeded to mop the toilets. As he stepped out of the toilet, he shuddered involuntarily. This happened to him both at home and in the school. There was nothing he could do to control these spasms. Then, picking up a stick with a cloth tied to its end, he dusted the school bell — a long piece of iron that hung from the ceiling outside the Staff Room. This rectangular bar of iron had a hole towards its bottom which held a one-foot iron rod. Whenever the bell had to be rung, Rangappa would pull out the rod and clang it against the bar. The suspended iron bar stopped five feet above the floor, out of normal reach of any child but within striking distance of a normal adult. It was a modified piece of a railway track, one that Rangappa had personally got done and contributed to the school.

After dispensing with his duties in the school building, Rangappa limped across the ground to the water tap, turned it on and dragged the hose a.k.a. the train. It was a silly joke, created and consumed only in his mind. The hose was metres and metres long, with several pipes attached to one another with connectors. This part of his job — watering the plants and trees — took time. He had to drag the lengthy and heavy hose all along the compound wall, spray less water around the plants which were more in number, spray more water around the trees which were fewer, while maintaining all along a cheerful conversation with the birds that chirped questions at him (for which he had no answers), tweeted answers at him (to which he hadn't posed questions) and sang general news about their lives which he acknowledged with a nod from time to time.

All in all, this little universe was in balance — for him, the birds, the plants and trees, the flowers and fruits, the three teachers, the thirty-odd underprivileged children, and the Begurs.

A railway signalman for nearly twenty years, life had dealt Rangappa a very cruel and painful blow. Two years earlier, after a frugal dinner, he had boarded the Bangalore Mail at Mogga. He was travelling to visit his married daughter, and in the middle of the night, someone had pushed him out of the running train. He had lain close to the tracks the entire night, until someone the next morning in another train heading towards Mogga had noticed a body. That train had been immediately brought to a halt, his unconscious body picked up, and delivered straight to the railway hospital in Mogga. It was a freak incident. Based on his sketchy recount as well as police complaints of some women who had lost their mangalsutras on this very journey, the public had pieced together the sequence of events on that fateful night: *Sometime around midnight, as the train was hurtling towards Bangalore, all the passengers in his compartment had been fast asleep. The train would have been close to Arasikere, probably just having passed it. The town of Arasikere was similar in its mood and modesty as the rest of the towns along this line – Mogga, Bhadravati, Tarikere, Birur, Kadur, Tiptur, Tumkur. But in recent times, for reasons unknown, the stretch around Arasikere had become infamous for theft. One of the compartment doors was surely left unlatched and a thief had gotten in. After expertly snatching gold chains off sleeping women, he headed to the door to get off at the next stop.*
Meanwhile, Rangappa had woken up to relieve himself. As he stepped out of the toilet sleepy-eyed, he barely noticed someone standing at the open door. But the thief panicked. In the madness of the moment, he pointed outside and told Rangappa that someone was calling him. Caught unawares in his sleepy state, Rangappa paused briefly at the door and before his mind could register any sense of what was going on, he was pushed out.

Two years and seven surgeries later, he was back on his feet. Though it had taken time and effort, it was a miraculous recovery. That's what everyone in his life uttered frequently. He himself felt so, but at times also felt if it was ridiculous to have his life back without a livelihood. The railways had offered him a compensatory desk job, but he had sworn off the railways. The mere sight of a train created trauma. The only fortunate thing was, by then his son had got into the railways as a welder in the loco-shed and they could continue to reside in the railway quarters. The local newspaper had covered his story including his negative sentiments towards continuing to work in the railways.

After a few weeks of trying to figure out the remainder of his life, Rangappa had been approached by Begur. Perhaps, this man had read about Rangappa's plight in the papers. Everyone in Mogga knew about the Begurs but this was the first time Rangappa had interacted with one. The Begur family had recently built a school and were looking for a caretaker. It had sounded a bit odd to Rangappa that he was being offered the position. The Begurs could build anything and hire anyone; they owned so much land that in and around the town of Mogga, they had Mother Earth on their side. But the way in which the meeting had transpired made Rangappa genuinely feel:
`Karma is a coin. Sometimes you lose, sometimes you win, without ever knowing when it is being tossed in your name, and by whom.'

Begur had appeared at his doorstep after parking his moped. The family owned tillers, tractors, trucks, and an Ambassador car but he had ridden down to the railway quarters on a TVS 50. After removing his Bata chappals, he had knocked on the door and walked in with laden hands. Big-built and soft-spoken, Begur had handed over three small sacks filled with potatoes, lemons, mangoes, and rice, mumbling that it was all grown at home. Along with that, he had handed over a book, `Swami and Friends' by R.K. Narayan.
"Reading heals the mind." He had said.
No one in Rangappa's family had ever read books but he and his wife had nodded vigorously at his comment.
After gulping down a tumbler of water, Begur had made his offer:
The school wasn't too big; just three classrooms, a Staff Room, and two toilets. It was in the heart of the town, less than two kilometres from Rangappa's house. It didn't need much effort but yes, it required someone to attend to things. The salary would be the same that he was getting from the railways.
It was a godsend and Rangappa had happily agreed, thanking Begur profusely. He had even tried to touch Begur's feet, but his surgery-sodden spine had slowed his movement. Begur had jumped up and shuffled back with a considerable frown.

On the very first day itself, Rangappa had walked into the school premises owning it more than the owners, in his heart, of course. He was diligent and dutiful. He had voluntarily taken on more tasks. On a couple of occasions when Begur had planned to hire a gardener, and a peon, Rangappa had dissuaded him.

"Begur Sir, I can manage it. But if you meet someone who is either less fortunate than me or more needy, we'll hire that person."

He saw Paratha Sarathy Sir, usually the first, cycle down the bund. He limped back to the tap to turn it off. He would resume watering the plants once the classes started.

(8)

CYLINDER

At four years nine months, three feet five inches and sixteen kilos, he stood facing the building. It was his first day of school though it had been operational for a few weeks. He had been unable to attend owing to jaundice.
Sniffing the air deeply, he looked up at Begur and smiled.
"This looks and smells like the farm."
Smiling, Begur pointed to one of the classrooms.
"That's where you need to go. Class will start in five minutes. You sit in the third bench on the left. Make friends and have fun. I am going to the Staff Room."
Clutching his schoolbag, he looked around and noticed several kids staring at him, some from close quarters and others from a distance. The usually noisy ground held only silence and stares. Suddenly, he heard a whisper from behind.
"Cylinder!"
It was laced with shock, not sarcasm. He turned and saw a group of

three boys a few feet away, one among whom had uttered. A bright smile lit up his face. This made them terribly conscious, and they responded with what could only be termed as sympathetic smiles. They knew about this boy who lived with Begur Sir. They knew his story. Well, not just them but most of the children knew.
"Hi! My name is Cylinder. Nice to meet all of you."
Cylinder grinned with genuine joy. Everyone looked baffled.

Rangappa clanged the school bell and the children hurried towards the classroom, in little clumps. Some overtook him, some consciously stayed behind, and no one walked alongside him. They were yet to figure him out, one whose tragic past they were familiar with and who had reacted strangely to that instinctive whisper.

Entering the classroom, he took his place and smiled at the boy next to him who responded with an unsure smile. Murmurs and whispers floated around but died down as soon as Partha Sarathy Sir walked in. He taught mathematics and science and was the sternest of the three teachers the school employed. He knew as much about the boy as the children did—nothing less, nothing more. Begur characteristically had informed the staff about his arrival without giving out any additional details.
Paratha Sarathy Sir signalled at him to stand up.
"We have a new student. From today, he will be one of us. He will introduce himself and I want all of you to …"
"Sir! He is Cylinder." A few boys from the back benches yelled before he could finish his sentence.
Partha Sarathy Sir looked aghast.
This was the thing with children; they learnt taunting without being taught. It was innate.
He was about to yell at them even as Cylinder stood up and grinned.
"Good morning, Sir! Good morning, friends! My name is Cylinder."
Paratha Sarathy Sir had an enigmatic look, more enigmatic than the subjects he taught. Some of the children instinctively smiled brightly while some looked stupidly confused. Unknown to the teacher and the students, the boy was indeed called Cylinder, ironically.
How did this come to be? Wasn't he aware that it had something to do with his past; a terrible mishap that had occurred on the farm? Well, he knew

every bit and it didn't bother him one bit.

Begur's parents had resolved that the child would be brought up without letting it peek behind at its ghastly past. Begur had obviously disagreed with them. Not just that, he had had a vastly differing point of view. He held the position that the more starkly the child heard about it while growing up, the lesser the impact would be when he grew up enough to understand it. It was just his instinct, not backed by any proven theory.

Riding on this, since the thirteenth day of the calamity, he had started uttering the word `Cylinder' in between any story he was reading out to the child. The very first time he had used it, the child had gurgled. It was apparent that he liked the sound of it. Begur's bizarre theory of quasi-parenting seemed to work. He increased its usage and after a point, arrived at a pattern. Every time he finished reading an excerpt or narrating a story, he would wait for a few moments and utter, "Cylinder".
It signalled the end.

For reasons peculiar to the adult mind, the child loved the sound and invariably made happy sounds upon hearing it. As he discovered speech, Begur would finish a story and wait, and the child would say, "Cylinder", and smile. This word became to the child what `Amen' was to a priest.

As he developed cognitive abilities, Begur started calling him `Cylinder'. One day, when the child questioned him why he was addressed as that, Begur reversed the reasoning, one that he had deftly implanted in his narrations over time.
"Since the time you were small, for some strange reason, you used to utter this word frequently and feel happy. So, one day, I decided to call you Cylinder."
It seemed logical and funny, and he had smiled generously at Begur.

Begur's parents were appalled and cross with him, but they couldn't do much about it. They had very little control over the two children who spent most of their time inside The Airport. The best that they could do was not take part in this idiocy and address the child as `Cylinder' despite Begur's urging that they, and everyone else on the farm, do so.

"The earlier, the better." Begur would often say.

But his parents continued to address the child as simply `Child'.

When he was a bit older to understand bits and pieces of the complexities of life, Begur had sat him down one evening and explained things about his parents, their past, the events of the fateful night, and the aftermath. Typical of him, Begur had explained everything in great detail despite his parents' insistence that he should never do so. Cylinder had listened eagerly and tried hard to recollect. But those were such distant, infant memories that he had drawn a blank.

Though he was the central character in this particular story, he felt far removed from it and consumed it as yet another story full of drama (a young man and a woman, both of whom had no parents met on a farm), romance (they liked each other and got married), suspense (they took a really long time to have a child), and tragedy (they died in a fire when their cylinder burst).

At the end of it, after a few moments, realising that the story was over, he had customarily said, "Cylinder".

"Yes Cylinder! That's what happened. Now you know." Begur had replied with a big smile.

As he grew up, his mind held hundreds of memories piled up over the years, and in each of them, the word `Cylinder' meant only happy associations and fascinating tales. The combined might of these memories effortlessly dismissed that one tragic reference. He loved the word. He loved being addressed as one. He wasn't particularly fond of being called `Child'.

As Partha Sarathy Sir wrote down elementary arithmetic questions on the blackboard, Cylinder with his effervescent smile, added to the cheerfulness inside the classroom; rather multiplied it.

(9)

BOOKS VERSUS BOOKS

Cylinder's time now got divided between books and textbooks. He turned out to be a decent student, grasping the basics of subjects. He neither disliked nor was particularly fond of any, other than English. But he found the English classes utterly basic and boring. He studied sparsely, managed his homework decently, and spent most of his time reading books from The Airport.

"Child, you need to put that book down and concentrate on your textbook. If you don't study well, how will you read and understand the books inside The Airport?", was a common refrain that he heard from Begur's parents.

"Textbooks have information. These books have imagination.", was his common retort.

He was now at that age where he had moved to the next stage of consuming literature. All along, he had only heard stories from Begur but now he read by himself. Digging into Begur's childhood collection of comics, he gorged on words and illustrations — Amar Chitra Katha,

Richie Rich, Champak, Chandamama, Archie, Suppandi, Shikari Shambu, Chacha Chaudhary, Phantom, Mandrake, Naseeruddin Hodja, Mickey Mouse, Flash Gordon, Akbar & Birbal, Tenali Raman, Winnie The Pooh, Asterix, Tintin etc.

Every month, he discovered and fell in love with something new. Some, he understood completely. The earlier system continued side by side. Begur would still tell him stories from the books he would be reading as also add his random tidbits about whatever comics Cylinder would be into.

"Repeat after me.", said Begur as he saw Cylinder reading Uncle Scrooge.

"An. Throw. Po. Mor. Fi. Zum."

After repeating slowly, not once but several times, Cylinder asked, "Who is that?"

"Not who but what. Anthropomorphism is taking human characteristics, emotions, thoughts, and applying them to animals, things etc."

Cylinder thought hard trying to process it. Begur elucidated.

"Uncle Scrooge is a duck but he talks, behaves and thinks like us. Understood?"

Cylinder looked animated.

"Can I try and teach the ducks on the farm?"

Begur looked alarmed.

"Don't! We cannot create another Animal Farm!"

He was play-acting. Cylinder looked stumped again. After a hearty laugh, Begur went on and on about this classic. Uncle Scrooge was forgotten for a while and the conversation moved to Napolean, Old Major, Benjamin, Stalin, and communism.

These were beautiful times for both. It opened up newer experiences for the child and re-opened childhood experiences for Begur.

The only ones who didn't find this agreeable were Begur's parents. "How much is three into seven?" Begur's mother asked Cylinder as he sat with them, reading a comic. He thought for a bit.

"Bracia B, Karcia B, Marcia B, Garcia B. Who are they?" He counter-questioned her.

She looked at him and shook her head in ignorance and annoyance. This random counter-questioning about irrelevant topics and stories reminded her of her own son when he was younger.

An impatient Cylinder exclaimed, "They are the Beagle Boys! That's what they are called in Poland."

"Whatever. Wherever. Today, you'll finish your homework, and eat your beetroot at dinner." She said wearily.

It was no surprise that in school, he quickly became the favourite of many. Initially, it was because he belonged to the owner of the school. But soon, the real reason established itself. He was simple, like most of them. He was always joyful, like some of them. This in itself, was good enough to make him one of them. On top of that, unlike any of them, he had stories, hundreds of them, of every kind. Beyond all this, he was ever generous. He did whatever was asked of him, laughed at whatever jokes were cracked at him, and happily parted with whatever eatables he had with him.

One day, while Partha Sarathy Sir was talking about oxygen, his mind went floating about. He had a thought. He felt that if everyone in school could read all the books that he read, life would be much more beautiful. They would have so much more to talk, think, laugh and argue about. Suddenly, he had an idea. It excited him but also made him nervous.

That evening, after dinner, when he was sitting inside The Airport with a Phantom comic and Begur was sitting with a fat book, Cylinder cleared his throat.

"Begur Sir, can I ask you something?"

Begur was so immersed in his book that he turned around and blurted the line he was reading.

"One lawyer with his briefcase can steal more than a hundred men with guns."

Cylinder smiled. He was used to Begur's idiosyncrasies.

Begur immediately regained his presence of mind, shut The Godfather, and looked at Cylinder with a gaze so riveting that Cylinder felt unnerved.

Clearing his throat again, he mumbled, "Can I carry all these comics, ummm ... not all but a lot of them ... at least some of them, and give them to my friends in school?"

Begur went weak in the knees and couldn't think straight. Cylinder had asked for his most prized possessions, his wealth (inherited and built), his life itself. He would rather let someone stab him over and over again but not let the assailant bend a page of any of his books. At the same time, he had always wished that more people read books. He often used to tell Cylinder, "What oxygen is to the body, books are to the mind."

At times, he would also wish that everyone read everything he read. He felt trapped between the two opposing forces. Leaning back in the chair, he adjusted his disjointed mind. After several rounds of turning positive and flipping negative, Begur finally said, "Yes. We shall take the books, the children's books, to school. We will keep them in the Staff Room. Make sure the children don't take them home. Make sure they don't fight over them. Make sure they treat books with as much care as mom and dad care for their deities. Make sure everyone reads. I'll tell the school staff to create a `Reading Period'. Thirty minutes each day."

Cylinder looked delighted even as Begur added, "Read along with them. Make them read aloud. And make fun of none just because you know more or you know better."

Cylinder was so overjoyed that he punched Begur gently on the side of his thigh, saying, "We will build a small airport."

The next day, they packed thirty-odd comics, and Begur, after deliberating, picked up six novels across authors and genres.

"These are for the teachers. Even they ought to read beyond their textbooks."

As they entered the school compound, earlier than usual, Cylinder proudly carried the bag containing the books. He was brimming with excitement to see the other children see the stack of comics. At the same time, he felt an inexplicable feeling of being a grown-up, carrying novels for his teachers.

(10)

FAT BOOKS

During the second week of the mid-term break, Cylinder, without letting go of comic books altogether, graduated to reading books without pictures. It happened instinctively, and in the beginning, he found it burdensome. Picture books were fun, vivid, full of colour, action and emotion.

Sitting on the divan with a spread of comics, and a novel in his hand, he looked at Begur sitting at his desk immersed in a book. He wondered how Begur kept reading fat books without pictures, one after another, day after day. He had just started to read his first and was already feeling weary. He would read a page, shut it, read a comic book, and open his fat book again. Yet, he felt a strange draw, a strong one towards them. For as long as he could recollect, his eyes had seen Begur immersed in books without pictures. His ears held words, big and unfathomable, that Begur would read out from time to time. His nose held smells of books that contained no pictures. Since the time he was small, really small, he had wanted to grow up and be like Begur.

A few days earlier, Begur had seen him ambling along the perimeter of the room, scratching his head, scanning the bookshelves, wondering which one would be his first fat book. Begur had then pulled out a stack of novels and handed it to him.

"Most children in the world, at some point, will grow up with head lice and Enid Blyton. Start with any of her books and you won't rest till you've read them all."

After looking at the front and back covers, Cylinder had settled on `Five Go To Finnston Farm'.

As the break progressed, Cylinder got comfortable and started enjoying fat books. He and Begur made plans that when the school reopened, they would try and do the same with the others; move them up the reading scale.

The second term started, and books moved from The Airport to school; more comics and the first batch of novels. Cylinder opened up this new world to the others, talking animatedly about The Five Find-Outers, The Secret Seven, The Famous Five, St. Clare's and Malory Towers, The O'Clock Tales etc. He hadn't read them all but knew of them from Begur. The children found these stories equally fascinating. Some managed the transition while most were still happy with comics. Soon, anyone seen reading a fat book and not a comic, was seen as more intelligent.

Over a weekend, as Cylinder sat enjoying his third Enid Blyton novel, Begur was immersed in a riveting tale of fraud and revenge. Though the book had come out a couple of years earlier, in 1976, he had finally managed to get a copy of it through Roy, his Reading classmate, who had sent it to Mogga. This first book by a new British author, Jeffrey Archer, titled `Not A Penny More, Not A Penny Less' was turning out to be spellbinding. The only sound inside The Airport was that of a page being turned, either by him or Cylinder.

Suddenly, Begur let out a chortle.

"Where where you?"

Cylinder looked up in surprise.

"What happened, Begur Sir?"

Begur repeated the phrase and chortled again.

Cylinder thought awhile before asking, "Is there a mistake in the book?"

Begur instantly shook his head and went back to his own thoughts.

Out of the blue, the phrase `Where where you?' continued to ring in Begur's ears. He didn't want to miss out on a single word of the book and decided that he would rather attend to the phrase before getting back to Jeffrey Archer. In all these years, something like this hadn't happened. Nothing could trespass his mind when he was involved in a book. But since the time he had started spending time in the school, he felt that a small portion of his brain had begun to take in things outside of the pages. In a sense, he was getting pulled back to his own childhood experiences. He was spending time with children, discussing comics and Enid Blyton, remembering his favourite characters, quotes and random trivia. For once, the child in him and the adult in him divided portions of his time between them, every day. It was a wonderful feeling.

He was hearing this phrase after a very long time.

`Where?' and `were' sounded the same from every child's mouth. Not just this, but tens of improper pronunciations:

Question mark was `koshen mark'.

Full stop was `fulis stop'.

Comma was `calm-a'.

W was `dub-li-you'.

Honest was `haa-nest'.

And so on. The children of Mogga went along merrily twisting syllables in any way that seemed convenient and comfortable. It was a regional thing and Begur got that. He found it cute but wanted it to be correct. He decided that the children could do with a bit of tongue training.

The following week, Begur introduced a new period in school. Rather, he tweaked the `Reading Period' to `Reading Aloud' period. This was divided across six students who got five minutes each. They were expected to stand in front of the class and read out from a fat book of their choice. While everyone looked towards Cylinder to start off this new, difficult and embarrassing period, Begur decided that it would take place in alphabetical order.

Tension filled the classroom as Begur announced, "Today is the first session of this very important period. Every student will read out one paragraph of a fat book, along with the punctuation marks. You know what those are. Some of you call them `puncher marks'. That's okay for now. Soon, all of you will get it right. Also, there are no marks for this period. Nobody will stand first, nobody will stand last."

The classroom looked hither and thither trying to spot the ones whose names started with the first alphabet.

Begur added, "Since we are kicking off this new exercise, it's fine if all of you read out the same passages from the same book. But going forward, I want to hear from more books. Otherwise, this will begin to sound like a temple where the same mantras get uttered every day. So, let's begin. Who's first?"

The six children whose names started with `A' squirmed nervously. This was the first instance in their lives when they disliked their names and wished that they instead started with X, Y or Z. The little boy, Abhimanyu, for once felt angry with his parents for having named him after the son of Arjuna, one of the most celebrated heroes in Indian mythology.

He shuffled up to the front of the class, focussed on the book in his hand while cursing his own name under his breath. Clearing his throat a few times, he started cautiously.

"Secret Seven Adenture. Ee-Nid Blyton. Chapter One. A Secret Seven Meeting."

He heard Begur Sir clear his throat, looked up and saw the entire class staring at him with collective tension. Only Cylinder looked excited and gestured to him that he was doing great.

"The Secret Seven So-see-ety was having its you-su-al week-aly meeting. Itis meeting place was down in the old shed at the bottom of the garden be-long-ing to Peter and Jaan-et. On the door where the letters SS painted in green. Peter and Jaan-et where in the shed waiting. Jaan-et was skoo-zing lemons into a big jug making lay-monday for the meeting."

"Lemonade!", said Cylinder under his breath.

Abhimanyu threw a nervous glance at him and was met with a covert thumbs up sign.

"On a plate lay seven ginger bis-cutes and one big dog bis-cute. That was for Scamper, there golden spa-ni-el. He sat with his eyes on the plate as if he was afa-raid his bis-cute might jump off and dis-hap-ear."

Having reached the end of his ordeal, he stopped, breathed for the first time in a few minutes and looked at Begur Sir. The entire class had their eyes on him.

"What's left?", asked Begur.

"Uh! Nothing, Begur Sir."

"Isn't there a puncher mark right at the end?", asked Begur deliberately mispronouncing it, like the children did.

This made the class laugh. There was less tension in the air now. Abhimanyu smiled in relief.

"Yes sir. Elec-shun mark." He said emphatically despite knowing that he was way off the mark. He was also aware that he had got several words wrong. He looked at Begur Sir expecting him to point out all the mistakes.

"Well done.", said Begur pulling out a few packs of Parle biscuits from his bag and handing them to a relieved Abhimanyu.

"Give one to each student while saying aloud, `Please have a bis-ket.'"

As Abhimanyu gleefully went about his task, Begur smiled and thought, `One word at a time. After this, no one in this class will ever mispronounce this word.'

As time went by, the `Reading Aloud' period created confidence in abundance, and corrected pronunciations of several words. It also got the children familiar with different books and characters.

(11)

THE SWEEPER

It was a Friday afternoon and the children had been through all their classes except the last one for the week. This was the weekly special. Every Friday, the regular classes ended at 3:00 PM, and after a recess of fifteen minutes, the special class would start and end at 4:00 PM. While the school curriculum was conducted by the three regular teachers through the week, this class dealt with a vague subject called `Et Cetera'.

The children didn't know what it meant. In fact, most of them couldn't even pronounce it. They liberally called it `Extra'. It worked in their minds since this was the special, extra class. That being said, every kid looked forward to it for several reasons. It had no set syllabus. There was no homework or tests, no right or wrong answers. With the fundamental scholastic rules out of the way, the children enjoyed it even more though they mostly understood nothing of what was spoken about. Every class threw up something totally different, having no connection with what was covered the previous

Friday. The class discussed poetry and plays, random trivia, oddities of the English language, obscure facts of history, philosophy etc. These classes were always filled with surprises, stupid answers and a great deal of laughter.

Once the school had been running smoothly for some months, Begur had decided to conduct these special classes. This was in variance with his character and more than anyone else, it had surprised him the most. He liked interacting only with books, not people, of any age, barring Cylinder. Also, despite being well-educated and the most well-read man in Mogga, he had never once felt the urge to teach. Therefore, when he had decided upon this, even he could not fathom why he felt so. Perhaps, it was a latent need to let out all that he read since he had no one else to discuss it with, other than Cylinder. This was his catharsis chamber. And so, he spoke about things that were worthy of being posed to university students, not underprivileged kids in a primary school.

The children were extra conscious of the recess time since Begur Sir didn't like anyone being late. It was merely one more of his oddities. They trooped into the classroom a few seconds before 3:15 PM and settled in their seats. The myriad conversations halted abruptly as Begur Sir walked in carrying a book, like he always did. Since this was the last class of the day, the floor was amply dusty and his Bata chappals rustled against it. He was a heavyset man who walked with a shuffle. Taking in the class, he adjusted his thick-framed spectacles.

"I will write down the answer. I want you to tell me the question."

The entire class looked on in anticipation since this was the reverse of what happened in any regular class. Picking up a piece of chalk, he started to write something on the blackboard when two boys skidded to a halt just outside the classroom door. Murmurs and peals of laughter filled the classroom. These two boys were notorious for being impish. They bent the rules the most and got punished the most. Begur Sir stared at them for a few tens of seconds while they stood panting and trying their best to look regretful.

"What is the time?" He asked matter-of-factly.

"It is three o'clock and twenty minutes, Sir!" Several voices yelled in unison.

Above the blackboard was a Favre-Leuba wall clock. There was an air of comic excitement. All the children including the two boys waited expectantly for the impending punishment.

Begur Sir's idea of punishment too was totally out of tune with what was practised in schools everywhere. Once, he had punished a student by making him sit in the teacher's chair, face the class and think of a word that rhymed with `purple'. Students in reputed universities in the motherland of the English language would have failed let alone this classroom of disadvantaged kids in an embryonic stage of learning the language. More so, none of the children even had a vague notion of rhyming words. That entire session had gone in the entire class scrambling their minds in collective ignorance. It had turned out to be a community punishment though the intent was to penalise only the errant boy. All through those forty-five minutes, Begur had leaned against the table, immersed in `The Life of a Useless Man' by Maxim Gorky.

On another occasion, he had punished a student by asking him to loudly utter Asterix (once), followed by Asterisk (twice). He had chalked these words on the blackboard and the student had to repeat it in a loop for two minutes. That had also led to collective participation with much tongue-twisting, mind-bending confusion. Towards the end of two minutes, it had created an animated classroom of kids yelling `Hastix' continuously. He had smiled back at their bright smiles of triumph and had got down to his lessons.

Begur Sir asked the two boys, "So what is your choice of punishment today?"
This was a recent thing that he had started. He allowed the student to choose his own form of chastisement. Begur's belief was that when one chose one's own type of repentance, it caused less bitterness and more betterment. His readings of Socrates, Nietzsche, Bertrand Russel, Immanuel Kant, Dostoevsky etc. had made him spend considerable time thinking about the concept of punishments.
Did this methodology work for grown-ups and serious crimes?
Begur wasn't sure but for tender, yet-to-be-formed minds and hearts, this was a worthwhile experiment.

When he had first offered this novel alternative, the initial set of students had all chosen options from the well-established menu of classroom punishments.

"I will stand up on the bench, Sir!"

"I will kneel down in front of the class, Sir!"

They could not think out of the box. It had made him smile thinking that while the human mind is a master of astonishing creativity, it is also a dim-witted slave to pattern. At some point, he had made the kids realise that they could punish themselves in more inventive ways. Rather than kneel in front of the classroom, he had once suggested to the errant student that he could clean the Staff Room while the class was on. Astonished, the errant boy had gleefully run to serve his punishment. Since that day, the kids had begun choosing school chores and tasks.

After some thought, the two boys responded that they would sweep the corridor and ran to the Staff Room to fetch the brooms. The class turned its attention back to Begur Sir who stood lost in deep thought. Nearly a minute passed. Some of the children exchanged glances and pursed their lips with amusement. Begur Sir was known for his lapses of concentration.

Suddenly, he asked the class, "What is time?"

A few earnest voices yelled, "It is three o'clock and twenty-five minutes, Sir!"

He stared at the class and asked again.

"I didn't say, `What is the time?' I said, `What is time?'"

The class remained silent, confused. He wrote down the question on the blackboard and stared back at the class. The children kept staring at the question. Saying that they had ten minutes to think about it, Begur sat down, opened his book and got immersed in it.

After several moments of silence, blank faces turned sideways to look at other blank faces. Whispers and murmurs started. Many of the students looked eagerly at Cylinder. If there was anyone who could figure out the catch in the question, it was him. After all, he lived with Begur Sir. Cylinder felt the pressure and tried to get his head around this esoteric question. Unable to make head or tail of it, he shook his head vigorously and looked outside.

The two boys were merrily sweeping the corridor. Suddenly,

he had a wide grin as his mind served up an illogical amalgam of the sequence of events. Turning to the others, he whispered, "Time is a sweeper."

It seemed perfectly logical and everyone joined in. The classroom resonated with the chorus, "Time is a sweeper! Time is a sweeper! Time is a sweeper!"

Everyone clapped and laughed triumphantly. The two broom boys grinned. Begur Sir looked up from his book and slowly broke into a smile.

(12)

OLD JUNGLE SAYING

Life on the farm, and in Mogga, carried on as usual for everyone. But for the children who attended Chennamma Begur school, it had become extra joyful and adventurous. While textbooks stretched their minds upwards, uncomfortably at times, the other lot of books unlocked their minds, and tongues, in unexpected directions.

Every day, they babbled about Suppandi, Superman, Shikhari Shambu, Spiderman and other superheroes. They picked characters, formed camps, argued more, sketched more (some traced while some drew freehand), laughed more during the day, and dreamt more at night. Some of the introverts began to talk more and some of the extroverts became more glued to books. They gobbled up fables, folklore, fiction, fantasy, in no particular order. Every day, the great minds of yesteryears kept feeding the fertile and fervent minds of the present day. As expected, some of the characters and superheroes came to life among the children.

Adil was one of the strongest boys in school and a bit of a daredevil.

He could scale any wall, scamper up the mango and jamun trees for fun, jump the farthest, do a somersault and land on his feet. When someone chucked a ball of paper at him, big or small, even when it caught him off guard, he would always catch it effortlessly, smile and throw it back. He had never once missed a paper ball.

During the Games Period, most of the children indulged in Kabbadi, a popular game in the region. One person (the rider) would cross the centre line, walk into the opponents' court uttering `Kabbadi, Kabbadi' and confront them, whose job was to snare him and not let him get back to his side of the court. The rider's job was to somehow touch one or more members of the opposing team and rush back. If the rider managed it, the ones who got touched would go out of play. But if the rider got pounced upon and held back, he went out of play. It was a game of strength, skill and subterfuge. Since riders went in solo against more people and had to come out triumphant, it wasn't everyone's cup of tea. Only the best and the blessed became champion riders and built their reputations (bigger and quicker) compared to the defenders. There were legendary riders across the region, across time periods and age groups. Even the best of them, at some point or the other, had been vanquished on a ride or two, or more. But at this point in time, in Chennamma Begur school, Adil had been unconquered. Even when the entire opposition, all seven players, would pounce on him, grind him to the ground, twist parts of his body and drag him back from the centre line, he would somehow crawl out or leap out of the tangled mass, touch the centre line, and walk to his side of the court with a shrug of his shoulders. Naturally, he had earned the sobriquet, Spiderman.

Another kid, known for his naivete came to be called Suppandi.

The collective left brain of the school, which dealt with academics was left behind by the right brain. The three teachers felt this. Despite the rules, children were found reading comic books and fat books at all times. They were caught reading under the trees, in the toilet and even during regular classes. The lower part of the blackboard, the desks, and the textbooks regularly carried ill-drawn outlines of Mickey Mouse, Mowgli, Hanuman, Spiderman, and dogs that appeared in comics. On top of this, they found that the homework books lacked the sharpness of answers.

One day, as the teachers sat in the Staff Room correcting the homework books, one of them suddenly stopped and stared hard at what had been put down. One of the children had scribbled something so hastily that it was difficult to make out. He held up the book for the other two to see.

They squinted, struggling to make sense of the line. After some effort, Paratha Sarathy Sir managed to crack it.

Phantom's hands quicker than eye can see.
                – Old Jungle Saying

"Who's this?", asked the other.

"Who else? Cylinder.", said the first.

When confronted, Cylinder smiled and apologised.

"Sorry Sir. I love that saying and wanted to use it somehow. I promise I will not do it again."

He was made to kneel in front of the class for an entire period.

The explosion of childhood imagination and impishness became a serious concern and the teachers decided to raise the issue.

"Begur Sir, we know reading is good. But the children are spending more time reading those books. It is affecting their studies."

Begur smiled.

"These books or those books, it doesn't matter. As long as they read, they will grow up to be better people. Trust me. Textbooks will give them better marks. Storybooks will give them better minds. In the long run, the latter will matter more."

Nodding in agreement, the teachers furthered their argument.

"We think Cylinder should stop getting more books to school. Begur Sir, he's your boy and you've brought him up in a different way. Let him read as much as he wants to, but the poor children should focus more on studies."

Begur smiled.

"I respect your thoughts. But ... and I am not saying this because the school belongs to my family but ... you do what you are supposed to do, and let the children do what they like to do. Trust me, what's happening is better for every child. As regards Cylinder being my boy, let me tell you this. He might have grown up with me but that little fellow is his own man. He reminds me of Kim."

"Who is Kim?", was but a natural question that came from one of the teachers.

Begur smiled.

"Kimball O'Hara. Kim. Rudyard Kipling. I'll ask Cylinder to carry it to school tomorrow. Read it, one by one. It'll take you to magical places and people all over India, before India became India as we know it. The British Rule and Undivided India. It'll take you to Lahore and Tibet, Cawnpore, Shimla, Lucknow, Patiala and more. Facts and figments of imagination fused into a fantastic tale. Beyond all that, it'll transport you to your own childhood, back to the magic and awe that filled your minds when you were small."

The three teachers gulped and gaped at Begur as he got up and shuffled out of the Staff Room.

School life and shenanigans carried on. At the end of the year, the class sat for their exams. Some did well. Some struggled in some subjects. Adil writhed and wriggled to the cross-over line and heaved a sigh of relief. Cylinder smiled through what he knew, shrugged off what he didn't, and made a list of books he would carry to school in the new term.

(13)

ORIGINAL WRITING

The school had completed two years. Newer batches of students had been enrolled. More classrooms were being utilised. The library held many more books, both academic and otherwise.

Rangappa's workload had increased but he still refused to take on additional help. His morning ritual of touching the school gate with his forehead and thanking the Lord continued. Getting additional staff wasn't an issue and Begur had proposed this to Rangappa and the teachers several times. They had declined saying that everything was fine and easily manageable. More than once, the teachers had mentioned, "Begur Sir, this has nothing to do with lessening our load. Two more batches, fifty-odd more students are not at all a strain. Plus, it's fun to teach children, especially the underprivileged ones. But you should seriously consider teaching. The children seem to have maximum fun during your sessions."
Each time, Begur had shrugged it off.
"I am not a teacher. I know only one kind of books. I was never much

into the other kind. Somehow, I managed and grew up to be what I am. Well, yes, I can conduct my random sessions now and then but beyond that, you are the ones who'll feed and grow these young minds."

The first batch of students were now super-seniors and behaved so. While they moved up the hierarchy of children's literature, they also indoctrinated the newer batches of kids into the habit of reading. Begur now conducted the `Reading Aloud' period for the junior class and had instructed the seniors to carry on with theirs, even in his absence. He would sit through some of them, now and then.

Among the seniors, some had blossomed into bright students. After tasting comics and novels, they had gone back to textbooks. They preferred facts of science and figures of mathematics over fiction and fantasy of storybooks. They were looked up to by the teachers, especially Partha Sarathy Sir. Cylinder obviously didn't figure in this group.

Some liked both sets of books. At appropriate times, they would read their schoolbooks and marshal their minds to hold everything within. At other times, they would read novels to set free their overworked minds. They had their own standing among the teachers and the students. Cylinder didn't figure in this group either.

He belonged to a handful of the third group who disliked schoolbooks. In fact, he was their leader. These children loved playing around with words and stories, ahead of their age. Obviously, Cylinder was instrumental for any zag or leap towards newer, unfamiliar books, concepts and authors. Surprisingly, Abhimanyu, the little kid who was the first to perform in the `Reading Aloud' period, who mostly looked nervy and nerdy, belonged to this set. This group enjoyed its own admiration, as abundantly as the first lot but not as consistently.

One day, during lunch, as the children sat in clumps based on collective interests and camaraderie, Cylinder held up a spoon to his little gang. They smiled instinctively knowing that he was going to say something crazy, interesting, fun ...

With a barely concealable smile, Cylinder asked, "Whose class do we have after lunch?"

The others found it straightforward and one of them responded offhandedly, "Paratha Sarathy Sir" even as Cylinder excitedly spoke over him, "Sartha Parathy Sir."

They looked at him confused as he shook the spoon in his hand. He was re-enacting what Begur Sir had done at the dinner table the previous night.

"Spoon.Er.Is.Um."

Cylinder declared the word, breaking it into parts for the benefit of his gang. As he explained what it meant and how it worked, their minds wouldn't sit still.

Over the next few weeks, these boys had such a blast that they became the envy of others. They seemed to have a secret language, one they indulged in, one that sounded familiar but didn't make sense. They would shout out sentences, write on chits and pass them across to each other during class, and titter.

Baths is moring.

Band up on the stench.

They even sparred with spoonerisms.

Fylinder, you just carted.

You mook like a lonkey.

Cylinder told his gang that they should share it with the rest of the class. Some of them weren't too keen (it was their trick, their treat) to which he characteristically responded, "When more people do it, it's more joyful."

There was something about Cylinder that set him apart from children of his age, something that neither he nor the others could discern. While most people of his age used the word `fun' for most things, he preferred `joy'.

The class tests got over and the results were announced. At the dinner table, Cylinder announced to Begur's parents, "I mailed in faths."

Begur laughed gleefully even as his parents knitted their eyebrows in confusion. When Begur explained, they knitted their eyebrows with concern.

A few weeks later, Cylinder shared an idea with the class that was met with excitement. Instead of the `Reading Aloud' period, he proposed a new one called `Original Writing'. By now, a few members of his gang had begun to scribble their own little stories. Cylinder, despite his early adoption, exposure and access to books hadn't taken to writing. He was happy to just read and listen to all kinds of stories.

"Abhimanyu! Abhimanyu! Abhimanyu!" The entire class chanted his name.

The little boy, who was now older and a shade bigger, walked up to the front of the class. Holding up a sheet of paper that had writing on both sides, he began reading out a story that he had written:

The Secret Seven.

Peter. Janet. Jack. Barbara. George. Pam. Colin.

It was their summer holidays.

They were sitting in the park, eating biscuits and drinking lemonade.

Scamper, the dog was playing happily.

They were bored.

George and Pam kept saying that they need a new adventure.

Suddenly, Colin said, "Do you know what my grandfather used to tell me?"

The six of them looked at him. Scamper stopped playing.

Colin said, "Did you know that my grandfather was in India for a long time?"

It took the class by surprise. They had no idea that Colin's grandfather had been in India. They stared at Abhimanyu who developed a hint of a smug smile and continued reading:

Barbara said, "No Colin. That's news to us."

Eagerly, Jack asked, "So, what did your grandfather tell you?"

Colin replied, "My grandfather used to say that India is the land of adventure."

The others looked at him wide-eyed.

Scamper started running around excitedly.

Peter and Janet said excitedly, "Let's go to India then."

The class stared at Abhimanyu. Between all of them, they had read several books of The Secret Seven and were familiar with all the stories and yet, no one had come across a story that was set in India. There was pin-drop silence.

"Fact or fiction?", asked a highly excited Cylinder.

Several others echoed his sentiments.

"Fact or fiction? Fact or fiction?"

Abhimanyu smiled.

"That is for all of you to decide."

He turned the page over. The class couldn't wait to hear more. Displaying the kind of creativity that Enid Blyton had been blessed with, he read out his last paragraph:

So, The Secret Seven come to India.

After solving cases here and there, they finally come to Mogga.

There were shrieks, whistles and thumping sounds of fists on desks. Abhimanyu folded his sheet and pocketed it.

The class yelled, "We want more! We want more!"

"Next time.", said Abhimanyu, smiled and walked back to his seat. He walked tall, feeling as powerful as the one he had been named after. Moans and groans of disappointment got drowned in the thunderous applause.

In the adjoining classroom, Begur, who was conducting the regular `Reading Aloud' period for the junior batch, broke into a smile. He knew that something beautiful had taken place.

(14)

TICK. TICK. TICK.

It was a regular day on Begur Farms, late in the evening. Begur's parents were downstairs, occupied with their own chores. Begur and Cylinder were upstairs, immersed in their own books. Begur's grandfather's Grandfather Clock downstairs was occupied with its own tick and tock. In this tiny universe, a cosmic assessment of things (big and small) would have carried only ticks, no crosses.
Chennamma Begur Primary School. Tick.
The underprivileged students. Tick.
Rangappa and the three teachers. Tick.
Cylinder and school life. Tick.
[Everything about the school was in balance. Chennamma would have happily described it so. Moreover, she would have been happier with what else the school had managed to achieve.]
Mickey Mouse. Little Lulu. Tick. Tick.
Panchatantra. Tinkle. Tick. Tick.
Chandamama. Champak. Tick. Tick.

Mandrake. Flash Gordon. Tick. Tick.
Suppandi. Shikhari Shambu. Tick. Tick.
Bahadur. Chacha Chaudhary. Tick. Tick.
Phantom. Spiderman. Superman. Tick. Tick. Tick.
The Secret Seven. The Famous Five. Tick. Tick.
Noddy. The Five Find-Outers. Tick. Tick.
St. Clare's. Malory Towers. Tick. Tick.
Enid Blyton. Roald Dahl. Charles Dickens. Tick. Tick. Tick.
[Different batches of children stood at different levels. The senior-most batch which Cylinder belonged to, obviously stood at a higher level, and Cylinder at the highest. Everyone and everything stood in balance.]

Unknown to anyone, the only one out of balance was Cylinder. Something had been gnawing at him for a while. He liked everyone — Rangappa, the teachers, his classmates, juniors. He was friendly with most and deeply connected with a few. Yet, he had been experiencing a vague sense of hollowness. Nothing about the excitement of school life or the comfort of farm life made him feel special — truly, deeply. Nothing filled him with an abundance of joy the way books filled Begur.

He had been ruminating about this vagueness for a while creating more vagueness in his own mind. He had finished his fourth term final exams with clarity in some subjects and happenchance in others. This was the end of Chennamma Begur Primary School. Now, he would have to move to a different one. For the past six months, Begur's parents had been discussing with Begur if he should be moved to a school in Mogga or sent to a boarding school. He wasn't sure what they had decided upon.

Presently, sitting inside The Airport, he tried hard to enjoy `Five Go To Billycock Hill' but was unable to concentrate. He shut it, opened his notebook, and wrote down:
Phantom. Batman. Superman. Spiderman. Bahadur.
[Fight criminals. Protect people.]
The Secret Seven. The Famous Five. The Five Find-Outers.
[Solve mysteries.]
He stared at the list and a few thoughts swirled around in his head:

`They do what they are good at. They love what they do. What is it that I am good at? What is it that gives me joy?'

(15)

SCHOOL TO SIGNAL

A few days later, it was yet another regular day on Begur Farms. It was half past seven in the evening and dinnertime was an hour away. Begur's mother was busy in the kitchen while his father was occupied with the ledger of the farm's accounts.

Begur was in The Airport deeply immersed in `Papillon' by Henri Charriere. He had read the sequel `Banco' years earlier but had somehow skipped this widely popular and contested, semi-autobiographical novel by the Frenchman. While Henri had said that 75% of the details were accurate, several critics had put down the veracity of it to a mere 10%. According to them, the rest was partly imagined and largely inspired by events in the lives of his fellow prisoners.

Cylinder gently stepped into the room and stopped a few feet behind Begur. He felt confident yet confused and nervous. As he cleared his throat to catch Begur's attention, it let out such a weak hiss that even his ears barely managed to hear it. His mouth was so dry that it held no saliva, only jitters. After waiting for a few seconds, he cleared his throat again with concentrated effort. It let out a strange, louder-than-required noise.

Begur turned around and looked piercingly at Cylinder. Cylinder looked piercingly at Begur, not out of intent but he knew not what the right mien was, to break the big news.

"Begur Sir, I love books, but I don't like textbooks. I don't want to go to school anymore."

There was silence. The pressure cooker in the kitchen let out a high-pitched whistle. Silence again. It let out a second one.

Rubbing his chin, Begur said, "Hmmm! I thought you would study hard, go to a good college, fall in love with the languages, read extensively, travel, observe, feel, imagine, and someday, write books."

Cylinder managed to conceal his relief and excitement. The relief was that Begur hadn't blown his fuse upon hearing that he wanted to discontinue his studies. The brewing excitement was in convincing him about what he really wanted to do. He was quite sure he had to play this out step by step.

"Begur Sir, there's no guarantee."

"Guarantee of?", asked Begur confused.

"You've done all of that, but you haven't written a book."

Begur instinctively laughed at this supremely sincere yet scathing remark.

"You are right, Cylinder. Maybe I was born to be a reader. I have never once felt the urge to write. I am happy spending this lifetime just reading. Perhaps, out of my theoretical seven lives, I do have a few left and in one of them, I might come back as a writer. Who knows?"

Cylinder beamed upon hearing this karmic probability.

"Begur Sir, I will be the first to read your book. I am sure it will be beautiful."

"How will you read if you don't complete your education?", countered Begur in a sincere, not scathing manner.

"I can read, to some extent. But somehow, I understand books. I mean stories, not textbooks. Begur Sir, I don't want to go to school anymore."

Begur rubbed his chin again.

"Hmmm! So, what will you do? Just be at home? Work on the farm? Milk the cows, water the crops, till the land, make biogas, run errands, drive the tractor, help mom and dad, harvest the crops? Or just sit and read books like me all day? I mean try and read, since you will be a school dropout."

Yet again, Begur's tone carried sincere curiosity, not sarcasm.

"Begur Sir, farm life is good. I can do everything you said. But I want to do something different."

Cylinder stood in anticipation while Begur sat in silence.

"What do you mean by different?"

"I don't know.", said Cylinder trying his best to sound genuinely ignorant.

"Then think. Let me also think. The day we find it, we'll discuss. Till then, attend school or if you dislike textbooks as much as you think you do, attend to things on the farm."

Cylinder nodded obediently.

As Begur turned his attention back to `Papillon', Cylinder intervened.

"Can I ask you something?"

Begur turned his gaze towards him again.

"Big Sir had once told me that many years ago, before I was born, you had opened a bookstore. Why?"

Cylinder's seemingly innocent question yanked Begur's thoughts back in time. In 1968, four years before Cylinder was born, Begur had opened a bookstore triggered by something he had read. A faraway smile crossed his face as he muttered, "Oh! Collective joy, Cylinder!"

Cylinder knitted his forehead trying to decipher what it meant. Begur knitted his forehead trying to remember where he had read it but couldn't. But the words had stayed with him, and he reeled them off from memory.

"The power of collective joy is most fundamental to human nature. Without it, we'd be lost, forlorn, perhaps even become demented. What then is this force? Imagine, you read a book that enthrals you. You love it so much that you just cannot stop talking about it. Now, for a moment, however improbable it may sound, imagine that you are the only person to have read it. Rather, the only person to ever read it. Therefore, you'll never be able to discuss it, gush over it in unison, re-read it with others. This could wreck you in ways you probably haven't thought about. The power of collective joy is fundamental to everything—poetry, songs, music, dance, sports, movies, books, food, places etc. It's truly magnificent."

Begur's eyes were aflame, orange in colour. Cylinder's eyes were aflame too, blue in colour.

[While a normal person is likely to say that orange is brighter than blue, a student of thermodynamics will say just the opposite. Blue might look more placid but burns at a significantly higher temperature. The common man has misread the candle flame for eons.]

Begur suddenly stopped and looked at Cylinder to check if the boy was getting the full import of what he was saying. Cylinder stood nodding gently, with a half-smile and a knowing look. Feeling assured, Begur carried on.

"If collective joy wasn't so fundamental to our existence, where then is the need for fan clubs and book clubs? Or even religion for that matter. I'd assume that even religions spread as fan clubs, albeit with much stricter do's and don'ts. There's also collective pain and for that, we have clubs we call support groups which provide succour. But here's the thing, in my modest understanding of things. The absence of collective pain will kill us, one at a time. The absence of collective joy will destroy us, as a race."

Cylinder nodded vigorously with a smile as if he understood every word.

"Then why did you shut it after 6-7 months?"

Begur smiled weakly.

"It failed miserably. In a good month, and there was one, six people visited and two books got sold. It's not that the people of Mogga aren't into reading. They are avid readers of newspapers, magazines and vernacular novels. After all, this is the land of the most celebrated writer, Kuvempu. But my anomaly is English books. Unfortunately, there aren't enough takers for it yet."

Cylinder looked equally disappointed. Having grown up surrounded by Begur's collection, English books were his kink too.

"So, the people didn't come to the books!" He stated decisively.
Begur pursed his lips and nodded.
"Cylinder, I am quite certain that in the future, say when you are of my age, this town will have ample readers, several book clubs, and some fine writers too."
"It won't take that long.", said Cylinder with authority.
Smiling at the boy's innocent optimism, Begur began to turn away towards his desk when Cylinder blurted, "Begur Sir, can I tell you what I want to do? I want to sell books. I want to be the bookseller of Mogga."

Begur froze in mid-action and stared at the boy whose face was aglow with a 60-watt smile. Within a few seconds, it got overpowered by Begur's 100-watt smile. It looked as if Begur was the child and Cylinder, the adult.
Weighing a few thoughts, Begur said, "Nobody understands me. Nobody will understand you. Mom and dad will never agree to this. They will scold you, and scold me three-fold. That is for me to handle. Your classmates will think that you are a loser. That is for you to handle. But time will take care of everything. If this is your calling, so be it. I will re-start Alexandria Book Store, and you Cylinder, will be its proprietor."
Cylinder unleashed more of his concealed scheme.
"Thank you. But there's no need for a store, Begur Sir."
"Then? What? How?", questioned Begur like a minor.
It was the adult's turn to respond, and he did.
"I will sell books on the street, in the street ... whatever is the correct thing to say."
The overeager child called Begur said, "Cylinder, you are confusing me, exciting me, and also making me think of you as an absolute idiot."
The composed adult said, "Begur Sir, if people don't come to the books, the books will go to the people."

The idea and articulation thrown up by Cylinder's native intelligence left Begur speechless. He stared blankly at Cylinder for what seemed like minutes. Cylinder's firefly-luminescent eyes stared back at Begur's blank stare.

"But, where on the streets?"

"Ohio.", said Cylinder without further elaboration.

Begur looked utterly lost.

After waiting for a few moments, Cylinder decided to give Begur Sir a clue.

"Remember what you had told me once. About the first traffic ..."

"Ho ho ho ho ho ho ho! You irrational, arbitrary child! Just like me, you are not made for the ways of the world.", said Begur in a booming voice and continued to laugh.

[Some years earlier, Mogga had got its first traffic signal, and in one of their conversations, Begur had mentioned to Cylinder that the world's first electric traffic signal had been installed in Cleveland, Ohio. The word `Ohio' had stuck in Cylinder's mind.]

With their imagination fired up, Begur got up, walked to the window and stared into the darkness across the farm. Cylinder walked up to one of the book shelves, gazed at hundreds of books and excitedly started making a list of the titles he would carry. Begur's mother's voice rang from downstairs telling them that dinner was ready. Cylinder scampered down after thanking Begur. Begur stood still at the window for a few more moments.

"If people don't come to the books, the books will go to the people."

He muttered to himself, involuntarily.

With a beatific smile, he turned and walked towards the staircase.

(16)

THE THREE-PARTS CASE: PART 1

The next morning, when it was breakfast time, Begur's parents sat at the table waiting for the two to come down. They saw Cylinder running down the staircase with a stack of books, followed by Begur. Begur's mom began to serve as Cylinder ran towards the table and said excitedly, "Which book would you like to read? Which one will you buy? If you are not sure, let me recommend something good. But read you must."
"First eat, then play." She said matter-of-factly.
Cylinder didn't respond.
Begur said matter-of-factly, "This boy has become a man."
"What is that supposed to mean?", asked his father matter-of-factly as he took his first bite.
"Some things mean nothing to some but will mean the world to others.", replied Begur cryptically.
  Begur's parents realised that something was afoot. They looked at Cylinder who looked at Begur who looked at his parents.

"Now, this boy has everything; everything but joy. And so, he has a small idea. Actually, it's a big, bold idea. And the thing with any big, bold idea is that no one can judge whether it's sensible or supremely stupid. Only time will tell."

His parents stopped eating.

"Now, let me break this down into three parts so that we all can be logical about it. The first part is quite simple. He doesn't want to study further. He does not like schoolbooks.", said Begur taking his seat.

Cylinder nodded earnestly while is parents looked shell-shocked.

"What do you mean he doesn't want to study further? Has he completed his Master's already? He is ten years old. What is this nonsense?" His father said, alarmed and agitated.

"Which is why I am trying to make sense of this situation.", said Begur sounding his best to be on his father's side of the argument.

His mother jumped in.

"So, what does he want to do? Become a superhero. Wear his underwear over his shorts and go flying across Mogga."

"Mom, you are close to the truth. He wants to be a superhero of a different kind. Nothing under or over-the-top." Begur tried to pacify her.

They had already lost their composure. In these few minutes, the conversation had jumped the sequence of logic and the required strictness of enquiry.

[Both were mild-mannered and mostly kept to themselves and their work. One could argue that this was unusual, especially of people who owned and ran a large farm, dealt with several labourers, transporters, wholesalers etc. It was unusual but not unlikely. They had been blessed with much wealth, and that usually made people feisty, aggressive, domineering, greedy, entitled to their views etc. Well, mostly but not always. It did have another side to it and Begur's parents belonged to this negligible minority. They were tolerant, placid, generous, and blessed with much simplicity and goodness. Both disliked conflict and confrontation of any kind. On several occasions, without an extra word spoken, they had had settled money negotiations in favour of a greedy labourer. On the other hand, a needy labourer had always been given more than what was agreed upon or even fair. Over the years, some of the near-and-dear ones on both their sides had received enough and more and had become distant. Their parents, Original Sir and Chennamma, had been equally generous and good natured but had also been firm and equitable in their dealings. In this regard, these two had suffered a generation loss, so to speak. As regards Begur, he had no dealings with anything or anybody, except books and Cylinder.]

Begur dug into his breakfast. Cylinder followed suit. The parents sat with knots on their foreheads. Finally, Begur's father spoke.

"Let's step back a bit. How can we let him not study further? We let you be whatever you wanted to be, but we made sure, and you made sure, that you got a good education. We must do the same for him. Otherwise, we will be ruining this boy's life."

Begur nodded obediently and took another bite. It seemed that he agreed wholeheartedly. His parents waited. They wanted to be sure that this illogical conversation had reached a logical conclusion.

"Sometimes, I wonder if he's a boy or a book." Begur said looking up at them.

They stopped short not knowing what he meant while he swallowed a bite.

"What are the chances of two orphans walking into our lives? Wait for nearly two decades to produce a child, and within months leave behind an orphan? Who grows up being named after the biggest tragedy of his life? And is happy about it. Which child decides so early on about what he or she wants to do? He's only ten and the first few chapters of his life already read like a book."

His parents' thoughts got strewn all over the place. Every time they managed to start a clear-cut, logical discussion, Begur would start talking about things fantastical. He continued, taking the conversation to an even higher plane.

"I don't believe in religion, rituals and the rabid worship of names and corresponding forms. Therefore, let me just say `cosmic power', whatever that be. I feel that some higher power has sent this boy with a special purpose. It is only right that we let the rest of his chapters be written as is ordained."

This turned so metaphysical that neither his parents nor Cylinder had any idea other than the feeling that the argument was flowing in Begur's favour.

"So, what is part two?", asked his mother.

His father hastily added, "Let's hear part two but we'll come back to part one."

"Well, this boy here loves books of my kind. More importantly, he says it's a joy to see more people read books. Now, this is a position that's different from mine.", said Begur and suddenly swung the conversation towards Cylinder.

"Just so that we have understood you correctly, tell me. If you had a choice between reading more books like me and making more people read books, what would you prefer?"

"Making more people read books.", said Cylinder.

Begur's parents had begun to find part two of the conversation as confusing as the first and before they could comprehend and question further, Begur rounded off with, "So, Cylinder has decided that he wants to become a bookseller."

This was no legal courtroom drama; more of a breakfast table family drama. Nonetheless, it had arguments (subtle and grand), objections, clever manipulations, red herrings, false moves of submission, tactical questioning of plaintiff and defendant etc. It was no surprise that Begur was a big fan of Perry Mason, the legendary literary lawyer who had a penchant for unusual, difficult or nearly hopeless cases.

"Anyway, there's time. We'll discuss in more detail.", said Begur and turned back to his food.

So did Cylinder. Begur's parents ate in silence chewing over all that they had been served. The case was adjourned.

(17)

THE THREE-PARTS CASE: PART 2

As the two headed up to The Airport, Cylinder whispered to Begur, "So, have we won the case?"
"Not yet, but consider it done." Begur smiled.

Inside The Airport, Begur took his little client to one of the corner shelves, one that was dedicated to a single author, one that held over sixty books. Begur gazed up and down in admiration. Seeing him, Cylinder did the same. After many moments, Begur's head which had been moving up and down, began to move sideways slowly in disbelief.
"Erle Stanley Gardner! A master of crime and detective stories. One of the best-selling American authors of all time. The king of pulp. The creator of Perry Mason. A writer so prolific that even a reader like me would find it difficult to keep pace with him."
"Begur Sir, then I am definitely taking his book on my first day.", said Cylinder with a big smile.

Everyone settled into the routine of the day. Begur's parents attended to their duties downstairs still dumbed into silence. Upstairs, Cylinder sat excitedly on the floor making a list of titles he would carry. Begur sat at his desk looking out of the window, thinking of the case. Around half past noon, the pressure cooker began to whistle downstairs. In some time, these two would be summoned for lunch. In all these years (pre- and post- Cylinder), Begur would head down at the very last minute. Today, for the first time, he got up earlier.

"Cylinder, I can see you are making your fourth list. Nothing is good or bad, right or wrong. Every list is beautiful. Keep at it. I am going downstairs."

His father, sitting with the local vernacular daily heard heavy footsteps, looked up and saw his middle-aged son walk down the staircase. Begur walked up to his dad, smiled and put his hand on his shoulder. This was a rare move. At the slightest of nudges from Begur, he effortlessly stood up and walked with him to the kitchen. Begur's mother, in the midst of her cooking, looked at her husband and son.

"Dad, mom, I know both of you are carrying confusion and conflict. Tell me."

"How can a child of ten drop out of school? It's absurd.", said his father.

"Dad, let's indulge him. For all you know, it might be a passing fancy. He might get bored of it within a few weeks or a month. He might want to run back to school even before the new term begins."

His mother smiled and nodded. For once, Begur spoke sense and simplicity.

"What happens if he decides to continue? Even if he gets bored of it, what happens if he loses interest in studies? Have you thought about his future?", inquired dad.

"In an ironical way, he is the most blessed one.", said Begur softly. "Unlike any of us, he has nothing to worry about; excess wealth or the lack of it. He has no past, and his future is taken care of. He can always work on the farm and fend for himself even after we are gone. Haven't we already decided to bequeath a small piece of land to him, just like we have decided for some of the other labourers?"

With love and respect not usually seen in his eyes, he put his arms around his parents and reminded them of something they had told him years earlier:

"There will be no more Begurs after us. And we have often wondered what will happen to all this land. It's simple, son. We will distribute it among all the labourers, the ones who've tilled and toiled for us. And if we are reborn as labourers on this land, they will hopefully treat us as well as we have treated them."

Begur had said that their worldview was simplistic, idealistic, fatalistic, and that their idea of giving away land was simply fantastic. This was the one thing that the three agreed on wholeheartedly.

His parents grudgingly nodded. Even in the worst circumstances, the boy would be taken care of, even in his old age. Begur had more to add.

"Dad! Mom! Beyond all this, I feel he has been sent down for a special purpose. A purpose that'll bring him joy and spread joy among hundreds of people. Trust me, he'll become the most popular and loved man in Mogga in time to come. The Begurs will be forgotten at some point, but Cylinder, I tell you, that boy will be remembered for ages."

They shrugged and for the first time since breakfast, smiled at him. They felt calmer.

"If the Great Almighty has a grand plan, one that we don't understand but he can see, let's go along and see." Begur's dad remarked to his wife.

She nodded and said, "Lunch is almost ready."

Begur yelled, "Cylinder! The bookseller of Mogga! Come down for lunch."

He scampered down with a few lists. Unlike the mood at breakfast, everyone was relaxed now so much so that Begur's mother quipped, "So, what will you do with all the money from selling books?"

"Buy more books.", beamed Cylinder.

"What will you tell your friends? Won't they make fun of you?", asked Begur's father.

"As long as I am having fun, it does not matter." He said with maturity rare for his age.

Serving Begur, his mom remarked, "You started a bookstore when you were an adult. Look at this child! He's years ahead of you in his thinking."

"That's true. Only this time, there will be no bookstore.", said Begur with a smile.

They were caught short again.

"So? Is he going to sell it from school? Not a bad idea. We can build a little store on the premises.", said his father.

"We will call it Chennamma Begur Bookstore. It will be so befitting. She read schoolbooks when she had to and enjoyed storybooks later on. Unlike this extra smart child." His mother added.

Their comments were met with silence.

"Sorry for stealing your thunder. You two are not the only creative people in this house. Just because we don't read books, don't think we can't think.", said his mother with a smile.

"This is not creative. It's actually quite logical. Anyone could have figured this out.", said his father with a smile.

Begur let out a deep sigh.

"Finally, we come to part three."

He turned towards the boy.

"Cylinder, this is the final piece. And I would want you to say something. Tell them what you told me."

Cylinder hastily swallowed the food in his mouth and nervously cleared his throat.

"If people don't come to the books, the books will go to the people."

There was confusion at the table once again. Begur explained Cylinder's logic; the `where' of it but before he could come to the `how' of it, his parents went ballistic. They spoke simultaneously with so much shock that it was difficult to isolate their individual words but collectively this is what they said:

"A ten-year-old boy standing at a traffic signal? Carrying books? Sun, rain, cold, dust! Whole day? Begging people to buy? Buses, two wheelers, autos, tempos! Sitting on the footpath? Stray dogs and cows. Thieves and beggars. Lunch and evening snacks? How much will he earn per book? Do we need the money? If he wants joy, let's open the biggest shop in Mogga, make him the owner and employ as many people as needed. He's a child, you are a well-educated man, but there's no difference between the two of you! Let's not do this nonsense! Where will he urinate?"

As more words and emotions tumbled out of their mouths, Begur focused on his own thoughts.

When he had decided to take up the case, he had instinctively known three things:

1. That he would have to break this up into parts.
2. That every part would be challenging.
3. That part three would be the most difficult part of the case.

[In fact, this was the part that had stumped him the most as well.]

He gingerly cut in.

"Both of you are absolutely correct in your thinking. I agree with everything that's troubling you. Just so that we all look at it logically, let me break this up into three parts."

They reigned in their words out of sheer shock. How could anyone on this planet even have a logical counter to their absolute bare-boned logic?

Begur surveyed their faces for several seconds before speaking.

"The traffic signal is in the heart of Mogga. In fact, it's only a few hundred metres or so from school. Cylinder has been walking to and back from school, carrying his bag. He'll do the same, carrying a little more weight one way. That's Part One. He'll carry sandwiches for lunch and biscuits for snacks, like he's been doing. That's Part Two. The traffic signal always has a traffic constable. Plus, most people in Mogga know him or know of him. I don't see anything untoward happening to him. That's Part Three. Everything else—dogs and cows, urinal, sun and rain, buses, mopeds—is a part and parcel of his profession stroke passion. I am confident he'll take them in his stride. What say, Cylinder?"

With a wide smile, Cylinder nodded vigorously. Begur's parents lost The Three-Parts Case.

(III)

THE SIGNAL

(18)

TWENTY RUPEES

On the morning of his first day as a bookseller, Cylinder was as excited as a well-made kite on a breezy spring evening. By 9:00 AM, he was done with breakfast. His snack box was packed and placed next to his water bottle. Begur's parents went on about an exhaustive list of instructions, each of which received a mechanical `Yes!' from him. An oversized schoolbag had been bought, the kind that was more suited for students in high school, the kind that could comfortably hold about fifteen books, a lunch box and a bottle of water. The first stack of books for sale that he would carry into the open world sat on the table. They had been handpicked by Begur. He and Cylinder looked at them, smiled at each other, and Begur began to place them neatly inside the bag.

It was decided that Cylinder would reach the signal around 10:00 AM when the townspeople started to move about. What still hadn't been decided was whether Begur would drop him off or Cylinder would trudge the distance. Begur was of the opinion that Cylinder should carry himself and his books. Cylinder had no issues with that. Begur's parents had been insisting that for the first few days, Begur should take him there and bring him back at an appointed hour to which Begur had responded impishly.

"What happens if the first few days run into a week, then into months and years?"

His parents had dismissed it outrightly.

"We'll see then. This stupidity will be over in a few days. Then, all of us including Cylinder, will have the rest of our lives to laugh about it."

Begur had then posited a more real reason.

"A bookseller knows books, not comfort and luxury. If Cylinder indeed wants to be one, he better get used to the reality of his trade."

"One day at a time. On the first day, you'll take the child." His mother had said.

Between Begur and Cylinder, there had been no discussion about an appointed hour of return. Begur had merely told him, "You come back whenever you feel tired or bored or frustrated. If you manage to sell all your books before midday, then come back for lunch, rest, rejoice and we'll pick books for the next day. And don't stay till sunset. People mostly buy books during the day with plans of reading at night."

Between the two, everything was sorted.

As Begur finished packing, Cylinder enquired, "Is it in order? Should I hold them the same way? Can I change the order now and then? What should be on top, and at the bottom?"

"I don't know. The town will tell you.", said Begur.

The previous day, Cylinder and Begur had spent considerable time selecting the titles. They had so many books on their minds that short-listing them to what could fit in Cylinder's arms was an extremely confusing task. Cylinder was unable to stick to any list of his and kept jumbling them up.

"Begur Sir, you are the expert. You decide."

Begur didn't look sure either.

"I was never a bookseller. I only waited for book buyers."

Rubbing his chin, he searched his mind for a formula that could work. The obvious one was a list of the popular titles—a few classics, and some of the recent ones. But in the absence of a vibrant reading culture, he wasn't sure whether that would work. It would certainly take a few weeks before they could arrive at a winning pattern. Suddenly, he had an idea, one that excited him very much. From what he could remember off the cuff, he pulled out specific titles as Cylinder looked on curiously. With the smile of a child, Begur placed the books in front of Cylinder.

1. The Case of The Velvet Claws — Erle Stanley Gardner
2. The Mysterious Affair at Styles — Agatha Christie
3. The Sun Also Rises — Ernest Hemingway
4. The World is Full of Married Men — Jackie Collins
5. The Year of The Intern — Robin Cook
6. Carrie — Stephen King
7. The Mystic Masseur — V. S. Naipaul
8. Grimus — Salman Rushdie
9. Untouchable — Mulk Raj Anand
10. Pebble in the Sky — Isaac Asimov

Mystery, pulp, sci-fi, horror, drama, Indian writing … it was a decent mix. Cylinder hadn't read any but was familiar with most of them.

"What do you think?", asked Begur.

"I don't know. I'll try.", said Cylinder sounding a bit unsure looking at the stack.

"Hmmm! I can replace some of them if I spend a little more time doing my homework. I just plucked out the ones I remembered.", replied Begur, his mind still running in the background.

"What homework, Begur Sir?" Cylinder's curiosity was aroused.

"Do you know what these titles are all about?" Begur's eyes became big, and he bobbed his head like an excited child.

"The first book. The debut novel of each writer. Since tomorrow is your first day, I thought, why not start with these?"

Cylinder got excited and clapped. Suddenly, the stack assumed greater significance in his head. He picked each book, read the title and the name of the author, erroneously at times, and stacked them back neatly in the same order.

"Some … well, most of them are great writers. There are one or two newbies too. Like Salman Rushdie.", said Begur.

"I was about to ask you, Begur Sir. Who is he? Is he a Pakistani?"
"Ahmed Salman Rushdie. He was born in India. In Bombay, but lives in England."
"Is he also a great writer?" Cylinder asked earnestly.
"I don't know. He wrote his first book a few years ago and I happened to read it recently. So, he was top of mind. That's all. I liked some parts."
"Okay. What does Grimus mean? Is it the name of a detective?"
"Oh no! He doesn't write mystery. His writing is more mystic. It's sci-fi, fantasy, fairy tale etc. An eclectic combination. Whenever he writes his next book and I read it, I'll be able to explain him better. I don't know what Grimus means. If you want, we can change that book to something else."
"No, let it be. I wanted to ask you something more important. How much do I sell each book for? I have no idea.", said Cylinder.
"Oh ho! In our excitement, we forgot the most elementary thing, my dear Cylinder. Good that you asked me. Let me think."
"Begur Sir! You just spoke like Sherlock Holmes."
Begur smiled at Cylinder's sharpness while pondering.
"Price of each book? Hmmm! Actually, every book is priced differently. It depends on the reputation of the author, the publishing house, where it gets published, the size etc. But let's keep it simple. Cylinder, sell each book for twenty rupees. Since you want more people to read, we shouldn't price it higher. At the same time, it shouldn't be priced as low as a jackfruit. Books don't grow on trees, just like money."

At 9:50 AM, Begur started his moped. Cylinder climbed and sat behind him. Begur's parents placed the bag of books between the two while repeating some of their instructions.
"Yes, yes. I'll be fine. You eat on time and rest. I'll see you in the evening.", said Cylinder as if they were children and he was the adult. He felt like one indeed.

The morning air was crisp as they rode towards the signal. The town was up and about. Cylinder kept looking at people they passed, mentally marking some of them as potential customers. Suddenly, a question popped into his head.
"Begur Sir, what should I do if someone says fifteen rupees or

ten rupees?"

Begur decelerated a bit mulling over this realistic query. As they neared the signal, he said, "Cylinder, twenty rupees! Not one rupee less. But if someone walks up, recognises a book, either the author or the title, and says that he or she has been dying to read it … if one indeed shows awareness and desire, give it away free."

Cylinder smiled into Begur's back.

(19)

A WASTE OF TIME

The traffic signal stood in the heart of Mogga surrounded by most of the important buildings in town—the Mogga Police Station, the District Court, the R.T.O., the Fisheries Department, the Silk Board and the Nehru stadium. There were a few large tracts of empty land that belonged to one government department or the other, provisioned for expansion when the town would grow bigger and busier. A majority of the townspeople passed through the traffic junction each day.

When it had come up three years earlier, there had been much excitement. It had become the talk of the town, a wonderment to people, Cylinder included. For the first few weeks, several children had sacrificed their leisure-time games to just stand at the signal and watch the workings of it. Families from the surrounding villages had made special trips to Mogga to feast their eyes on the orchestra between lights and vehicles. Every single denizen of Mogga, from the wealthiest to the most destitute felt a tinge of pride. The traffic signal was symbolic of their small town having taken a big stride and stepping into adulthood.

Begur brought the moped to a halt at the signal and as Cylinder got off with his bag, wished him luck. A young, skinny traffic constable with a big smile greeted him though they had come face-to-face for the first time.

"Hello, Begur Sir. My name is Chikkanna."

Begur wished him back.

"Hello! You'll have company from today".

Smiling at Cylinder, he rode off as soon as the signal turned green.

Chikkanna looked down curiously at the little boy with the big bag.

"So, you are Cylinder. I've heard stories about you."

"Who has told you stories about me?"

Chikkanna skipped the question and instead remarked, "School project, eh? Don't worry. I will tell you everything about traffic and lights."

"Lifetime project." Cylinder said with a big smile, taking him by surprise.

As Cylinder made himself comfortable under the tree that adjoined the signal, Chikkanna ambled across to the other side of the traffic junction. Cylinder pulled out a cap from his bag, adjusted it on his head, balanced the stack of books on his left arm, held it firmly with his right hand and looked around eagerly. As a few vehicles stopped, he proposed, "Books! Books! Detective stories! Mystery! Humour! Science Fiction! Many more. Only twenty rupees."

Some looked at him uninterested while some smiled at him indulgently and sped off as soon as the signal turned green.

Chikkanna walked back and saw Cylinder with his stack.

"Have you been punished by Begur Sir?"

"No. I've been blessed by him.", replied Cylinder taking him by surprise again.

Turning negligent towards his duty, he began to ask Cylinder questions, trying to make sense of him and his situation. Cylinder spoke gleefully about his life, stopping every now and then to sell books when the motorists stopped, or a pedestrian walked past.

"Books! Books! Perry Mason. Latest. Greatest. Salman, first book. Only twenty rupees."

As the day unfolded, so did their conversation. Chikkanna would blow his whistle every now and then, exchange pleasantries and news with some passers-by, walk around the traffic junction at regular intervals and come back to Cylinder with more questions. At one point, he looked at the stack of books and looked as blank as a traffic light off-duty.

"Who are all these people? I haven't heard of any of them. Have you read them? What do they write about?"

Cylinder got excited but the moment he began to respond, Chikkanna picked up the top book from the stack and looked at it absentmindedly.

"Rich people. Books are only for rich people."

Cylinder had nothing to add.

"How long does it take to read any of these books?" Chikkanna asked him.

"Begur Sir will finish a book in one or two days. I have also started reading fat books. I take four to five days, sometimes a week. I can read faster but then I don't want the book to end. Then there are people who take weeks or even …"

Cylinder's response was cut mid-way by Chikkanna with his next question.

"And how long does it take these people to write these books?"

Cylinder thought awhile.

"It depends. Many months. Sometimes, many years."

Chikkanna smiled.

"See! I told you. Both, those who write and those who read, have to be rich people. You think ordinary people like us have so much time to waste."

Cylinder was taken aback. He suddenly didn't like the traffic constable anymore. How could somebody consider books a waste of time? He went back to his spot under the tree even as Chikkanna got busy blowing the whistle at three people on a moped who jumped the signal and rode past laughing at him.

"Serves him right!" Cylinder muttered to himself.

Suddenly, Cylinder saw a big, white car, the biggest he had ever seen approach the signal. Throwing a quick glance at the traffic lights and seeing that it was about to turn red, he balanced his stack just as Chikkanna straightened up and saluted the car that halted in front of him. Seeing this, Cylinder felt unsure and stayed back, staring at the car. The windows were rolled up and he could not make out who was inside. Chikkanna stood smiling at the car till it moved away.

As he turned around, Cylinder asked him, "Who was that? Your boss?"

Chikkanna tut-tutted.

"Boss? You think my boss can even dream of a Contessa. He is the big boss of Mogga district, Huchche Gowda Sir. He has so much money that money doesn't stay in his house. He has nine rooms but still there's no room for all the money. So, it is put here and there — plantation, sugar factory, trucks, liquor. He's also started a temple, and a school. Very big man. Very rich."

Cylinder looked overawed. He swallowed his dislike for the constable and asked him eagerly, "Next time he comes by, can I sell him my books?"

Chikkanna smiled with warmth.

"Of course, Cylinder. Do that. He might buy all your books in one go. He has all the money and time to waste."

This time strangely, Cylinder didn't feel that Chikkanna was being ignorantly sarcastic and began chatting with him freely again.

"So, who has told you stories about me?"

"Oh! New News Nagaraj. Have you heard of him? He's the best English reporter in town. He works for Malnad News. You should read his articles. They are better than any book, I can tell you."

Though Cylinder's fixation was to find readers, he got excited the moment he heard about a writer. He didn't personally know a single good writer other than his ex-classmate, Abhimanyu.

"Chikkanna, please introduce me to him when he comes by."

"I'll do that. He keeps crossing the junction often. He's a very busy man, always looking for stories. He writes beautifully. He also reads. I am sure he will be interested in your books.", said Chikkanna.

"You've made me curious about him, both as a writer and a reader.", said Cylinder with a smile.

"If he finds you interesting, he might just write about you. New News Nagaraj is like that. The only problem is that our town is too small for his talent. The day Mogga runs out of stories, he will move to Bangalore or America.", said Chikkanna sounding like his confidante.

Despite their differences about the matter of books, the two had struck a rapport. The age difference didn't come in the way of conversations. They kept attending to their duties while talking about varied things. Towards the evening, Chikkanna knew about the boy's liking for his unusual name, details about his school days, The Airport, tidbits about some authors and books, and why Cylinder had chosen to do what he was doing. Most of it seemed surreal to him.

At ten minutes to 5:00 PM, Cylinder packed all his books.

"I didn't manage to sell anything today but had fun. It was nice meeting you. See you tomorrow."

"Same here, Cylinder. Don't you worry. I am with you. We will soon start selling." Chikkanna reassured him with a big smile as Cylinder hoisted his bag, looked in either direction and crossed the road.

(20)

HIGGINBOTHAMS

As the clock struck five, Begur shut his book and stood up. For a little over an hour, his parents had been repeatedly asking him to go and fetch the boy. He was about to turn away from his desk towards the staircase when he saw Cylinder walk in through the farm gate. From this distance, his bag looked laden. A minute later, he stepped inside The Airport.
Before the words 'So, how was your first day?' could roll out of Begur's mouth, Cylinder asked, "Begur Sir, if I need to order more copies, can you do it?"
"How many did you sell? Which copies do you want?", asked Begur surprised.
Cylinder responded animatedly.
"I tried but couldn't sell a single book today. But the good news is that I will start selling soon. Chikkanna doesn't understand books at all. He thinks it's only for rich people. I explained many things to him. I don't know how much he understood but towards the end, he got excited

and promised me that he'll help."
Begur smiled.
"Good. He's quite a character. You keep talking to him about books, authors, characters etc. Lend him books. Let him also get into the habit of reading. The traffic signal is a good spot. It will happen."
Cylinder nodded.
"I can already feel it. You know who I saw today? Huchche Gowda Sir, the big boss of Mogga district."
"You address someone as `Sir' when he has a mind greater than yours, or a heart bigger than most. Not because he has more money.", said Begur sharply.
This came out of the blue. In all the years, Cylinder hadn't heard Begur talk about the rights and wrongs regarding this simple, heavily used word. He stood unsurely, trying to retract or modify what he had said.
"Actually, I saw his car, not him. It's so big that all the books on four or five shelves can easily fit in. The next time he comes by, he might buy everything and ask for more. That's why I asked you about more copies, Begur Sir."

Cylinder was taken aback to see teardrops rolling down Begur's cheeks. It was the rarest sight.
Wiping them off, Begur said, "I am sorry, Cylinder. But I've been a troubled man today."
Cylinder patted his arm trying to comfort him without knowing the source of his botheration.
"Begur Sir, I am not lying but it didn't bother me at all. I didn't feel bored or frustrated. I didn't feel the heat or hunger. I really enjoyed myself. Please don't worry about me."
Begur's response was on a tangent.
"I silently prayed that you would sell all the books. At the same time, I desperately hoped that you wouldn't sell any. I am sorry. You see, they are all personal copies, some belonging to my grandfather. It's not easy to give them away though I have decided on it with a heavy heart. I will get used to it. You start selling and I'll order more copies."
Cylinder stood looking at Begur for several moments, unsure of what to say.
"Remorse is momentary, satisfaction is eternal. We will spread joy,

Cylinder. Go on, wash up, eat something and settle down.", instructed Begur with a smile.
"Begur Sir, is it Salman Rushdie or Rooshdie?"
"I say Rushdie."
With two things (more copies and unsureness about the name) out of the way, Cylinder scampered down, freshened up and sat with Begur's parents telling them tales from his first day at work.

A little later, he came running up.
"Higginbothams! Higginbothams! More copies, Higginbothams!"
Begur looked at him with astonishment.
`How the hell did he know this name? Not just that but he also pronounced it perfectly!'
Begur surmised that the little fellow was good with long words, and at times struggled with very short ones.
"How do you know Higginbothams?", asked Begur.
"I have heard you call him regularly. Every time you want a new book, you pick up the phone and say, `Hello, Higginbothams?'" Cylinder said before adding, "I like the name and it's stayed with me. Where does he stay?"
"Abel Joshua Higginbotham. He now lives in Heaven. God bless his soul.", said Begur enjoying the confusion on the little fellow's face.
He then proceeded to tell Cylinder whatever he knew about India's oldest bookstore.
"Abel Higginbotham was born in Kerala, grew up with missionaries, worked on a merchant ship and when he was in his early twenties, moved to Madras. There, he began to manage a bookstore run by missionaries which largely sold religious books."
"I don't like religious books.", interjected Cylinder.
"Neither do I but having said that, religious books are also supremely well-written stories of adventure, drama, injustice, curse, romance, revenge, greed, infighting, betrayal, the good, the evil, and the inevitable. They carry an incredible array of characters created with extraordinary imagination. Facts fused with fiction and fantasy, to varying dosages. They are such an amalgam that it becomes impossible to separate the real from the surreal. Beyond all that, they contain everlasting wisdom."

"Tell me about Higginbothams.", said Cylinder impatiently.
"Yes. So, while managing the bookstore, he discovered his love for books. He also displayed an unusual knack for sourcing them. Sometime in the mid-1800s, the missionaries decided to shut the store and Higginbotham bought it from them."
Cylinder sat glued as Begur continued.
"He moved it to Mount Road in Madras. The first Higginbothams store. From there on, it became popular. He started publishing books as well, became a prominent man and before his death, was the Sheriff of Madras."
"When did he die?"
"Around 1890, I think."
"Okay. What happened then?"
"His son took over and the store became bigger. They opened a store in Bangalore and set up bookstalls in various railway stations."
"A railway station is also a good place to sell books.", said Cylinder excitedly before correcting himself, "But Mogga has only two trains during the day."
"The traffic signal is the best place.", said Begur.
"And then?"
"At some point, the son also died. Somebody in Madras bought the store. It's been going strong. It is still the best place for books."
"Begur Sir, can we open Higginbothams in Mogga?"
"We can. But only when lots of people start reading and buying."
"I agree. Otherwise, Mr. Higginbothams in Heaven, sorry, Mr. Higginbotham will not be happy.", said Cylinder, sounding like a half-baked seer.
Begur opened his diary, looked up the telephone number of Selvaraj, the contact person at Higginbothams and showed it to Cylinder.
"Whenever we need new books or extra copies, let me know. I will pick up the phone and say, `Hello, Higginbothams? Can I speak to Selvaraj?'"
Both laughed and settled down with their books.

(21)

THE LEGEND OF TEMPO TONY

Days began to roll over and a routine fell into place for everyone—Cylinder, Begur, his parents. After the first few days of carrying the same titles, Begur and Cylinder made newer sets, comprising some books from the first list.

After a few weeks, at Cylinder's growing insistence coupled with Begur's own conviction, Begur stopped ferrying him to the signal. Between the two, they managed to assuage Begur's parents about their silly concerns of him getting kidnapped, suffering a sunstroke, being run over by a bus, getting gored by a bull, becoming a hunchback etc. He now trekked both ways, joyfully. He preferred this as it gave him time to think about the authors and the books he was carrying, as also form sales-slogans around them.
"Anything missing from your home? Take home Sherlock Holmes."
It also gave him time to rehearse and rectify his pronunciations.
"Alexandre Duma. Duma, Duma."
"Roo-al. Roo-al. Roo-al Dahl."

The routine became a comfort even for Chikkanna. He would land up on duty every morning and a little later, Cylinder would walk up joyfully and greet him. They would spend the entire day exchanging random stories from books and the lives of people in the town.

The previous week, Cylinder had made an offer.

"Chikkanna, which book or books would you like to take home? Choose anything. There's no charge for you."

Having asked him a few times at regular intervals and Chikkanna having remained uninterested, Cylinder had decided to decide on his behalf.

"I suggest you start with short stories. Here is Timeless Stories for Today and Tomorrow. All the stories have been chosen by Ray Bradbury. Amazing stories, by him, Franz Kafka, Roald Dahl, Sidney Carroll and others."

After thinking for a few moments, Chikkanna had said, "Tch! Reading about foreigners and their world has no connection with our lives. It is a waste of time."

Shaking his head intensely at this illogical belief of his ill-informed friend, Cylinder had made his second offer.

"I disagree but it's okay. Then, you should take The Guide by R.K. Narayan. This is set in south India. All the characters think and speak like us only. You will enjoy it."

After thinking for a few moments, Chikkanna had said, "Tch! Reading about ourselves when we live it every day? It is a waste of time."

Exasperated, Cylinder had forcibly shoved a book into his hand, knocking down his whistle. It was `Casino Royale' by Ian Fleming.

"This is for young men like you. It has everything. Start reading and you will want to be James Bond."

Presently, as they stood, Chikkanna hadn't read a single page. A few weeks had gone by and Cylinder hadn't sold a single book. Yet, both were optimistic and happy in each other's company.

"I haven't seen Huchche Gowda Si ..."

At the very last syllable, Cylinder altered his sentence.

"I haven't seen the Contessa car since that day."

Chikkanna nodded and spoke with the mien of a guru.

"Do you know what happens when you become very big in a small town? You start travelling and meeting big people in big cities. He must have gone out of town. When he comes back, we will know. His car will glide across the signal."

'Chikkanna isn't as dumb as I thought he was.' Cylinder thought and smiled to himself.

They stood comfortably, looking around, without anything to do or talk about. Minutes passed and the silence between them was peppered with the sounds of passing vehicles. In a little over a month, their friendship had become so strong that even when they said nothing to each other for periods of time, neither of them felt conscious.

Cylinder picked up a thread of conversation about the book he had lent to Chikkanna the previous week.

"Do you know what 007 in James Bond stands for?"

Chikkanna shrugged, looking unfamiliar and uninterested. Cylinder pursued the line of talk.

"James Bond has many fancy cars, better than the Contessa. And his driving skills are legendary."

Chikkanna raised his eyebrows fleetingly. Cylinder's hunch was right; possibly the topic of cars and bikes would evince some interest in a traffic constable. He searched his mind for more trivia across books.

Just then, a battered tempo pulled up at the signal, laden with sacks of potatoes and plastic chairs. Even though the signal was green, the driver (a greasy, unkempt, weary-looking man in his late 20s) stopped the vehicle. Cylinder instinctively knew that there was no point trying to sell to him.

Chikkanna greeted him fondly.

"Tempo Tony! All good? Where to?"

With a big, bright smile, he replied, "Here and there, dropping off things as usual. All good with you? Take care. God is great. He'll look after everyone."

Throwing a glance towards Cylinder, he waved at Chikkanna and rolled across the signal just as it turned red.

Chikkanna turned towards Cylinder, eyes big with excitement.

"Tempo Tony! Once upon a time, when I was growing up, when you were not born, he was the James Bond of bikes. Ask us, the old-timers and we will tell you amazing stories of his skills."

Cylinder got highly curious.

'How could a beaten-up looking driver of a beaten-up, awkwardly designed three-wheeler called a tempo be an erstwhile champion rider?'

As his curiosity rose, so did his excitement. For once, he had seen Chikkanna excited; excited about stories, fact or fiction, irrespective of it. If he could get Chikkanna to narrate his story, it meant that Chikkanna could be cracked open to reading stories from the mightiest minds across the world.

Feigning an extra dose of excitement, Cylinder said, "Sounds fascinating. Tell me please."

Between then and evening, between their individual duty calls, between facts and fabrication that had happened over time, Chikkanna relayed the legend of Tempo Tony.

[As a kid, Tony was different from the rest. Given a choice between a visit to the ice cream parlour or the zoo, he would opt for a roadside garage. Automobiles fascinated him. He understood vehicles more than textbooks, ever eager to watch numerous mechanical parts function in unison. He loved the sound of engines and could reproduce them with his mouth quite precisely—Luna, TVS 50, Bajaj M80, Bajaj 150, Hero Puch, Vespa, Yezdi, Ambassador, Fiat, Mahindra tractor. Well, his tongue and vocal chords carried separate lanes for each of them. While other children sang nursery rhymes to neighbours and relatives (at the insistence of their parents), Tony came to be known as the 'mimicry artiste of motor vehicles'.

By the time he was in Class X, he had innately figured out how to disengage parts and put them back again. Compared to people much older than him, he was not only a better reader of bikes but also a better rider, taming two-wheelers at will, making them wheel and kneel any way he liked. Not surprisingly, his academic ride had been punctured all along. Pushing and perspiring, he had managed to reach Class XII. Thankfully, back then, the rules (both traffic and academic) weren't too stringent in Mogga.

After pre-university, some of the boys in his group who belonged to better families came in possession of bikes—Royal Enfield, Yezdi Roadking, Rajdoot 175. But Tony was the master and they happily lent him their bikes so that he could demonstrate what their possessions were capable of. He would conduct 'bike theatre' every now and then. When they would enthusiastically try some of the stunts and end up ruining a part or two, Tony would expertly fix those. They owned the dogs but he was the handler, so to say.

He held the double distinction of being the fastest rider as well as the slowest. He could sit still on a running bike and make it stand still for nearly a minute before losing balance. He would then move it ever so slightly and regain stationary balance, and repeat it till the onlookers got bored or the bike owner had to go home. Among a certain section of the youth in Mogga, he was loved and revered; nothing less than some of the big matinee idols of the time.

Thereafter, life whizzed past him rapidly in fourth gear. After the twelfth standard, a lot of his friends and fans moved on and got busy with other pursuits. They would meet Tony occasionally, reminisce about their sunny days over a cup of shared coffee and at some point, leave hurriedly. His glory days became a fading part of his growing up years when the heart and mind soared over small actions and big thoughts, ignorant of life's realities. He was left idling. His life had turned from a magnificent motorbike to a miserable moped. Fate had dealt him an alliterative downgrade.

He got admission into Raju Mechanic's Garage. He spent hours each day with grease and spanners fixing car tyres and radiators, cleaning carburetors and bike exhausts while humming or whistling popular songs that played from an assembled Blaupunkt system placed on a greasy stool in a corner. Raju Mechanic was a decent employer, and they shared a good rapport. He would lend a hand in the complicated cases but usually left most things in Tony's expert hands. With a sincere and skillful lieutenant to handle the day-to-day, Raju Mechanic stepped onto the next rung of his business ladder, focussing more on trading second-hand vehicles.

After working for four years, Tony had decided to get back on the road. He felt it was liberating to be moving around and listening to songs than being stuck inside a tin shed. With his meagre savings, he had purchased a second-hand tempo and started ferrying anything for anyone.]

Cylinder stood fascinated till Chikkanna completed his story. He then looked towards the traffic junction hoping to catch a sight of the tempo. Chikkanna kept staring at him with a daring look eagerly wanting to hear who among the two (James Bond and Tempo Tony) was the bigger icon. Then, both shook their heads with disbelief and smiled at each other, the kind of smile that two people sometimes indulge in, the kind that's not meant for one another but for a third party.

Cylinder suddenly realised that it was time for him to head back. Both had no idea how and where the afternoon had whizzed past. He bid farewell and crossed the road.

(22)

THE FIRST SALE

Two days later, as the two stood at the signal, Chikkanna suddenly pointed with his eyes and Cylinder turned behind. He saw an elderly man in a crisp, white half-sleeved shirt and a white dhoti walking towards them. His head was covered with white hair, and he had three white lines drawn across his forehead, customary of Tamilian brahmins. He was carrying a white cloth bag with vegetables. Along with that, it looked like he also carried an air of self-importance.

Chikkanna quickly slipped in a sentence before the man came within earshot.
"Don't say anything till he addresses you specifically."
Before Cylinder could process it, the man was next to them. He stood looking at the traffic. Cylinder assumed that he was waiting to cross the road. The signal turned red but the man stood still, surveying the air. Cylinder was confused whereas Chikkanna had a hint of a smile. After a minute or so, the man said, into the air.
"What is wrong with the traffic department, I say!"

Chikkanna didn't respond.

"Tch! Tch! Tch! A traffic signal with a traffic constable? What sense does it make? Shouldn't it be either-or? Or are we paying too much tax?"

He looked squarely at Chikkanna who looked towards the road and so he turned and looked squarely at Cylinder.

"Oh, young fellow! What are you carrying? Books, I see! Have you been put to work, I say!"

Because of Chikkanna's directive, Cylinder had held back his tongue. But now that he had been addressed specifically, he let himself speak.

"Yes. But not by anyone. I decided on this myself.", said Cylinder looking him in the eye.

The elderly man found it impressive and made an expressive face.

"You decided to sell books at a traffic signal? In Mogga? At your age? Where are you from? And where do you want to go? Where have you got these books from? Do you even know what you are carrying?"

Cylinder smiled.

"I come from nothing and I am going towards nothing. In between, if I can get people like you and Chikkanna and many others to read and feel joy, then I would have done something."

The chutzpah of his response blew the elderly man's mind. He stood dazzled for moments where each moment felt like a long-drawn one. Equally astounded by his little friend's powerful words, Chikkanna blew the whistle, not knowing how else to display his appreciation. A few motorists turned towards him wondering who had bent the traffic rules.

"Show me what you've got." The white-haired man said and proceeded to check out the books.

"Airport by Arthur Hailey. I know this fellow. He writes well-researched books. New York, John F. Kennedy Airport, and the snow-storm. Yes. I've read it."

"Lincoln Airport, Chicago." Cylinder corrected him.

The man gave him a hard stare before deftly side-tracking the point.

"Yes! All those airports are named after Presidents. What else do you have? Oh! The Fountainhead. A great book. I only wish the print was bigger. Still, I have read it two and half times already. I like how it ends."

"Then there was only the ocean and the sky and the figure of Howard Roark.", said Cylinder crisply.
"What did you say?"
"That's the last line of the book.", said Cylinder crisply.
The man decided to change the topic from titles to the titles-holder.
"I haven't seen you before. Since when have you been selling books?"
Cylinder gave him a bright, disarming smile.
"Yet to sell. I have been here for some weeks."
The elderly man sympathised.
"It is difficult, little fellow. In a place like Mogga, there are two kinds of people. The ones who don't read at all."
Saying so, he cast a glance towards Chikkanna safely assuming that Chikkanna was a non-reader. Cylinder nodded with amusement and Chikkanna smiled foolishly.
"And the other kind, the ones who read, would have read pretty much everything." He added nonchalantly.
"Have you read The Bourne Identity? It's a recent one. A bestseller."
Cylinder held it up. The man took the book and looked at it.
"Robert Ludlum. Hmmm! Gunnar, my boss from Sweden used to talk about his books. Thrillers, I believe. He is one author I am yet to read. Currently, I am looking for something a little light-hearted."
He bent down and peered at the titles.

Chikkanna hurriedly signalled to Cylinder not to waste his time. Cylinder smiled and signalled back that he was in control. He was not yet sure what to make out of this man who was older than Begur Sir and seemed to know books decently well. He found it invigorating that he had finally met someone who was familiar with them.
"What is a young fellow like you doing with Harold Robbins?" The man looked up at Cylinder.
"The young fellows, the old fellows ... all fellows will like his books.", riposted Cylinder, by now thoroughly enjoying his one-on-one.
"Hmmm! I am too old for his books. But I have had my share of them. What else have you got? Let me see."
He peered at the stack again.
"Ah! P.G. Wodehouse! Now, that's my man. Jolly fellow he is!"
By now, Cylinder was convinced that this man knew his books.

Begur Sir also loved Wodehouse. He would regularly read out lines from his books, tell him tidbits about the man, explain his writing and wit. So much so that Cylinder had been fooled by a particular quote of his and it had taken Begur some explaining to make him understand what Wodehouse had meant. Upon clarity, Cylinder had liked it to the point of memorising it. He decided to unleash it on the elderly man.

"Yes. P.G. Wodehouse. He started writing before he was five years old."

The elderly man looked at Cylinder unsurely.

"Nonsense! P.G. Wodehouse is great but this is total nonsense. Before five years? Before the age of five, he must have been writing ABCD!"

Cylinder patiently heard him out and then added sincerely, "He has himself said it."

"What has he said?", said the half-sleeved-white-shirt man, a little worked up.

Cylinder paused, maintained his veil of sincerity and quoted P.G. Wodehouse.

"I know I was writing stories when I was five. I don't remember what I did before that. Just loafed, I suppose."

The elderly man stood confused, fooled as thoroughly as Cylinder had been. Not wanting to push it further, Cylinder broke into a big, silly grin.

"P.G. Wodehouse is great. His books, and his quotes."

It slowly dawned on him. His smugness left him, looked in either direction and crossed the road. With a weak smile, he patted Cylinder's back.

"How do you know so much about books?"

"I have spent all my life with them.", said Cylinder.

"He is Begur Sir's boy.", chipped in Chikkanna.

"Oh ho ho ho! Now, I get it. Very nice. Good to meet you. What's your name, son?"

"Cylinder.", said Cylinder.

The elderly man was stumped again, with this most unusual name. But by now, he was so unsure of this child that he decided not to question him further. Instead, he introduced himself.

"People call me ISV."

"Nice to meet you, ISV Sir. So, what have you decided on?"
"You tell me what I should read."
Cylinder looked at his stack, thought and held up `One Hundred Years of Solitude'.
"Have you read this?"
"Gabriel Garcia Marquez. No, strangely I haven't heard of this author."
"Oh! Then you must. It's not light reading but it's the right reading for someone of your intelligence. Begur Sir says it is a must-read."
Trusting the boy's judgement, ISV took the book.
"How much?"
"Only twenty rupees, ISV Sir."
"That's all? Let me give you twenty-five rupees. You deserve it."
"Not a penny more, not a penny less." Cylinder said and smiled.
ISV shook his head rapidly to rearrange its insides. Handing over twenty rupees, he thanked Cylinder, picked up his bag of vegetables and slowly walked off. After a few steps, he turned around and threw a glance at the little fellow and saw Cylinder re-adjusting his stack.

Chikkanna blew the whistle thrice to celebrate the first sale. Some motorists and pedestrians slowed down and looked in odd directions. Then, the two looked at each other with smiles as wide as the footpath.
"Litttle felllow! Nowww, you have become biggg!", said Chikkanna beaming, stressing on all the right alphabets for emphasis.
After managing to swallow his smile, Cylinder asked, "Who is this man, ISV? Do you know him?"
"He's a good old uncle who thinks he is the big boss of Mogga. Ha ha ha ha ha! Not by money, but by mind. He takes himself so seriously that a lot of us find him funny. But you were something else today."
Chikkanna's attention suddenly got diverted as he spotted an ice-candy seller on a tricycle near the signal.
"Oye, Vasu! Give two orange candies. I am treating Cylinder today. He is a cool fellow."
Slurping on ice candy, the two continued to speak about the big moment, re-enacted parts of the exchange with ISV and laughed.
Suddenly, Cylinder got a little thoughtful.
"Today is a big day. And it's not even midday. I have the rest of the day. Who knows? I might end up selling more today. At the same time, I am

also very eager to run home and break the big news to Begur Sir. He will be so happy! What should I do, Chikkanna? I am confused."

"Do that. Now that you've sold your first book, you'll sell more. You have your entire life. Go!"

For the first time, Cylinder was home before lunchtime. Begur looked up from his desk and looked surprised. His parents looked towards the farm gate and were thrilled. Lunch was almost ready but then Begur's mother decided to make payasam, a regional sweet delicacy. They sat down for a hearty, happy meal, hearing Cylinder's story in all its smallest details.

"So, how was the first sale?", asked Begur.

"It was challenging, took time, but I enjoyed it.", said Cylinder.

Begur stood up and for the first time in his life, served food. He served a ladle of payasam into Cylinder's bowl.

"Cylinder! This is for the first sale."

He then served a second helping.

"And this, Cylinder, is for the first sale being that of Gabriel Garcia Marquez."

(23)

PERCENTAGE RAVI

It was mid-morning on a Wednesday. Cylinder was standing at the traffic signal with his stack of books. To be precise, he was standing while his books sat on the pavement. He had kept the pile down since there was sparse traffic. `Fountainhead' sat right on top as it was smaller in size (not thickness) compared to the rest he was carrying. For now, Cylinder stood alone.

Chikkanna had informed him the previous day that he would arrive late since he had to take his mother on her annual pilgrimage. Chikkanna had meant it as a joke. Of course, he was blessed with his own sense of humour, as is every person. The pilgrimage was a trip to the Syndicate Bank. Once a year, his mother had to appear in person in front of the bank manager and sign a few documents so that she would continue to receive her late husband's pension.

To while away time, Cylinder decided to indulge in one of his pastimes. He pulled out a scrap of paper from his shorts pocket, smoothened it and stared at the exotic, lengthy name: Alissa

Zinovievna Rosenbaum. He began trying to memorise it, breaking it down into manageable parts as per the convenience of his tongue. Though he kept faltering each time, he seemed hopeful. It was a peculiar pursuit, a useless one. Remembering this name would make no difference whatsoever to his life or that of others. But strangely, it made him feel special. If he could possess this trivia, it was riches that even the most well-read or the wealthy wouldn't own. Clearly, this was an eccentricity that he had picked up from his master — Begur, the Master of Oddities.

Several months earlier, Begur had been telling Cylinder about one of the most popular and powerful books, `Fountainhead', a masterpiece, no less. Cylinder was agog all through as Begur spoke vividly and vivaciously. At the end of it, Begur, with a smile that reflected an obscure joy, had said, "Cylinder, what a piece of work! I hope you read it someday, and make several people in Mogga read it too. And here's something else that you'll enjoy. The world knows her as Ayn Rand but not many people know her real name, Alissa Zinovievna Rosenbaum."

Begur had then beamed like a child. Cylinder had been equally fascinated, with the cake as well as the icing. He had requested Begur to write it down so that he could memorise it.

He heard the familiar sound of a moped approaching the signal, looked up to his right and saw Percentage Ravi. Sputtering to a halt, Percentage Ravi greeted him and said matter-of-factly, "Chikkanna will be late today. He's at Syndicate Bank. Today, the queue is at least 13% longer."

Cylinder smiled back knowingly.

"So, Cylinder, what percentage of books have you managed to sell this week?", asked Percentage Ravi matter-of-factly.

Cylinder managed to hold his giggle and responded that the week was still young and barren. The two of them chitchatted for a while as the traffic lights went about their monotonous loop of duty.

The town had numerous people named Ravi but the most well-known was Percentage Ravi. No one addressed him by his moniker; they simply called him Ravi. But in any third-party conversation, if there ever was a reference-confusion and someone asked, "Which

Ravi are you talking about?", the responses were always pivoted around him:

"Not Percentage Ravi! I am talking about Giridhar's son, Ravi."

"I am talking about Percentage Ravi only. Every day, who else covers the length and breadth of Mogga three times more than the city bus?"

Though he wasn't accomplished in any sense, physically or intellectually, he had become a frame of reference as far as the name was concerned. Every now and then, in conversations across the town, his name would crop up, sometimes accompanied by:

"But why is he called Percentage Ravi?"

[Growing up, Ravi had been a dud. His highest score in any subject was a measly 49 percent. That too, just once; a miraculous aberration. In 14 years of academics, he had never hit the halfway mark. His norm was leading the ascending order in every class he was a part of. On some occasions, his percentage had been lesser than his shoe size. Some people in the town surmised that his prefix was a result of his depth-defying scores, but that wasn't true.

The only child of a Syndicate Bank clerk, he had always been happy-go-lucky while his father had always been a worried man. At the age of 18, Ravi had somehow managed to scrape through his pre-university exams. His father had sat through 33 years of banking career and now stood face-to-face with retirement. A die-hard Syndicate Bank enthusiast, his dream was to see his son land a job in this hallowed institution. He would have been overjoyed if Ravi could clear the Bank Clerk Exams but his track record delivered no hope. So, he had sat Ravi down and charted his future.

"Son, God has a plan for everyone. So does Syndicate Bank."

There was a way Ravi could work for the bank without clearing any exam. His father spoke about an amazing, life-altering concept that Syndicate bank had pioneered, and rounded off with, "You will do extremely well as a Pigmy Collector."

Years earlier, the bank had introduced the Pigmy Deposit Scheme, a savings plan for petty traders, shopkeepers and daily wage earners. The aim was to help inculcate saving habits to fund their future requirements: weddings, buying a moped, expanding business etc. It was a well-thought-out social experiment. Money, as little as five rupees could be deposited on a daily basis. But the unique characteristic of this scheme was that a bank agent collected the money daily from the account holder's doorstep. Syndicate Bank had been looking for more foot soldiers. Ravi had accepted the idea wholeheartedly. He felt it was a novel profession, a noble one even. His father had happily bought him a Suvega, a nondescript, not-so-popular, low-on-maintenance but a hardy 50cc moped that ran around effortlessly as long as its rider wanted to.

Ravi, along with two other fresh recruits had attended a training session at one of the branches. The bank manager had spoken about life (ups and downs, present and future), money (earnings, expenses, savings, investment, inflation, growth), and their role in helping people manage these two inextricably linked concepts. Naturally, the word `percentage' had cropped up time and again. For once, Ravi had been the most attentive in class. He was drawn to both, the subject and the speaker. The veteran manager had proceeded to talk about what it required to be a successful Pigmy Collector.

"If you don't meet your target every day, your target will never meet his target."

In one word, it was `diligence' and this had filled Ravi with pride and purpose.

Ravi had walked out feeling several times taller than what a part of his job title meant. Since that day, his conversations about anything had begun to carry a high percentage of this very word.

"Today, there's less salt in the sambar. But it's okay, mom. One can always increase the percentage but cannot reduce it."

"Dad, your percentage of white hairs has gone up considerably. It's time for you to retire and relax. Now, that I have a good job, I will take care of everything."

Within a couple of months, the town had begun referring to him as Percentage Ravi. Soon enough, he had heard about it. Rather than feeling peeved, he had felt good. Percentage was an important part of life, and he was determined to grow its significance even more.

The other unusual thing about Ravi was that he was blessed with `zero percent' ego. As in academics, his natural ability in matters of ego was the poorest. He never felt any snub, however incidental or intentional. Perhaps this was karmic but it was this trait that made him the most qualified for the job, more than anybody. He would reach his target's place of business, smile, make small talk, tell tall tales, gossip with whoever had time to spare, wait his turn patiently, collect a small amount, bestow wishes, and fix up time for the next day. Very early on, he understood the strange reluctance that people felt while handing over money despite having decided on wanting to save, invest and grow it. They would prioritise work over him. Everyone felt that earning was more important than saving.

Javra, the cobbler, did this with alarming regularity. He would make Ravi wait till he had repaired a hard sole, which took time. But Ravi would have no qualms. He would lean against his moped humming a movie song (or a kirthana) depending on his mood, or sit peacefully on the footpath next to Javra, watching him mend a piece of cheap footwear.

His profession demanded that he meet several people every single day. From half past ten in the morning till seven in the evening, he zipped across the town meeting his targets. They were of all sorts: tonga owners, mechanics, arecanut traders, pani puri vendors, paan shop owners, notaries, a few priests, a butcher, an idol maker, tempo drivers, cobblers, tailors etc.

One of his most unusual customers was a pickpocket. That was his side business, known only to his close friends and Ravi. His main activity included selling movie tickets, lottery tickets and last-minute bus tickets to Sabrimala, the venerated temple town in Kerala. Warped though it was, the pickpocket had his own logic for being Ravi's customer.

"There is one simple rule in life. Money never stays in the owner's pocket. Every time I pick a pocket, I become the owner of that money, and the rule applies to me as well. I spend it on unwanted things. It is better to give it to you so that someday, I can stop picking pockets."

Time went by and Percentage Ravi unwaveringly stuck to his template of life, without burden or boredom. Every morning, he would head out feeling as excited as he had been on the first day of his career. He would do his usual rounds and in between also meet potential customers with this line:

"What percentage of your daily earnings are you saving?"

He was always seen crisscrossing the town, humming, smiling, waving at and wishing anyone he went past. On a regular basis, he met more people than the local legislator. As a common sight to the townsfolk, Percentage Ravi was perhaps second only to Cylinder. One stood in the same place every single day while the other flitted around nonstop. In the bigger scheme of things, both were as insignificant as an atom but equally fundamental too. Begur had once told Cylinder that he was the nucleus, and Percentage Ravi, the electron of Mogga.]

Cylinder and Ravi heard the familiar sound of Tony's tempo. It clattered to a halt at the signal. They exchanged greetings. Tempo Tony fished out a crumpled 5-rupee note from his greasy pocket and handed it over to Percentage Ravi.

"Here is today's Pigmy. I am heading to Navile to bring back 300 kilos of clay for the Ganpati season. I'll be late."

The signal turned green. Tempo Tony inched forward after nodding a goodbye with his Colgate smile. His teeth were the only part, of him and his tempo, that had retained its original lustre. Percentage Ravi smiled back warmly at his childhood classmate, and now his customer.

"Cylinder, life has its own plans for everyone. Look at Tony! When we were growing up, all of us wanted to be like him."

As a matter of habit, he checked the time on his HMT watch and started his moped.

"I have to be at Ikram's Butcher Shop in five minutes. I'll see you later."

(24)

WOE IS ME!

Cylinder raised his stack to cover his eyes from the sharp glint of the sun. It was mid-morning on a hot summer day, the sort of day that tested the poise of people whose livelihood depended on outdoor work. For Cylinder, it had nothing to do with earning. Rather, it was the yearning to spread the joy of reading among his unenthusiastic populace. After the first sale, life hadn't been fair to him. Despite his earnestness, he hadn't managed to sell anything. While he stood physically at the signal, emotionally he stood somewhere in between on the scale of `isms'. From optimism, he had slid towards its unsavoury adversary and was currently in that tricky in-between region: scepticism.

Holding the stack up hurt his arms more than the sunrays hurt his dartful eyes. As he lowered his arms, his eyes froze.

Across the road, he saw a most unusual sight. A boy, roughly his age, a shade taller, stood with a stack of books. The signal turned red, a few motorists stopped but Cylinder could not take his eyes off the boy.

After what seemed like several minutes, the honk of a passing moped registered in his brain, and it resumed its functioning. Cylinder stared hard at the stack the boy carried. Squinting his eyes, he tried to guess the titles that occupied the boy's hands. Starting from the bottom of the pile, he moved his eyes up, one book at a time. The books looked larger and thinner, leaving Cylinder confused. His eyes then moved up to the boy's face. It looked cheery, lit up, just the way Cylinder's own face lit up every time he held good literature. For once, Cylinder could not read his own mood. He paused, reflected and stood confused.

Logically, his instinct said that he ought to be happy; that he needed to be encouraging as well as feel encouraged. In the history of this humble town, he had been the only one who had chosen this most daunting and odd vocation. And now, here was another boy following in his footsteps. Tomorrow, there would be a third. And then another, followed by many more—young boys and girls, young adults, grown-ups, retirees, the well-to-do, the failures of the town—all sorts of people standing at corners with stacks of books of their choice, selling to hundreds of avid readers. In a hundred years from now, the people of Mogga could well be heard saying occasionally, "Oh, Cylinder! It all started with him. Our own little literary prophet."

He looked away from the boy, rather disturbed. He carried a strange concoction of emotions in no particular order: anger, envy, sadness. His thoughts were as haphazard as the traffic in the town. Placing his books on the pavement, Cylinder interlocked his fingers and stretched his arms in the direction of the boy. He wanted to take a closer look at the titles. The moment the signal turned red, he darted across the road.

"Ay! What are you selling? How come? Just like that? Do you know the names of the authors, and their works? And, what's your name?"

The boy's answer to everything was a mere smile even as Cylinder looked at his stack and frowned. He was carrying a stack of magazines—weeklies, monthlies, fortnightlies, in English and the vernacular.

"Huh! These are magazines, not books." Cylinder muttered allowing himself a half-smile.

"What's the point of standing at the signal with magazines?" He posed with authority.

"People need to read.", said the boy.

"Of course, they need to! But they should be reading literature! Works of the finest minds on the planet, not magazines!", rasped Cylinder uncharacteristically.

"That's for the people to decide." The boy said with a full smile.

The signal turned red again. Leaving the red-faced Cylinder, the boy stepped onto the road, peddling magazines to motorists.

"Mirror, The Week, SportStar, India Today, Sudha, Taranga, Woman's Era, Femina, Cine Blitz. Full timepass! Take it, take it!"

A few motorists glanced at the magazines with familiarity and interest.

"Waste of time! Waste of time! Don't waste your money!", yelled Cylinder from behind. "I have real books. On the other side."

He darted back to his stack.

An hour later, three quarters past noon, the traffic had lessened. The sun was feasting on the asphalt. Cylinder was sweaty and felt subtracted. His normal effervescent self had evaporated and he knew it wasn't the sun's doing. He sat under the tree and opened his tiffin box. Biting into a sandwich, he glanced across the road. The boy put down his stack of magazines, sat under a tree, opened his tiffin box, pulled out a sandwich and cheerily waved at Cylinder. Cylinder wavered momentarily and didn't wave back. He was having a confused day.

At this moment, a pedestrian walked past the boy, paused, walked back a couple of steps and looked at the magazines. Sandwich in one hand, the boy spread his stack with the other. Moments later, the pedestrian bent down, picked up a magazine, pulled out a note from his bush-shirt pocket, paid the boy and walked off.

Across the road, a swirl of thoughts arose.

`Which one? English or vernacular? Current affairs or a movie magazine? A weekly or a monthly? Tch! Whichever! How does it matter? That pedestrian is silly! Wasting his money and time on writing that's fit for serving savoury snacks by street cart vendors! Instead, he could have walked down my side of the road and bought something that would be worthy of bequeathing.'

As he bit into the sandwich, his thoughts let go of the boy and focussed on it. He enjoyed the meal, followed by a glug of lemonade. Refreshed, he felt less regretful about the boy and spoke to himself, as a neutral umpire.

`Cylinder, why should you bother about him peddling pedestrian writing to pedestrians? If they indeed have value, wouldn't Begur Sir dedicate several shelves to them? Let him sell his read-and-throw magazines. Here today, gone tomorrow. Both, the boy, and his books ... I mean, I didn't mean books. Books are those that carry mankind forward. And books are what you are carrying. Settled? Now, finish the rest of the lemonade and get ready before traffic picks up.'

He turned into his old self again. With gusto, he picked up his stack of books and stood, waiting for motorists to stop. On the other side, the boy displayed sloth. Despite his meal break, he continued to sit on the pavement, in the shade.

Over the next hour, several groups of motorists stopped and sped away. Not one carried even a dull curiosity about the goldmine that Cylinder was carrying.

"Woe is me! Sigh! Alas! Woe is me!" Cylinder uttered and smiled.

On days that he couldn't sell a single book, Cylinder would resort to this mantra to humour himself and keep his enthusiasm intact.

Sometime in the third week of his new life as a bookseller, when he hadn't managed to sell even one, he had gone back utterly demoralised. That evening, Begur Sir had spoken to him at length.

"Cylinder, you've chosen your calling. And you say this is what gives you joy. That's beautiful. But remember, there will be several days, even weeks when you'll find none. You'll feel tired and troubled, three times over. But you cannot let that derail your ride. In such moments, what do you do?"

Begur had paused before elaborating.

"Just tell yourself, `Woe is me!' Do you know what it means?"

Before Cylinder could shake his head, Begur had said, "It is from Shakespearean times. It is an over-dramatic, often comical way to express sadness or disappointment at an unfair situation. Say this to yourself to turn mild tragedy into mild comedy. Sigh, breathe, and get

back to your purpose."
Instantly, Cylinder had loved the sound and the sense of it. That night, he had gone to bed with his secret weapon, uttering it several times and smiling in the darkness.

A couple of days later, a gang of four loutish teenagers astride a motorbike were seen approaching the signal. They clearly looked like mischief-mongers. They were passing through that age (the stage between obedience and grown-up responsibility) when the only idea of fun is at the expense of others. Chikkanna had his back to them, busy helping an old woman with directions.

"Chikkanna! Oye Chikkanna!" Two out of the four had yelled.

Chikkanna had turned around instinctively.

"Four by two! Four by two!" All four had yelled, cackled like hyenas and gone past the red signal. This was the local way of saying: `Four people on two wheels.'

Chikkanna had blown his whistle hard and run after them in vain. Fuming and cursing, he had come back to his spot. This idiotic prank had happened a third time in a week and he was frothing. Cylinder had realised that there was no logical response to this: the senselessness of youth and Chikkanna's helplessness.

The best one could do in in this situation was not get worked up but laugh it off.

He had then supplied his magic mantra.

"Chikkanna, just say `Woe is me' and smile. Nothing else."

Chikkanna's frothy expression had turned into a frown while Cylinder had sported a knowing smile.

At present, Cylinder had the same knowing smile but couldn't sustain it. He saw another man buy a magazine off the boy who continued to sit in a sloppy posture. Within half an hour, three more magazines had flown off the pavement. Soon thereafter, two more pedestrians stopped and bought magazines.

By early evening, the boy, despite any interest or effort, had managed to sell all his magazines except one. He decided to call it a day. Picking up his tiffin box and water bottle, he crossed the road, walked up to Cylinder and handed him the magazine.

"Here! Please keep this book. My gift to you. You've been such wonderful company."
Smiling, he turned around and darted across the road.
Several moments passed. A minute, no less. Cylinder stood with a blank mind, magazine in hand.
`Woe is me!' He thought but couldn't get himself to utter it.
The day had gone beyond, way beyond the potency of his mantra.
Deeply disturbed, he hurriedly dumped his books into his bag, buckled it, hoisted it, picked up his lunch bag and left without bidding goodbye to Chikkanna who had gone to relieve himself.

Begur was at his desk, reading. He looked up and saw Cylinder flounce through the farm gate, up to the house.
"The boy and his walk don't go hand in hand.", remarked Begur to himself and smiled.
Cylinder stormed up the staircase, entered The Airport and sat glumly on the chair. After several beats, Begur turned around to look at him. Cylinder was sitting head down, magazine in hand.
"What ails thou today?", enquired Begur using an outmoded phrase.
Cylinder held up the magazine.
As Begur looked at him questioningly, Cylinder burst forth narrating the events of the day, with special emphasis on things that were troubling him.
"What does it take to sell magazines? Spread, sit, sprawl and sell? Is that how literature gets sold? Tch! Does the seller even know what he's selling? Does he know about all the stories inside? Does he know if they are worth reading?"
He paused for breath, and it did seem that he wasn't finished yet but Begur took over and addressed the room.
"All ye masters! Did you hear that?"
Looking around the room, he made eye contact with every shelf.
"Today, a wonderful thing called `life' happened to Cylinder. The very `thing' that you've all drawn your stories from. For the first time, he experienced competition. Even better, he lost. He now knows that life will forever not be a dreamy, rosy world."
He then smiled at Cylinder who responded with a scowl.
"I am more pained than troubled.", said Cylinder.

"And what's caused that?", enquired Begur.

"How can people prefer magazines over books? What depths of the mind does a magazine article explore? How can the wit of Mark Twain and P.G. Wodehouse lose out to information and news? How can everyday writing be more popular than brilliant writing? This is not fair!"

Cylinder's eyes carried more hurt than his words conveyed. Begur sat back in his chair carrying a smile wide enough to touch the armrests.

"The best doesn't always win. Some of the finest writers have found no recognition, no purchase. They have spent a lifetime living a thousand deaths, surrounded by successes of mediocrity. Whoever said life is fair? A lot of the time, it isn't, Cylinder."

Cylinder relaxed his scowl while Begur did the same with his exaggerated smile.

They looked their normal selves again.

"You are merely a seller of their work. If you feel so pained, imagine how broken they would have been? It pains me too but that's life and you learn to live with reality."

Cylinder listened intently as Begur carried on.

"Writers! The choosers of the loneliest profession that I know of. A pursuit glorious enough to push the mind beyond one's own assumed limitations, and at the same time, cruel enough to squeeze one's heart and throw it into a dustbin of despair. Hemingway captured the travail of a writer with these masterful words:

There is nothing to writing. All you do is sit at a typewriter and bleed."

Begur paused to let the words worm their way down Cylinder's young mind.

"Cylinder! In my opinion, a writer needs to be as foolhardy as a rock climber. One chooses to conquer a sheer blank wall, and the other, a blank page. And, if it doesn't work out, one is fortunate to have a sudden, painful death. The other, on the other hand …"

"… neither dies nor lives." Cylinder promptly completed the sentence and smiled.

He no longer felt troubled or pained by what had transpired. He was joyful again. Whether it was Hemingway or the rock climber, one knows not but the magic of writers filled his mind and body with tiny spasms of reverence and delight.

"Wash up and eat something.", said Begur.

A lively Cylinder stood up and the magazine fell from his lap. He picked it up and flipped through the pages.

"Begur Sir, do you know what a magazine contains?"

He didn't say it as a question for which he was looking for an answer. Instead, he posed it in a way such that he would provide it.

Begur looked at him curiously.

With the authority of a best-selling author or a notable critic, Cylinder told Begur, "Magazine writers. They are like hill trekkers. Who knows? One or two of them might become champion rock climbers in the future. I will wait for that day. And from tomorrow, I look forward to seeing that magazine boy."

He smiled, turned around and began to walk towards the staircase.

"Sorry, Cylinder. I hired that boy only for a day."

Cylinder stopped dead in his tracks, turned around and looked at Begur with marble-wide eyes.

"Now, I am convinced that nothing will crush your spirit.", remarked Begur with a wry smile.

Cylinder burst into a spirited laughter, ran back to Begur and hugged him.

"Begur Sir, you are the best."

(25)

SCIENCE OF THE SIGNS

"Hello Shastriji!" Chikkanna wished the man who crossed the road and walked towards him. "That's a lot of files you are carrying."
"You know the amount of paperwork involved in buying a house.", replied Shastriji.
"But I thought you already have a house.", said Chikkanna looking surprised.
"I do. I am in the process of buying one more. Might as well when one can and give it out on rent. Who knows what the future holds?", replied Shastriji.
Chikkanna laughed with a shake of his head.
"Nice joke, Shastriji. If you don't know the future, who does?"
"Where is Cylinder? His books are here."
"Nature's call. He'll be here any minute." Chikkanna said, suddenly standing to attention as a traffic department jeep went past.
Shastriji looked closely at the stack of books.
"Two weeks ago, Cylinder had promised me a book. A magical book,

he had said. Since I was headed this way to the Registrar's Office, I thought of checking on it."

He had barely finished his sentence when Cylinder came running, full of beans.

"Hello Shastriji! I have been waiting for you for three days."

[Shastriji was primarily a palmist, a sought-after one. No one knew where he had acquired his knowledge but a lot of people believed in him. This lot was divided into two lots. The first, fewer in numbers, were the rich. With much at stake, they were always eager to know what their future held; how much bigger would they get, what pitfalls stood, sat or slept in wait. The other lot, big in numbers, were the not so-well-to-do from Mogga and the numerous villages around. With not much in hand, they always hoped that their `tomorrow' would be rosy. So, while some bet on lottery tickets, some landed up at Shastriji's feet, handing over money and their palms to him.

He had an interesting pricing plan: Five to Fifty. He foretold a person's future starting with five years and going up to fifty years, in multiples of five. He charged accordingly—five rupees for five years, ten for ten ... fifty for fifty. He had been asked about it on numerous occasions, and his response:

"It's taken me years of study. There's no point in applying my knowledge for anything less than five years. And if somebody can predict what can or will happen after fifty years, it's better to read a science fiction book than let me read your palm."

To most people, even the rich, this made him come across as erudite as well as unpretentious. It lent more credence to his craft.

While people opted for different packages based on their levels of curiosity and hope, most of the rich went for the maximum. Not just that, but they also displayed addictive behaviour. Despite knowing what he would have foretold, a lot of them would come back a year or two later and go for the maximum again, so that they would know their future by an extra year or two. He had been doing this for eighteen years but had gained a sizeable reputation since the past seven. Some of his critics used to say that his past was as sketchy as the future he foretold, but that hadn't dimmed his reputation or business.

Unlike some people in this trade, he didn't come from a lineage of palmists. His father had been a clerk in the Public Works Department. Shastriji had been a decent student and had finished his matriculation. He could have studied further and landed a government job but there were two things he had always disliked. One was a strange irritation with anyone telling him what to do. He much rather preferred being the teller. His other issue was with having to work for an entire month before seeing money. He would often think about it and get into discussions with friends.

"What happens if I work hard every single day and die on the 30th of the month? You say my family will get the money but how will I know it?"

At this point, the discussion would always get metaphysical, which most of his friends abstained from. The crazy confluence of his two primary issues had led him towards palmistry.

He could have chosen from several other options—a petty trader, a priest or something else. He had felt that being a trader was below his ego. His grandfather had been a priest and hence, this had conveniently sat on his career-choice list as soon as he was born. But priests only spoke about the past and he was a forward-looking chap. Also, scriptures and scruples were not his biggest strengths. Palmistry was a good combination of science and art, intelligence with intuition. Plus, he was good at talking, listening, and wasn't averse to reading.

He had then taken to books and articles about the subject. He had visited over forty palmists, all over the region to get his palms read. Observing their practices and preferences, questioning them at length, even borrowing books from a few of them, he had understood the basics and more.

Some chose to read the right palm for males, and the left one for females. They believed that the right hand symbolised Shiva and the left, his consort, Parvati or Shakti. The Chinese did the exact opposite with some logic of their own. Some were adamant that both palms had to be read since the left is what God gives us and the right is what we do with it—destiny and potential. He understood the variances between what was widely followed in the South Vs. North Vs. Chinese, traditionalists Vs. modernists etc. He had read up on the lines (head, heart, life) types of hands (earth, air, water, fire) the mounts, and finger shapes. He realised that there wasn't much to it yet enough to interpret, and more importantly, enough leeway to make people interpret it in many ways. He had launched himself as a palmist and after the initial struggle, had done more than well.]

A few weeks earlier, he had met Cylinder for the first time. After a brief, mundane conversation with Chikkanna, he had been introduced to Cylinder.

Shastriji had been eager to know why he was doing what he was doing. He had also checked out the list of titles without saying anything or buying anything. But that had been good enough for Cylinder; he had at least spent time looking at books. Chikkanna had obviously filled him in on Shastriji's background after he had departed.

During their second meeting, Shastriji had asked Cylinder to place the books down and show him his palms. After studying them for a while, he had turned to Chikkanna and said cryptically, "One day, this boy will stand head and shoulders above everyone else in Mogga."
When Chikkanna had extended his hands for a gratis reading, Shastriji had told him, "You come home and choose from the package."

Naturally, Cylinder had gone home and spoken about him to Begur. When Cylinder had told him about Shastriji's prophecy, Begur had mumbled that even at the moment, Cylinder stood head and shoulders above everyone else in Mogga. He had dismissed palmistry as a pseudo-science but had acknowledged the fact that the palmist was an intelligent mind. Anyone who showed even a remote interest in books was intelligent in his books.

A few days later, Begur had some news for Cylinder.
"There's a book that your palmist friend might be interested in. I would never read it and hence don't have it. But I can order a copy. It's not about palmistry but a related science if one can call it that. Tell him it's about sun signs. Also, tell him that it's the first book on astrology to feature in the New York Times Bestseller List, if that means anything to him. Check and let me know."
"Begur Sir, go ahead and order. I know he'll love it."
"Done. I'll call Selvaraj right away. And one more thing. Give it to him for free. He likes to read, whatever his kind may be."

When Cylinder met Shastriji a few days later, he had communicated this, and that had set the palmist's mind in motion. In the recent past, he had anyway been thinking of adding to his repertoire.
'Why just palms? Why not horoscopes? That will bring in more people. Plus, there are linkages between the two. Why not utilise my reputation in one to rub off on the other?'

"Please tell Begur Sir to get me a copy. I am willing to pay double the price. Tell him it's a business investment. He will understand." He had emphatically told Cylinder.

The book had arrived and Cylinder had been waiting impatiently for Shastriji.

He now pulled it out of his bag and handed it over to him.

"Shastriji, here is Linda Goodman's Sun Signs."

Shastriji took the fat book, flipped the pages, nodded and thanked Cylinder.

"How much do I pay you?"

Cylinder smiled and shook his head.

"Shastriji, you didn't take money from me to read the lines on my palms. How can I take money from you for reading lines in a book?"

As Shastriji walked away slowly, immersed in the back cover, Cylinder threw in a tidbit for good measure.

"Shastriji! Linda Goodman's sun sign is Aries."

(26)

ROBOT

Chikkanna sat on the plastic chair with his legs folded awkwardly and uncomfortably. Cradling the big steel plate in the ill-formed cavity of his laps, he feasted on rice pancakes. Between mouthfuls, he told his mom, Shantamma, that he would have one more, the fifth and final. She knew him inside out, already halfway into getting it ready, muttering that hopefully someday her food would show on his body. A traffic constable who looked like a traffic signal pole didn't sit right in her head. Perhaps, hours of being on his feet every day sucked the strength out of him. Also, he was only twenty-one and had always been small and wiry, unlike his late father.

[His father, Manjunatha Gowda had been a squat, potbellied man with a *Mahishasura* moustache. He had spent years in the traffic department. The errant riders of Mogga, prone to breaking traffic rules called him *Meese Mama* (*Meese* was moustache and a cop was often referred to as *Mama* in jest.) They would always look out for him whenever they intended to bend or break rules.

He looked domineering but was an affable man, usually letting off the offenders with a firm warning, followed by a big smile. Other than traffic rules, he was particular about only one thing. He was a mutton maniac.

"Make some mutton and anything else you want to." He would tell his wife every day.

Clearly, his salary did not allow him this extravagance. Tasked with managing the household with his not-so-handsome income, she would often tell him, "If you at least alternate between chicken and mutton, we can save some money."

Manjunatha disliked chicken. In fact, he disavowed it.

"Shantamma! Chicken is nursery school. Mutton is Ph.D."

His big boss, Mr. Alva, DCP (Traffic) had joked about him once at a departmental function. "Each one of us is born with a belly button. But Manjunatha is born with a belly mutton!"

All those assembled had laughed till their bellies had ached. Manjunatha had grinned and patted his big stomach. He had been genuinely happy to be at the receiving end of this joke, that too from a big man. To him, it demonstrated that he stood for something, other than merely managing traffic.

About three years earlier to the day, Manjunatha was at the Clock Tower managing the traffic; a menagerie of dawdling carts and tempos, zig-zagging mopeds and stagnant cows. All of a sudden, he was no more. His signal had turned red permanently. He had suffered a massive cardiac arrest. The defined set of events had played out—lamentation, commiserations and funeral rites. After a period of mourning, the wife and son stood face-to-face with their new reality. Chikkanna was eighteen years old and had finished his first year B.Com. Now, in the new scheme of things, they knew that the family's balance sheet would not tally. He would have to start earning immediately. But with a one-third degree, how and where would he land a respectable and secure job? Fate had dealt a cruel blow and perhaps feeling remorseful, immediately extended a helping hand. Since Manjunatha had died on duty, the traffic department offered Chikkanna a job. At an age when most of his friends and classmates were still studying, he became a figure of authority on the streets of Mogga. Once in a while, when he spotted a friend or two riding past him, he would deliberately blow his whistle, unnerve them momentarily, laugh heartily and get merrily sworn at.]

Shantamma served Chikkanna the fifth pancake, and a helping of chutney.

"If your father was around, he would have had mutton curry with pancakes too. It's a blessing you haven't taken after him."

Chikkanna finished his breakfast, placed the empty plate on the plastic stool and got up to wash his hands. Shantamma had already pressed his starchy white shirt and coarse khaki trousers. Picking up his plate, she shook her head with mild irritation and a great deal of concern.

"At least, keep the plate in the kitchen. Who will manage your household work in the future? Who will look after you when I am gone? I pray every day that you get someone who cares for you as much as I do. But life is only about hope and not guarantees. I want you to make a habit of at least doing your chores."

Unlike his mellow character, Chikkanna responded with farsighted confidence.

"Don't worry, mother! Like every other mother! You are Chikkanna's mother and Chikkanna will be taken care of!"

She retorted in the same vein, referring to herself in third person.

"Chikkanna's mother will always be worried about Chikkanna! What if your wife turns out to be a sloth, just like you? I want to at least make sure that you get into the habit of taking care of your daily tasks."

Chikkanna realised she was in one of her tetchy moods and tried to comfort her that his life was going to be fine.

"Don't worry, mother! Robot will be there to take care of everything!" He said matter-of-factly.

"Who?"

"Robot!"

"Who is that?"

"Hmmm! Automatic man, made of steel or aluminium. I will tell robot and he will do everything."

Shantamma looked as blank as the pan on the stove.

As Chikkanna was looping his khaki canvas belt, she rasped, "Why are you talking like you have had toddy early in the morning?"

From a deflective response in the informal conversation, Chikkanna got a little more actively involved. He searched his mind for the name that Cylinder had mentioned. After groping for a bit, tossing around different combinations in his head, he said confidently, "Hisack Hasimov! Genius! He says that in the future, robots will do all the work for us. Cylinder told me."

"Who told you what?"

"Oh ho! You don't understand anything, mother! Cylinder is a bookseller at the traffic signal where I stand. He keeps telling me amazing things. He told me about Hisack Hasimov and showed me his books. You can't imagine how our future will be."

Shantamma had lost him at the end of his second sentence.

"First of all, what kind of a name is Cylinder? And who is that ... whatever that strange name you said? I will tell you what your future should be like. Work hard, make enough money so that you can eat mutton every day, but not have it every day. Save that money, get married to a good, sensible girl and live happily even when I am gone."

"Where is my whistle, mother?"

As she handed him the whistle, Chikkanna reminded himself to fetch her BP medicines in the evening. He knew that she would work herself up over trivial things and so decided to comfort her once again, with something more familiar.

"Don't worry, mother! I'll start saving every month. I'll speak to Percentage Ravi."

As she started to dust the house, she muttered loud enough for him to register.

"I have lived longer than you in this town and haven't heard of any of these strange characters. I don't know what kind of people you are mixing around with."

With a smile of resignation, Chikkanna walked out muttering to himself, "I can easily manage Clock Tower traffic but I cannot manage her on some days."

(27)

JACKIE

"Richard Bach, Stephen King, Jeffrey ... Jeffrey ... Jeffrey Archer! Bestsellers at best price! Great writing, great reading!"
Cylinder was in the middle of the road moving amidst eleven potential customers employing four different modes of transport. He had twenty seconds before the signal would turn green and this lot would vroom off. There were six people on mopeds, Dr. Manjunath (the dentist) on his scooter, two people in an autorickshaw, and the businessman in his white Contessa. He had so much money that he could easily buy out Cylinder's entire lot of books. But he had not bought even one despite passing the signal on a regular basis.
Maybe, he didn't want the town to see him buying books at a traffic signal. Maybe, he bought them in big bookstores when he went out of town. Maybe, he paid people to write books for him. Or maybe, he was a non-believer in books. A book atheist?
Whatever his `maybe' was, he hadn't picked one from Cylinder and so Cylinder didn't even bother to showcase the bestsellers piled up in his

hands by pausing outside the rolled-up window. Instead, he snaked around the wheels of the mopeds.

"Take home groceries, jackfruit, but also a book."

He proposed literature to motorists some of whom were hauling home a jackfruit each. It was the season of the most adamant fruit, as obdurate as a hardened spy or a POW. One had to literally employ third degree methods before it would yield its truth.

No one seemed interested. They only looked out for the red light to turn green. He retracted from the road towards the footpath. His shoulders felt stiff, his hands ached and he wanted to lay down the books for a while.

As he stepped on the uneven footpath, he suddenly came face to face with Jackie.

"Jackie! Hurrrr! Hurrrr! Jackie!"

Jackie looked at him unflinchingly with her large, bovine eyes. Cylinder threatened her as seriously as he could.

"I will beat you if you come any closer."

Her lower jaw was moving sideways considerably. As usual, she was chewing on rubbish picked off the streets. She wasn't muscular or menacing but yes, she was moody. Most days, she was cow-like and docile but on some, she would get resolute about something. Cylinder saw her looking at his stack of books and desperately shooshed her away.

The previous week, he was doing business as usual. There was healthy traffic at the signal, a little more than usual. As the light changed to green, all the people except one pressed their respective horns with so much intensity that as if in fright, the signal stopped working. It started twitching between its colours in no particular sequence. This naturally led to disorder. Then, motorists waiting at the other three ends assumed their right to move. The honks increased manifold. At Cylinder's side of the traffic lights, Tony's yellow tempo had refused to start and this was the precursor to the chaos.

Tempo Tony was trying his best to get his livelihood back to life, but it kept making disgruntled noises. One could not blame it. It had always looked and sounded weary. It had spent years doing odd jobs for people in the town. It would ferry shamianas & folding chairs, goats & cattle during Ramzan, cement bags & bricks, broken-down mopeds, sugarcane, cases of liquor, Ganesha idols during the festive season etc. Whoever had designed the tempo had surely taken inspiration from mythology associated with the Lord of Obstacles and messed it up. While Lord Ganesha had the face of an elephant and a mouse as his mount, the tempo had the face of a mouse but the bodily expectations from it were that of an elephant. It was unfair. Anyone else in this tempo's place would have renamed himself `temper'.

Tony stood in the middle of the road looking troubled. He was wildly gesturing to other motorists that they make their way on either side of his vehicle. Chikkanna was blowing his whistle incessantly and adding to the cacophony. Cylinder put down his stack of books on the footpath, ran to the back of the tempo, yelled at Tony to get in and pulled Chikkanna's sleeve to lend a helping hand. Cylinder was small but wiry. His arms had strength from carrying books for hours each day. Chikkanna was built in accordance with his name. Unwittingly, his parents had been prophetic. If one blew at him with the same force that he blew his traffic whistle, he would fly across the traffic junction. But an emergency brings out the best in people and these two managed to move the tempo. As it started to roll with moderate speed, Tony worked his magic with the clutch and the gears, and it coughed back to life. Cylinder saw Tony's hand wave a thankful acknowledgement before it disappeared inside to steer the wheel.

Wiping the dirt off his palms on his shirt, Cylinder ran back to the pavement to pick up his lot of books. The light would turn red soon again and he wanted to catch the next set of literati. Or illiterati?

Shocked at the sight in front of his eyes, he instinctively pushed the cow with all his might. In the few minutes that he had been caught up with the traffic mess, this cow had stepped onto the footpath and was eating one of his books. Thankfully, Cylinder managed to snatch a few pages along with the back cover out of its mouth. He wanted to show Begur Sir the proof of this crazy but funny incident. The cow lazily chewed the rest of `Lovers and Gamblers' by Jackie Collins, preparing it for cud. Cylinder felt loss and mirth at the same time.

'If only the people of this town digested books as enthusiastically as this idiotic cow, my hands would ache a little less.' He smiled to himself.

Not that he knew its real name but since that day, he had renamed this cow, Jackie.

(28)

THE BIG MONSOON SALE

Water and paper.
Sworn enemies? Incorrect.
It needs dislike from both sides to qualify for that. It would be more rightful if we said `the squisher' and `the haplessly squished'. In any encounter between these two, one has the might and the other, unqualified to put up even a semblance of a fight. The paper, whether blank or carrying the mightiest thoughts of the mightiest minds stands nary a chance against water. Herein lies the irony:
Some of the greatest adventures in water — Treasure Island, The Hunt for Red October, Moby Dick, Robinson Crusoe, Sinbad the Sailor — were disseminated across mankind by paper. Millions, who had never seen a sea or sailed the high seas were in awe of it; overwhelmed by its beauty, brute strength, depth, vastness, equanimity, rage etc. Since the time of its birth, the paper has carried out enormous selfless service for water with no reciprocation. Even a fleeting meeting and water destroys it, out of ignorance and lack of gratitude

and remorse.

Cylinder wasn't weighed down by such ruminations but presently he was hampered. Monsoon had announced its arrival in Mogga. It usually lasted a little over six weeks, pouring much fertility on the land and much joy upon the populace. Bringing down the average temperature of the preceding months, it would also bring down the median blood pressure of Mogga. A detailed study of the records at the government hospital (McGann Hospital) would testify to this. But Cylinder's blood pressure had inched up. He loved the rains, like everybody else, but it stood (rather fell) directly in the way of his life's mission.

`How will I carry precious books now? How will I protect them, peddle them? I don't mind getting soaked but I will not let a drop, drop on any of them!'

Big Sir and Big Mother had proposed that he should take a break for the next two months and he had nodded vacantly. Minutes later, he sat on the porch, eyes fixed on the pelting rain while his mind was fixated on his conundrums.

`Okay, let me suppose that I will sell books for another sixty years. And every year, I lose two months. That is ten years. And if I assume that I will sell fifty books every year, then I will end up selling five hundred books lesser. If it was fifty or hundred, I could think about it but five hundred? No! Summer holidays for schoolchildren is fine but monsoon holidays for a bookseller makes no sense to me.'

His clarity made him feel like a victor. Cylinder smiled and held it for several seconds. Slowly, it curved into a frown, like a question mark.

`How do I do it?'

Picking up a bundle of polythene from the storeroom, he darted up to The Airport.

"Begur Sir, I cannot take a monsoon break. But please do not worry. I will not let any book get damaged."

Begur looked up from his book.

"Put the plastic down and come here."

As Cylinder walked up to the table, Begur smiled and held out the plate.

"First, have some onion pakodas, the perfect accompaniment to rain."

Big Mother had fried a massive quantity of these savouries, to be enjoyed by everyone on the farm. The combination of petrichor and the smell of pakodas was a divine feeling for every nose, not to mention the dance of tastebuds in every mouth.

Cylinder wolfed down a few and made a `thwack' sound with his tongue.

"Begur Sir, If I wasn't a bookseller, I would have probably sold pakodas and spread delight of another kind."

Both grinned like little children and polished off the plate.

"Run down and fetch another plate.", said Begur.

As Cylinder came running up with a full plate, Begur was sitting on the floor with a stack of books and the bundle of polythene. This was agricultural polythene, a staple on every farm. Transparent and lightweight, the farm plastic was thicker than regular polythene and way more durable. It served a variety of uses on a farm—setting up a greenhouse, protecting plants from insects, enhancing sprouting etc. One of the books had been fully clothed in it.

Begur taped it meticulously, stood up, walked to the window and held the book out. Within seconds, hundreds of droplets (some big, some small, just like the words inside of the book) fell on the book cover and rolled off. Begur wiped the water off using his shirt and checked the book closely. It was watertight. Cylinder smiled.

Begur held the book out in the rain again, shook it vigorously to shake off the water and asked Cylinder to move back a few paces. He then held up the book.

"Cylinder, which book is this?"

Though the water droplets had rolled off, there were irregular lines of water residue on the cover, making the title look a bit hazy.

"That's ... uhh ... ummm ... just a second, Begur Sir."

"C'mon, boy! The signal will turn green any second now."

"That's Psycho by Robert Bloch. Norman Bates, Norma Bates, Normal Bates. What a book, Begur Sir! Psychological thriller at its best." An excited cylinder squealed and beamed.

"Don't judge a book by its cover." Begur smiled and paused.

"That's a rich and rightful metaphor, as all metaphors are and one that is used quite repeatedly by mankind."

Cylinder nodded without being sure about where this conversation was headed. The monsoon dilemma had been solved and he was full of vim.

"We'll come back to our present issue but would you want to go back in time and know the origin of this phrase?"

"Tell me, Begur Sir.", said Cylinder avidly.

He had always been a sucker for trivia and now, unencumbered from the season's challenge, he was all ears.

Begur looked afar, jogging his memory.

"The earliest usage is in The Mill on the Floss by George Eliot, in 1860. In this classic, the character, Mr. Tulliver uses it while discussing another great book, The Political History of the Devil by Daniel Defoe, which came out in 1726."

Begur paused and looked afar again trying to recollect more when Cylinder piped in, "Oh! So nice! George Eliot was a great writer. Wasn't' he, Begur Sir?"

"George Eliot was a `she'", said Begur instantly.

"Oh!", said Cylinder instinctively. "But how can a woman be named George? This is confusing."

"Cylinder, that's her pen name. Her real name is Mary Ann Evans."

"But why would she choose a man's name as her pen name? That's confusing me."

"For a good reason. To kill the gender bias, Cylinder. You see, women writers weren't taken very seriously. She took upon this name to escape the stereotype that women writers are good with lighthearted romances and nothing more."

Cylinder pursed his lips nodding to himself, chewing on the piece of information.

"Begur Sir, I love all three. The storytellers, the stories they write, and the stories behind the storytellers."

Begur pursed his lips and nodded to himself, chewing on the line he'd just heard.

"Yes, Cylinder. You said it better than I ever can. All three are beautiful."

His thick lips, topped by a moustache (more brushy than bushy) stretched into a beautiful smile. In tandem, Cylinder's thin lips with no topping, stretched themselves.

"What were we talking about?", asked Begur after a few moments.

"Don't judge a book by its cover.", reminded Cylinder.

"Yes. Yes. That got sidelined. It started gaining popularity in the mid 1940s, thanks to a book by Edwin Rolfe and Lester Fuller, a murder mystery called Murder in the Glass Room. `You can never tell a book by its cover.', says one of the characters."

Trivia. Trivia. Trivia.

Cylinder relished them as much as the pakodas. Involuntarily, he made a `thwack' sound and smiled.

"Now, let's get back to the present issue.", stated Begur.

Cylinder turned confused. In his head, the issue had been sorted. The farm polythene had taken care of it.

"Here's the funny thing, Cylinder. The metaphor works beautifully but in its literal sense, it almost always fails. Most readers, potential book buyers, will judge a book by its cover. Front and back."

A look of astonishment covered Cylinder's face.

"That's so true, Begur Sir!"

"Now, in these heavy rains, with books clothed in polythene and clouded by water …"

The look of astonishment got replaced by clarity.

"Aaah! Why will anyone buy any book? I get it, Begur Sir."

Cylinder plucked the book out of Begur's hand, held it outside the window, wiped it against his shirt, placed it upright on the table, walked back a few paces, stood next to Begur, looked at it and nodded in affirmation.

"You know it's Psycho by Robert Bloch. To the uninitiated, the cover is nothing but a blotch.", said Begur and smiled.

"What do I do now?", asked Cylinder pensively.

"I don't know, Cylinder. We'll think of something. Come, let's wrap the other books."

The two sat down and got down to the task.

The next day brought in its quota of heavy rainfall. Chikkanna stood under the tree at the signal, covered in a large black plastic sheet from head to knees. The motorists sped by. The pedestrians scurried with their heads hidden under umbrellas. To varying degrees, everyone got wet, yet life carried on in its daily routine.

Cylinder walked up in a yellow raincoat, the colour of adolescent sunshine. He placed his bag under the tree, placed an umbrella over it and pulled out six water-proofed books. Chikkanna shook his head, amused.

"Cylinder! The umbrella will fly, not the books." He said and laughed. At the same time, he picked up a sizeable stone and placed it on the base of the umbrella's handle.

"In this weather, do you think the people of Mogga will be interested in buying books?"

"Begur Sir and I have worked out a plan. Let's see." Cylinder smiled.

He readied himself for the signal to turn red. As a few vehicles gathered in front of him, Cylinder held up the books joyfully and let forth his sales pitch, one that he had rehearsed several times the previous day.

"Monsoon sale! Monsoon sale! It's raining offers! Buy one, twenty percent off! Buy two, thirty percent off! Great weather. Enjoy a great book! Perfect with pakodas! Monsoon sale!"

(29)

THE WRITER WHO WASN'T

Cylinder looked out of the window staring at sheets of water. It was noon in the third week of monsoon, and it had upped its game significantly. It had been pouring relentlessly for over thirty-six hours causing the Tunga river to up its level and flood parts of the older part of the town. This occurred once every two years or so. Most establishments lay closed for the day, including government offices barring the very essential services. Most of the populace was forced to sit home, and that included Cylinder.

Begur sat in his chair excitedly unwrapping a new parcel that had arrived a few days earlier. Cylinder settled down with `The Sinister Signpost'. He had been on a reading spree of The Hardy Boys and couldn't get enough of them. Thankfully, The Airport held an extensive collection of them.
"Begur Sir, Franklin W. Dixon writes really well." He commented.
"Well, but he's not a real person.", replied Begur.
Cylinder looked puzzled.

"What does that mean?"

"Franklin W. Dixon is just a name, a fictitious name, a pseudonym. There are different writers who write The Hardy Boys books. You'll not know who the writer is." Begur said as he looked at his new book with childlike wonderment.

"But why is that? How can different people write The Hardy Boys? And why will they write and not put their names on the books? I am very confused, Begur Sir."

"That's the genius of Edward Startemeyer.", said Begur with a smile.

"Who's he?"

Having unwrapped his parcel, Begur got waylaid.

"Oh! One of the greatest minds of our times. I have waited for three months for this book. I have not been this excited in a while. Look at this!" Begur could not control his delight and held up his book.

"But who's Edward something?" Cylinder could not control his curiosity and held up his.

"I am sorry.", said Begur. "Edward was a prolific writer of children's literature. He was also a publisher. Some people say that he was to literature what Rockefeller was to oil."

Cylinder didn't understand the reference but didn't interrupt.

"Sometime in the early 20th century, he had an idea. He created The Hardy boys, Nancy Drew, and published them under the pseudonyms Franklin W. Dixon and Carolyn Keene. The first few books did well. And then he had a bigger idea."

Cylinder's eyes got bigger even as Begur carried on.

"He built a network of writers who would write stories around these characters. Now, why did he do this? For many reasons. This way, he could produce a huge number of books, in double quick time. The writers got paid a decent amount for their work. He continued to publish newer titles under the established pseudonyms."

This was deep and Cylinder took time to get his head around it.

"But Begur Sir, why would any writer agree to not having his name on a book? Isn't that what every writer lives for?"

"You are right but there is more to it. After the hardest part is done, which is the writing, begins the frustrating part. It is sometimes harder than the hardest part itself. It is not easy for a new name to be accepted.

There is no guarantee that a new name will be picked up by the public. When one is not recognised, it takes a lot — promotions, publicity, interviews, book tours — none of which is easy. Beyond everything, there is destiny. Do you understand? Therefore, once a name is established, it's best to stick to it."

Cylinder was still ingesting, and Begur carried on.

"From writers to painters to musicians to scientists and others, some of the most gifted and celebrated names today never made a name for themselves in their lifetimes. They were supremely talented at what they did. Perhaps, they didn't promote themselves well enough. I don't know. And even if they did, going by history, providence wasn't with them. They died unrecognised; some in penury, some ridiculed, and I suppose all of them broken-hearted."

Cylinder sat dazed.

"Such is life." Begur smiled weakly and turned back to his new book.

"So, who are the great writers who didn't get recognised?", asked Cylinder with a knot in his throat.

"Let me think. There are many. Some of the biggest names we hold up today as pillars of literature. Hmmm! Franz Kafka! He never got recognised till after his death. He was so anguished at the time of his death that he had asked a friend to burn all his work. Thankfully, the friend didn't do anything stupid. He got it published and the rest is history."

"Tch! Tch! Tch! Tch! That is really sad, Begur Sir. Who else?"

"Hmmm! Edgar Allan Poe! A master of short stories, mystery, and the macabre. He published them during his lifetime but never made money. He could not even support himself. That great poor man."

Cylinder sat downcast. Begur suddenly remembered another name.

"Henry David Thoreau! His books are on the shelf to the left of the mirror. He wrote beautifully about the importance of natural living, being one with nature. But it was only after his death that his books became an inspiration for many, including Leo Tolstoy and Mahatma Gandhi."

By now, Cylinder couldn't speak and Begur couldn't stop.

"Oscar Wilde! He died bankrupt. I think he made some money during his lifetime but got imprisoned for something that was no fault of his.

I'll tell you about that some other time. And he lost whatever money he had, paying the lawyers, trying to get out of prison. It's only after his death that his writing captured the imagination of the world."

Cylinder sat in silence for several moments.

"Begur Sir, this is gloomy. Please tell me about Edward."

"Oh yes! The Hardy Boys became hugely popular, and the public developed a healthy appetite for the writings of Franklin W. Dixon. Edward was intelligent enough to realise this. Therefore, he created a pool of talented writers who kept churning out stories. He became a millionaire, paid the writers well and above all, created a massive publishing machinery that attracted millions and millions of ..."

"Begur Sir, do you know who the real writers of The Hardy Boys are?" Cylinder cut in.

"Hmmm! I do know that a lot of the early books were written by Leslie McFarlane, a Canadian. After that, there were several others."

"I feel sad for Leslie, Kafka, Edgar, David and Oscar. Actually, Leslie is okay. He got money. But the others ... they never got anything in their lifetimes. Tch!", said Cylinder in a weak voice.

"Writing is not for the weak-hearted, Cylinder."

Cylinder nodded knowingly and opened his book searching for the page he was on.

Begur excitedly opened his. He was halfway through the first page when Cylinder piped in.

"Begur Sir, what is this new book that you are so excited about?"

Begur held it up, beaming like a star.

"Cosmos by Carl Sagan, one of the most marvellous minds of our times."

(30)

ARTIFICIAL INTELLIGENCE

The annual monsoon dance was over. It had retreated on time like a well-rehearsed professional stage artiste, making way for the next act.

It was mid-afternoon and naturally quite hot. There wasn't much movement on the streets. Even the trees hardly moved, perhaps directed by their own sense of guilt. If they moved, they would move the hot air around and this was innately contradictory to their purpose. It was that time of the day that tested the purpose and patience of people and things. This was the cosmic reality. Everyone, and everything was created with a purpose and then put to test, every now and then.

The traffic lights for instance, had been created with such a singular purpose that if they didn't adhere to it, they would be cursed and replaced. Hence, every single day of their long work hours, they operated with precision, almost always remaining sharp-eyed. But at this time of the day, the heat had diminished their zeal. With hardly any traffic to manoeuvre, they continued to work but without intent.

No doubt, their eyes carried their colours but upon keen observance, one could notice that they looked vacant, laden with ennui. With no potential book buyers, Cylinder kept staring at the lights, noticing the difference in their attitude. He could genuinely read and feel their mood. After all, no one had spent as much time with them as him, having started his working life literally under their eyes. Suddenly, something buzzed in his mind, and he looked down at his stack of books. He pulled out `2001: A Space Odyssey' and flipped its pages. He reminisced about the conversation with Begur a few months earlier.

On that day, Begur Sir had been excited having received his order of new titles, across genres. He smelled each book, smiled, handed it over to Cylinder, especially held back `2001: A Space Odyssey', smelled it deeply, and placed it on top of the stack.
"Cylinder, this is no ordinary read. Make sure someone worthy picks it up."
Cylinder had beamed feeling a new thrust. He had stared at the cover trying to gather what it was all about.
"Begur Sir, this looks like one of Asimov's books."
"It's by Arthur C. Clarke. I have seen him once."
"In America?"
"I have never been to that country, Cylinder. Arthur C. Clarke was an Englishman who lived most of his life in Ceylon. I have been there once, and was fortunate enough to see him eating breakfast in the hotel that I was staying in."
The author's geographical proximity had made the book even more special to Cylinder and he had looked at it again.
"Looks like it's about future and space."
"That's the setting but it's about something much more radical. I might not witness it in my lifetime, but I am sure you will be around to see the day we live with artificial intelligence."
"Artificial intelligence?" Cylinder had repeated the last two words with emphasis without knowing what it meant.
Seeking more clarity, he had looked up to Begur Sir who had such a faraway look that he could have probably peeked into 2001 and

beyond. Ever so slightly, he had shaken his head and uttered, more to himself, "I am not sure whether this will be a good thing or a bad thing but someday this will change everything."

Breaking out of his daze, he had looked down to see Cylinder looking up at him expectantly. For a while, he had wondered how to simplify an unimaginable concept such as this.

"Artificial intelligence is ... things ... umm ... machines having the intelligence to think like us. We won't have to tell them what to do. They will understand a situation and decide what needs to be done. That's what it is."

Cylinder's eyes had become as big as the traffic lights.

"You mean, my traffic lights will start thinking and then blinking?"

"Ha ha ha ha! Yes, Cylinder. One day, that'll happen. It's exciting and scary."

Cylinder had beamed and lovingly touched the book.

"Then, my traffic lights will become world-famous. People from all over will come just to look at them. And I'll sell hundreds of books."

Begur had smiled while Cylinder had carried on excitedly.

"My traffic lights are special. One day, they will have artificial intelligence, but they already have feelings. They get bored, excited, sometimes irritated also. I can see and feel it."

"Conceptually, that is AI Level 2 or 10, God only knows! Someday, they will start to think but the day they begin to feel, even God will not know what might happen. Apart from having a profession and a purpose, they will start having a point of view too. And what if theirs and ours don't match?" Begur had thought aloud.

Beyond this, even an erudite mind like his could not make sense of the magnitude of the magic and mayhem that would get unleashed upon the world. He had shaken his head vigorously to realign himself with the present as Cylinder had picked up his bag of books and jauntily walked out.

Presently, standing on the dusty footpath, Cylinder kept looking at the bored traffic lights and started a conversation.

"Someday, you'll have more intelligence than me. Then, you'll become more intelligent than Begur Sir. I cannot believe that but Begur Sir himself thinks so. But don't wait till 2001."

The light turned green and Cylinder smiled in acknowledgement.

"You can do it."

With nothing to do, he rearranged the order of his stack. Beads of sweat rolled down his body but it didn't bother him one bit. His purpose was to sell books. Given the nature of his trade, heat was his friend; his enemy was rain. As he waited with patience (and perspiration) for traffic to start flowing again, he saw Percentage Ravi on his moped at the other end of the traffic lights.

There was a striking similarity between the two. Both were resolutely sincere about their chosen professions. Both took their jobs seriously and themselves lightly. To most people, what they did seemed trivial, but they went about their occupations with God-like purpose. If one could sufficiently summarise God's purpose as giving people knowledge (and wisdom) and taking care of their well-being, both got covered between these two. One strove to make people read and the other drove them to save.

Percentage Ravi came to a halt in front of Cylinder and told him to get on the moped. In less than a minute, they stopped at Rahim's Sugarcane Joos Cart at the end of the road. Rahim, a frail man in his late 50s greeted them and picked up a stick of sugarcane. As he started turning the wheel, Cylinder asked him in hopelessness, "Rahim Chacha! When will you correct the spelling of Joos? Every time, I remind you."

Rahim smiled unconcerned and placed two glasses of refreshment on the tin counter. Percentage Ravi handed over a fifty-paisa coin. The two of them glugged gleefully and halfway down began sipping soberly. Both acts were reflex actions, the first more physiological and the second, a psychological slowing down since they wanted the juice to last longer. Percentage Ravi kept sipping and looking acutely at Cylinder.

Cylinder noticed it and thought that a man looked at another such-like in only two instances: either while expecting a crucial response or while wanting to ask a deep question.

"What is it, Ravi?"

"Cylinder, tell me something! For months now, you've stood at this traffic junction. Some days, you manage to sell a book. At times, you sell nothing for weeks. Why do you do what you do?"

With uncanny perceptiveness, Cylinder asked, "Ravi, is everything fine with your job?"

Breaking into loud, happy laughter, he replied, "Yes! Yes! Job is very good. I am doing very well. Now, I am a senior and next week, I have to conduct a training session for new Pigmy Collectors. I have prepared everything. But the most important thing is purpose, I feel. I can give them my example, but it has to be said in a nice way."

Cylinder smiled and then took a few seconds to empty his glass.

"I'll tell you my purpose. And you'll automatically know yours."

Percentage Ravi looked intently at Cylinder.

"If people don't come to the books, the books will go to the people. That's my job."

He said it with so much clarity and velocity that Percentage Ravi took time processing it while hastily asking, "And my purpose is?"

"Same, Ravi. If people don't come to the bank, the bank will ..."

"... go to the people! Every day!", said Percentage Ravi and hugged Cylinder.

They placed the empty glasses on the cart counter even as Percentage Ravi continued to beam like a bar of gold. Bidding goodbye to Rahim, they mounted the moped. Percentage Ravi dropped Cylinder back to his spot, thanked him and rode across the traffic junction.

`If I had Cylinder's natural intelligence, I would have become a branch manager by now.' He thought to himself.

(31)

COSMOS

Seen from outer space, from a staggering distance, the earth was a tiny, pale blue dot. On this dot, was an infinitesimally tiny, lush green dot: Begur Farms.

Life in this miniscule microcosm carried on the way it had always been. Begur kept devouring books at an alarming rate—new authors, new titles from established ones, one-book wonders, sleeper hits, anthologies etc. The books kept coming in, got relished and racked up on the shelves. He continued to narrate and read out stories to Cylinder whenever Cylinder wasn't immersed in his own books. Cylinder continued to read whatever caught his fancy. He continued to memorise trivia and practice pronunciations. He continued to place orders with Begur Sir for titles and copies whenever required and Begur would promptly call Selvaraj.

There was a small variation though. Now, stories flowed both ways. While Begur told him tales from books, Cylinder told him stories from the streets of Mogga. He interacted with a lot of them on a daily basis and had become good friends with many. They would stop by and spend time with him and Chikkanna—chitchatting, gossiping about things and people, cracking jokes, cackling, enquiring about new authors and daily sales, taking his opinion on random matters etc. Most of them weren't into reading but they always promised to bring more readers to him. Everyone encouraged and adored him. Apart from these regulars, nearly the entire town was familiar with him. He was a wonderment, an enigma but a beautiful one at that. They saw him every day in the same spot—forever present, forever smiling, forever helpful, forever excited about selling books.

Though the traffic signal was the most prominent spot, he had become a point of reference to quite a few. When people from the villages came into town looking for places or people, it wasn't uncommon to hear something like this:

"Go straight and you'll see a boy selling books. You cannot miss him. He's the only one. Turn left there and go straight for a furlong. You'll see a eucalyptus tree on your right. Right there, you'll see a house painted with green distemper. You cannot miss it. It's the only one in that line. That's Shastriji's house.'

On this particular evening, Cylinder came back home, changed and settled down in The Airport. Begur was at his desk immersed in a book, shaking his head every now and then. Seeing the back of his shaking head, Cylinder knew that whatever Begur Sir was reading was taking him on a trip. He didn't want to disturb him but at the same time wanted to indulge in some conversation. After a full day at the signal, there was nothing more rejuvenating than exchanging notes or indulging in banter.

"Begur Sir, is it the same book?" He asked.

"Yes. Cosmos." Begur said without looking up.

Cylinder vaguely knew that it meant the earth, the sky, the stars, the space and whatever else it held. Yet, he asked, "What does cosmos mean?"

Begur turned around with starlit eyes.

"Carl Sagan puts it beautifully. Cosmos is a Greek word for the order of the universe. It is the opposite of chaos."

"Cosmos. Chaos." Cylinder muttered the two words and smiled.

Cosmos sounded comforting. Chaos reminded him of those occasions when the traffic lights misbehaved.

"From the shake of your head, I could make out that it's as good as you had imagined. Maybe better."

Begur sounded as excited as Galileo, Kepler and Newton when they had made their discoveries.

"Heavy but heavenly. It's out of this world, literally and figuratively. I am eating one line at a time. Every page is a treasure trove of information and imagination, folklore and facts, the micro and the macro, distant past and the distant future ... This book is, what do I say? Simply putdownable. After every page, I am compelled to put it down and think about hundreds of things about this tiny, pale blue dot we call home."

Cylinder heard rapt in attention. He didn't get the essence of the book but got a sense of how deeply the book had impacted Begur.

"Once I am done, I will order a few more copies for the signal.", added Begur.

"Begur Sir, the only person I can think of who might understand and appreciate it as much as you is ISV."

"From what you've told me, he's quite well-read and knowledgeable. But why is he called ISV?", asked Begur curiously.

"Take a guess." Cylinder broke into a wide grin.

"It must be his initials ... ummm ... ISV ... hmmm ... I don't know, Cylinder. At this point, all I can think of is Interstellar Vehicle."

Both burst into peals of laughter.

"Venugopalan Vadapalani Venkataraman. That's his full name, Begur Sir.", said Cylinder.

"Oh! A Tamilian brahmin. Birth name plus the name of his native place plus his father's name. So, he'd be naturally called Venu.", surmised Begur effortlessly.

"What did you say, I say!", said Cylinder authoritatively.

It was so uncharacteristic of him that Begur looked at the little fellow who had a mischievous glint and was trying to form something in his racing mind.

"Cosmos is a fantastic read, I say! And that Carl Sagan fellow has a good mind, I say!", said Cylinder looking Begur squarely in the eye.

Begur looked at him fixedly, part fascinated, part lost, just like an average person looked while looking up at the night sky.

Cylinder didn't want to push the joke. With an apologetic smile, he began to offer an explanation.

"I am sorry, Begur Sir. I said what ISV is most likely to say. He thinks extremely high of himself and often refers to big authors as `that fellow', `this fellow'. He worked all his life at the matchbox factory in Mogga and retired as the plant manager."

"That's Swedish Match! A legendary company that's been around since the mid 1800s. Imagine! Of all the places, a company from Sweden has a plant in Mogga, of all the places.", said Begur with a smile. Cylinder returned one.

"They set up a plant here sometime in the 1920s. Since our region is blessed with fertile soil and surrounded by forests, we have an abundance of soft-wood trees needed to make splints and matchboxes. My great grandfather owned a lot more land and used to supply wood to Swedish Match. Anyway, I still haven't figured out the first two initials."

"ISV is for `I Say Venu'." Cylinder said with a grin.

"He got influenced by a Swedish manager of his and began to end most of his sentences with `I say!' According to ISV, it adds gravity and authority to anything. After a point, people noticed this peculiarity and started calling him `I Say Venu' behind his back. At some point, it became ISV and when he got to know about it, he was more pleased than pained and began referring to himself as ISV."

As Begur was piecing it all together, Cylinder reeled off lines that he had heard from ISV:

"Mogga is so mofussil, I say!"

"Have you got any new books, I say!"

"I can write better than this American fellow, I say!"

Both guffawed, running ISV's lines in their minds and holding their sides.

Wiping his tears, Begur said, "ISV is an interesting fellow, Cylinder. Let me order a copy. Give it to him for free. It's joyful to feed minds that expand like the cosmos."

(32)

WRITER'S BLOCK

"Give me something good to read, I say!", yelled ISV from several feet away, striding towards Cylinder. He walked up, placed the bag of vegetables on the ground and peered at the stack in Cylinder's hands. "Now that I am retired, I have more time, I say!"
"ISV Sir, you surprise me.", said Cylinder with a smile.
ISV looked up at him unsure what this wily, little fellow meant.
"Like most people in the town, you were born here and have spent your entire life here. But unlike most people in the town, you are a big reader of books. There are very few like you here." Cylinder added.
"My latitude and longitude are the same as the rest of Mogga, but my aptitude …", said ISV smugly without completing the sentence, another trick he had picked up from his erstwhile Swedish manager, Gunnar Karlsson.
"That's a great line, ISV Sir.", beamed Cylinder sincerely.
"So, what do you recommend today?" ISV asked.

"I have a phenomenal book for you. Cosmos by Carl Sagan. Begur Sir is reading it. He's already placed the order for another copy. Give me a few days."

"Carl Sagan! He's a gifted astronomer plus astrophysicist plus cosmologist plus astrobiologist plus whatnot! A great mind. I'd love to read it. At least, it'll be worth my time, I say! But till then, what can I read?"

"I can give you something similar."

Cylinder pulled out `Chariots of the Gods'.

[This was a worldwide bestseller and had created millions of fans for Erich Von Däniken, and his seemingly outlandish but highly plausible theories. The perspective was priceless; so were the innumerable pieces of evidence painstakingly studied, measured and collected from every region of the globe. It knitted postulates from mythologies (Indian, Greek, Egyptian, Peruvian etc.), drew summaries from history, paleontology, microbiology, architectural sciences, archeology etc. It presented cave drawings from China, France, Australia and various other regions. While the book had stirred massive interest and amazement among his readers, it had also stirred deep criticism among the scientist community. Carl Sagan had made a scathing remark, a mockery of the man and a butchery of his work.

`That writing as careless as Von Däniken's, whose principal thesis is that our ancestors were dummies, should be so popular is a sober commentary on the credulousness and despair of our times. But the idea that beings from elsewhere will save us from ourselves is a very dangerous doctrine – akin to that of the quack doctor whose ministrations prevent the patient from seeing a physician competent to help him and perhaps to cure his disease.'*
– Carl Sagan]

To Cylinder's utter surprise, ISV knew of him as well.

"That Swiss fellow! My manager, Gunnar, was an ardent fan of his books. His theories are quite thought-provoking, I say! Let me read Cosmos first and then I'd like to read his."

Cylinder wondered what else could engage ISV's mind. Suddenly, ISV's eyes darted towards the bottom of the stack.

"What is this book, I say!"

Cylinder followed ISV's finger and pulled the book out of the stack.

"Interesting book, ISV Sir! Very little writing but lot of meaning."

ISV took the book and looked at it piercingly.

Notes to Myself: My Struggle to Become a Person

Hugh Prather

The title held his attention. The first part connected with him instantly. Every day, he was used to making several notes in his little pocket diary, and his big mind. He flipped through the pages of what appeared to be an unusual book, the sort he hadn't seen before. As Cylinder had rightly mentioned, it had less words and more blank space. Each page carried just a quote. Some had merely a line while some carried a little paragraph. He flipped the pages again, stopping randomly and taking in what they had to say. One of the pages held nothing except the line:

It is enough that I am of value to somebody today.

ISV hmmm-ed and opened another random page.

What an absurd amount of energy I have been wasting all my life trying to find out how things 'really are', when all the time they weren't.

He hmmm-ed again and moved to another page.

Now that I know that I am no wiser than anyone else, does this wisdom make me wiser?

ISV began to get a drift of what the author was trying to say. It wasn't any different from what our scriptures told us. Our ancient texts were replete with such profound sayings, and ISV was only too familiar with them. Something switched on in his head and he re-phrased it in his mind.

Now that I know that I am wiser than a lot of others, does this wisdom make me make others wiser?

He smiled, flipped the pages and landed at another quote.

I don't need a `reason' to be happy. I don't have to consult the future to know how happy I feel now.

Then, he came across the line:

Selfishness is neither good nor bad – it depends on the way we are selfish as to whether it nourishes or injures.

ISV thought about this and felt that he needed to think about it more in order to corroborate or challenge it. He flipped through a few more pages.

There is a part of me that wants to write, a part that wants to theorize, a part

that wants to sculpt, a part that wants to teach ... To force myself into a single role, to decide to be just one thing in life, would kill off large parts of me.
ISV suddenly spoke.
"This Hugh fellow is talking some sense, I say!"
Cylinder nodded in agreement. ISV went back to the book, to yet another page.
The number of things just outside the perimeter of my financial reach remains constant no matter how much my financial condition improves. With each increase in my income a new perimeter forms and I experience the same relative sense of lack.
He smiled, looked at Cylinder and nodded vigorously. Cylinder had no idea what he meant but his nodding seemed as if Hugh Prather had put down exactly what ISV had been saying for years. ISV confidently flipped yet another page.
If the desire to write is not accompanied by actual writing, then the desire is not to write.
He shut the book, smiled to himself, fished out two ten-rupee notes from his shirt pocket and stuffed them into Cylinder's palm.
"Cylinder! Simple but interesting book. And because of this, there will be a better book, I say!"
He then turned around and walked off with an urgency.

ISV reached home, asked his wife to make him a cup of coffee, sat at his table, arranged a sheaf of papers and gallantly pulled out his pen. For most part of his life, he had had so many influential thoughts. Some were inspired by his readings and some, purely his own observations and reflections. He had often lazily thought about penning his thoughts but for most part of his adult life, matchboxes had taken precedence over memoirs. But now, he decided to work on the material that lay inside him. He opened the book and searched for the line that had stuck in his mind.
If the desire to write is not accompanied by actual writing, then the desire is not to write.
ISV smiled and muttered, "Well said, Hugh!"
Slurping on his coffee, he put down the title of his book.
Notes To Everyone
By ISV

He looked at it wondering if this was plagiarism but within a moment decided that it didn't matter. Every bestseller spawned a host of similar literature. It helped grow the genre. He was only borrowing a part of the title. The philosophy would be entirely his. He was quite confident that his musings would be far superior to that of Hugh's. After all, his understanding of life was much deeper and richer than the West. He decided (albeit prematurely) that during his interviews, he would openly acknowledge that Hugh Prather's book was the inspiration; rather, the catalyst.

What he particularly liked about Hugh Prather's book was its structure; a few lines on each page that spoke about some profundity of life. A reader could open any page and find something precious. It also didn't need explanations. Rather, it was the lack of context that made readers interpret in their own ways and derive rich meaning. Unlike a novel, this was easily doable. With seedlings of doubt out of the way, he focused back on the published book's title. It had an additional line:

My Struggle to Become a Person.

This added credence to the material inside. It made the reader feel that the quotes were not borne out of imagination but were indeed brought to realisation by the harshest teacher of all, the one we call `life'.

ISV wondered if his title needed something extra. But he had had no struggles in comprehending life. He had been blessed with clarity and perspective from a young age. He had always been a healthy reader, and the scriptures had taught him many a thing. He had the knack of looking at life from angles that others missed. So, he decided against having an extension. At that very moment, a quote sprang in his mind out of nowhere. He decided that it deserved a place on the cover itself. And so, on top of the title, a fair distance apart, in small lettering, within quotation marks, he put down the first of his sayings:

Books are flowers. Readers are bees.

He couldn't have asked for a better start. Feeling smug, he called out to his wife for another cup of coffee, much to her consternation. She muttered loud enough for him to hear that since he was now retired, her working hours would increase. But it didn't register as ISV was consumed by his own lofty thoughts. He moved the title sheet to the

bottom of the pile and on a fresh sheet, wrote:
It's a small thing but it's a big thing.
He couldn't remember when he had thought of this, but it had been with him for a long time. He also used it regularly. To ISV, this sentence was all encompassing. Over the years, he had churned many thoughts around it (things positive & negative, big & small, physical & psychological) and he knew it held true. Since he was finally publishing his thoughts for posterity, he ran through a random collection of things: a toothpick, a hot cup of filter coffee, a smile, a bloody cold, a pimple, a puppy, a melody, a snub, a gratifying trip to the toilet, a matchbox, Mount Everest (in relation to the cosmos). The line held true, without exception.

He moved this sheet to the bottom and wrote on the next:
There are two kinds of man in every man. One who likes familiarity, and one who likes variety.
He knew no one could argue with it. Yet, he thought for a bit. It wasn't a big deal for him to write like an Englishman or an American, but he felt that it would read nicer with a dash of local flavour. He re-wrote it:
There are two kinds of man in every man. One who likes same same, and one who likes different.

His wife restlessly reminded him that it was way past lunchtime. Without looking up, ISV said that he was full. She asked if he was referring to his stomach or his head and proceeded to eat. ISV moved the sheet to the bottom of the pile and wrote on the next:
Did God create man or man create God?
He was an adherent to all symbolic religious practices. But deep down, he was more spiritual than religious. He had the gumption to question the sanctified.

On the next sheet, he put down something that life had taught him, visibly.
Young people laugh at old people.
Old people smirk at young people.

Staring at a fresh blank sheet again, he thought of the psychologist Rensis Likert. His years at Swedish Match had exposed him to a tool that they used regularly for consumer surveys: Likert Scale. Juxtaposing this with psychology and philosophy, he wrote:

If five people think very highly of you, and five others think very poorly of you, where will you place yourself on a scale of 1-10?

He placed the six sheets in a sequence and read the lines. His own writing stunned him. It was wonderful material, indeed! Suddenly, he felt famished. He called out to his wife to lay out his food. She groaned, got up from the bed and began to serve him. He ate joyfully, deep in thought, and then lay down staring at the ceiling.

In the evening, after dispensing with some household chores, ISV occupied the chair at his desk. His mind was brimming with so many thoughts that he reminded himself to buy a bottle of Chelpark ink the next morning. The nib stood eagerly just above the sheet as he framed the words in his mind about what he wanted to say. Twenty seconds later, he put down his lengthiest quote yet:

Each one of us is born to make an impression. In our childhood, we use our innocence. In youth, we use our body. In our prime, our mind, and in old age, our soul.

He twirled the pen, read what he had just written, thought about it for a while and nodded robustly. He instinctively decided that the next quote shouldn't be too heavy. After rummaging through his thoughts (several of them), he picked one that made him smile. It was a line that that occurred to him years earlier on a trip to Madras.

Death is the greatest leveller. Followed closely by humidity.

He got up, walked to the bathroom, stood in front of the mirror and cursed his reflection.

"What were you doing all your life? Making matchboxes for mankind while a writer sat burning brightly within? You stupid fellow, I say!"

Charging back to his table, he picked up Notes to Myself and saw that it had 176 pages. At this rate, he felt he would write double of what Hugh Prather had, in less than half the time. He wondered whether to pack all of his philosophy into one book or save some for a sequel. The idea excited him. Without fuss, he thought of the title for his second book.

More Priceless Notes To Everyone

By ISV

Feeling buoyant, he yelled out to his wife for a cup of coffee and placed the pen with purpose on the next sheet of paper. The nib stood in the same spot creating a bigger dot as the ink spread. ISV gently scratched the inner part of his left thigh though it wasn't itchy. His toes were clawing at his Hawaii chappals without reason. After scratching the thigh, his left hand moved up and started scratching the side of his head, gently of course. From an upright posture, ISV leaned back slightly and capped his fountain pen. In a matter of seconds, he had run dry. He had had so many thoughts, so much eagerness and confidence, and inexplicably they all stood frozen. Absolute fertility turned into a frown. The dreaded `writer's block' had seized him. His thoughts behaved like stray plastic bags on the streets on a breezy day.

Over the next thirty-five minutes, he sat in extreme frustration trying in vain to frame his next quote. He then got up, walked out, switched on his Dyanora TV and settled down watching Krishi Darshan on Doordarshan.

(33)

NEW NEWS NAGARAJ

January 1st, 1984. It turned out to be a Sunday. The New Year woke up serving ladles of cool winter breeze. As a bonus, it also sprayed healthy sunshine on the town. Mogga was south of the Vindhyas and was exempt from the bitingly cold winds that swept across the north of India. The earth smelled fresh. The birds chirped incessantly, much more than they did on a regular morning. It seemed like they were wishing `Happy New Year' to everyone around.

The people of the town had displayed similar conduct hours earlier at midnight, and perhaps the birds had decided to let them get over with their excitement rather than do it in parallel and create commotion. It was their turn now. And just like their human counterparts, all the birds didn't sound the same. Some were mellifluous and some, cacophonous. Some sat in one place while some flitted around overexcitedly. Irrespective of their behaviour, it was clear that they too welcomed the new beginning with much gusto. The trees in the town swayed with extra latitude, swishing and wishing each other. They also showered down leaves, their confetti to welcome the New Year. Looking up at the elders, the plants and bushes jerked around like novices, happily so. It was a special day for everyone.

At around ten in the morning, the streets were mostly empty. Most people had woken up late and were stretching into the New Year. After lazing around discussing the previous night, followed by a late breakfast, they would make plans for the day and resolutions for the year.

At the traffic signal, there was hardly any movement. Chikkanna too had a day off. The only person there, cheerful and hopeful, was Cylinder. The first day of the year always made most people make big and brainy resolutions, and reading more was certainly a part of many a person's to-do list. Cylinder didn't want to miss out on these golden hours. Even if two or three people ended up buying a book, it would be worth his wait.

He saw Nagaraj, with a bounce in his steps, crossing the junction briskly and walking in his direction. Nagaraj always walked with a purpose, even in his dreams. Halfway through the junction, he waved at Cylinder and ran up to him.

"Happy New Year, Cylinder! I wasn't sure if you would be here today."

As they hugged, Cylinder wished him back.

"So? What's your New Year resolution?" Nagaraj asked.

"Fifty new readers.", said Cylinder without hesitation.

"Now, it's forty-nine. I am already here. I actually came out to buy a book or two and was hoping that you would be around."

"I said fifty new readers. You are already one.", countered Cylinder and added, "In my first year, from the middle of 1982, I managed to sell 18 books. It was a good start. Last year, I sold 87 books, and got 25 new readers. This year, I want to double that, the count of new readers. I think it's possible."

Nagaraj nodded with equal optimism.

"So, what's your resolution?", asked Cylinder.

"Same. Same." Nagaraj repeated for extra emphasis before adding, "Since the day I decided what I wanted to be, my resolution has been the same every year, every day, every hour."

He then looked Cylinder in the eye.

"To be the most respected and recognised journalist in the world. That's all!"

Cylinder smiled and nodded suggesting that it was such a realisable goal.

The key to Nagaraj's confidence lay in the phrase: `That's all!'

It worked as a psychotropic drug and was widely used (or abused) in this part of the world. One could say anything, however monumental, round it off with `That's all!', and the task instantly became doable, gettable, even surpass-able. Depending on one's proclivity, it wasn't uncommon to hear statements such as:

"I want to become the next Tata or Birla. That's all!"
"I want to be the next Bruce Lee. That's all!"
"I want one meeting with God. That's all!"
"I want to beat Don Bradman's record. That's all!"

There was an implicit rule that it should be applied only to things that were grand in thought or promised glory. Most people used it rightfully. Only the unwise applied it recklessly, for the mundane.

"I want ten lakh rupees in my bank. That's all!"
"I don't want any headaches in life. That's all!"
"I want biceps like Gym Krishna. That's all!"

[Nagaraj was an overzealous reporter with Malnad News, the local English daily. Though a cub, with a mere three years of experience, he was already the rising star. In fact, some of his colleagues had given him the moniker of `New News Nagaraj'. He had a knack for adding newness to news; such was his reportage.

Consummate in his mother tongue Kannada, but consumed by the English language, he had dreamt of a career in journalism since high school. After his graduation, he had a job offer from both the local dailies. The vernacular, Kannada Kesari, was more prestigious and popular. It had also been around for twenty-eight years longer. A placement with Kannada Kesari was a matter of pride. But English was his kink. That he would be a renowned journalist was a foregone conclusion in his mind, but he had a clear distinction between being an acclaimed Kannada reporter Vs. English journalist. He often daydreamed, seeing this distinction in the form of his obituary.

Upon his death, some-to-several publications would carry tributes about him. Herein lay the difference. As a highly saluted Kannada journalist, he would find mentions in every local publication. That would mostly be within the state and that wasn't dazzling enough for him. What about The Hindu, The Times of India, The Telegraph, The Indian Express? How about Daily Mail, The Independent, The Guardian, The New York Times, The Washington Post? Why not Izvestia and Pravda?

After all, he had chosen a profession called 'news'. So, purely being true to the acronym, if the four parts of the globe didn't give him a respectful send-off, then what good (or how great) was his life's work! The defining headline in his head, on the day of his death, read:

All his life, he wrote for newspapers. Today, all newspapers write about him.

Driven by this lofty dream, he had worked excessively hard by reading anything printed in English—from local pamphlets to international publications—whenever he could get his hands on them. With a cocktail of stimuli (from the ridiculous to the sublime), and a handicap of the language (while his hands worked on an English typewriter, his mind worked in Kannada), he had developed a strange but heady mix of his signature style of journalism: intriguing headlines, innovative acronyms, concocted similes, and other idiosyncratic usages. Any decent English journalist would twist 'n' fist oneself reading these but for the people of the town, his writing was evocative and entertaining.]

"So, what books are you carrying today?", asked Nagaraj looking at the stack that Cylinder had placed on the ground. "I have to write all my life, and for that I have to read all my life."
"I wish Mogga had more Nagarajs.", said Cylinder with a smile.
"Mogga can have only one Nagaraj.", said Nagaraj with a smirk.
"Of course. No one can be what you are. What I meant is, I wish more people got inspired by you and started reading more."
Cylinder pulled out a book, covering its cover with his palm.
"Talking of inspiration, this book will add a whole new dimension to your writing."
"Which one is it? Who's the author?", asked Nagaraj bursting with curiosity.
"Close your eyes, please!", requested Cylinder.
Nagaraj obliged. Cylinder flipped through the pages and pulled out a small handwritten note that he had placed inside. It was one of the author's innumerable quotes that captured his unique witticism.

He read out slowly.

"One of the poets, whose name I cannot recall, has a passage which I am unable at the moment to remember, in one of his works, which for the time being has slipped my mind, which hits off admirably this age-old situation."

Nagaraj's eyes shut tighter as his mind battled for comprehension. Moments later, shaking his head in defeat, he opened them and looked down sharply. Cylinder stood with a smile, his palm covering the face of the book.

"What was that? It was so intelligent that I didn't understand anything.", said Nagaraj looking out of depth. "Who is this author?"

"P.G. Wodehouse. A master humourist. His wit is wit-hout a doubt, as delicious as English bread. Begur Sir calls it Brit-wit. You can add more punch to your writing."

In a trice, it was out of Cylinder's hand. Nagaraj whisked it and punched Cylinder's arm gleefully.

"Wishful thinking, Cylinder, but I do think about it often. If I was born as an Englishman, I would have ruled the world.", said Nagaraj with a wistful look.

"I love my language for conversing but for reporting, I am biased towards English." He added quickly.

He then smiled as his mind was working out something spectacular.

"If I have to tell you the same thing in a different way …"

He paused and held back till he saw Cylinder's curiosity bubble up to the maximum.

"I prefer to talk like our river Tunga but I prefer to write like river Thames.", said Nagaraj with a smile as wide as both the rivers.

"Nagaraj! You are our P.G. Wodehouse." Cylinder said, masking his amusement.

Nagaraj beamed so brightly that the spirit behind the three mechanical and most used words on this particular day (Happy New Year) beamed across the planet. Slowly, the beam became a smile, then turned a bit soft, and then softer. Sun to moon.

He kissed the book, fished out twenty rupees from his pocket, extended it towards Cylinder but suddenly held it back.

"Cylinder, I am following up on an important case. I am sure our

Mogga police will solve it soon. They will solve it for the victims. That's their job. But what is my job? A reputed reporter's job?"
Cylinder thought but couldn't surmise.
"To solve it for the people. It is my responsibility to make every resident feel safe.", said Nagaraj emphatically.
"So, are you carrying any books about world-famous detectives?"
"Of course. I almost always carry Agatha Christie. Here is Five Little Pigs."
Cylinder pulled it out.
"One of the most loved literary detectives, Hercule Poirot."
Grabbing it, Nagaraj flipped through it briskly.
"Herculees Pirate! His first name is so familiar. His second is so intoxicating."
Pulling out two more ten-rupee notes, he thrust the four notes into Cylinder's shirt pocket. Armed with a book each by two of the finest British writers, an elated Nagaraj thanked Cylinder and ran across the traffic junction.

(34)

HERCULEES PIRATE

A few weeks earlier, sometime in the beginning of December, the Begurs were at the breakfast table. As his mother served everyone, Cylinder was busy with yet another book of The Hardy Boys. Begur sat with the local English daily, Malnad News. This was the only time of day when he squandered his intellect on everyday tripe. His eyes rested on a headline:
The Case of The Spring Shoes Gang.

This was quite a case—no witnesses, no leads, no recurrences after the first three burglaries, nothing at all except outlandish clues in the form of people's figments of imagination. Purportedly, it was a gang of 6-8 members from north Karnataka who had hopped across the state committing break-ins in various towns. They would hop in and hop out in the middle of the night, easily jumping as high as 15-18 feet in the air. On a single night, they had hopped over high compound walls of three homes, broken in, rummaged and ransacked valuables, hopped across the walls again, and were never spotted or heard of. The word on the street was that they had special imported spring shoes that helped them leap like Olympian high jumpers, with a fraction of the effort but double the effect. Three families had lost valuables along with their most valued possession: peace of mind. Beyond that, it wasn't a grave crime. But the fanciful nature of the burglaries had gripped the imagination of the people. It was the talk of the town, so much so that every conversation started or ended or got waylaid with a discussion of The Spring Shoes Gang.

A few weeks later, on December 31st, Dharmaraj, an unassuming policeman had nabbed three people completely by chance. He had found them highly intoxicated and in deep slumber, inside a stolen police jeep on the outskirts of the town. During their interrogation, one thing led to another, and they confessed to the daring burglaries, described their modus operandi, and laid bare the mythical beliefs that had gotten fabricated. They were locals, not from Mogga proper but from around, and possessed nothing more fanciful than Bata chappals.

Post the burglaries, these three louts had been on a merrymaking spree and in their euphoric state of revelry, brazenly driven off in a police jeep.

"Now, no one can look at us and say that we are on the wrong side of the law. We are the law, da." One of them had quipped, and all three had giggled.

They had then stopped to pick up a case of beer and parcels of biryani, driven to the outskirts, parked in the middle of nowhere and had settled down to celebrate.

"We've ended the year on a high. Now, let's get higher. Cheers, da." One of them had said and all three had giggled, and guzzled. At some point in the night, their bellies full of beer and biryani, they had passed out.

Presently, two days after they were apprehended, a day after New News Nagaraj had bought the book from Cylinder, the Begurs sat down for breakfast. Begur opened the newspaper, and the front page carried an emphatic and enigmatic headline:

Herculees Pirate Solves The Case of The Spring Shoes Gang.

There was an extensive article about this high-profile case, with a photo of the robbers (heads held low, Bata chappals held high) flanked by a few policemen among whom Dharmaraj stood out prominently.

"Duffers! It is Hercule Poirot, not Herculees Pirate!" Begur muttered under his breath.

After his instinctive disappointment, he managed a smile. At least, the town would now become familiar with the name of the legendary literary Belgian detective, the silly misspelling notwithstanding. It soothed his soul.

"He's quite a character, Cylinder. This New News Nagaraj.", said an amused Begur finishing his breakfast.

Cylinder beamed a silly smile.

"He is, Begur Sir. But he's also one of the most ardent customers."

Several of Nagaraj's colleagues, not to mention most of the readers, and the entire police department were unaware of this world-famous detective. Dharmaraj, upon whom Nagaraj had bestowed this sobriquet, hadn't the faintest idea. But it found much purchase and popularity among everyone. A highly discussed case had been cracked, the villains nabbed, and an inspirational hero had emerged. The town brimmed with confidence that no criminal activity however ingenious would go unsolved. A part of this confidence also came from the last line of the news story. While penning the article, Nagaraj was clear that he needed an arresting headline and an equally arresting end line. Between these would obviously be the factual details of the case. That didn't offer him much scope to use his creativity. Therefore, after much thought, he had ended the article in the form of a quote by Dharmaraj. The unassuming policeman had never uttered anything remotely similar though. It was simply a result of exuberant reporting.

`Sinning is their karma. Nabbing them is my dharma.'- Dharmaraj.

Consequently, three things happened in the town of Mogga:
1. Overnight, Herculees Pirate became a household name for detective work. Even when a few aware people in the town would pronounce it rightly, the others in the conversation would promptly correct them, incorrectly. The common minds always surmised that the newspapers knew better than the individual.

2. It transposed the original character's legendary case-solving abilities onto the unsuspecting Dharmaraj. Since that day, every popular and

complex case was assigned to Dharmaraj, and its reportage, to Nagaraj.

3. Cylinder started getting more enquiries for Herculees Pirate's books. He managed to sell a few copies of The Murder of Roger Ackroyd, Murder On The Orient Express, And Then there Were None.

However, while reading the books, the townsfolk continued to pronounce the name as Herculees Pirate. The minds had already seized the name long before their eyes fell on the rightful spelling. Behind this mispronunciation lay a fundamental reason, an oblique one.

Most people in the town rode bicycles. The three most prominent brands were BSA, Raleigh and Hercules. They were local brands, at least in the people's minds since these had been around for a long time. Except for a handful of relatively well-read, well-travelled citizens, no one had any inkling that all three had British origins.

BSA was the simplest to pronounce since it was made up of just letters. That it stood for Birmingham Small Arms was lost on most people; not that it mattered.

Raleigh was pronounced Rally, which was fair. One couldn't expect people in Mogga to pronounce it exactly as the folks in its town of origin (Nottingham) would, nearly 8400 kilometres and a thousand dialects afar.

As regards Hercules, the locals called it Herculees. For nearly two generations, this brand of cycles had become a part of their vocabulary and hence, it was difficult, almost impossible, to utter a familiar word and do a dead-stop one letter sooner. Hercule sounded incomplete, incorrect, incongruous.

As regards the second name, it was in all honestly, unfair on them. Not one person could properly pronounce the name of a staple north Indian bread which had been around for a few hundred years: parantha. They conveniently and confidently called it parota. Poirot was never to be what it was meant to be.

(35)

A.K.A.

It was past midnight, way past their regular bedtime, but Begur and Cylinder were sitting up inside The Airport, an occurrence that had never happened. It was a special occasion and both were excited in their own ways. It showed a lot more on Cylinder; he was particularly restless. Because of their mood states, they weren't able to sit with their respective books, immersed in the imagination of great writers. They had tried and given up. So, they sat and chatted about this, that, and the other—anything that kept them engaged till the impending moment. And that moment was maybe thirty minutes or perhaps three hours away. They had no way of knowing it.

And so, Begur began to tell Cylinder an interesting story behind a master storyteller.

"Samuel Clemens a.k.a. Mark Twain. In the 1850s, when he was in his twenties, Samuel Clemens was a steamboat pilot for a while. It was a boyhood dream of his. He loved the Mississippi river, and the paddle-wheel steamboat that he commanded. Later on, when words started flowing from his pen faster than the river, he chose his pen name which was influenced by his time on the river. `Mark Twain' is what the leadsman of the boat would yell frequently. It was a measure of depth. It meant that the water was two fathoms which is roughly twelve feet deep and indicated safety for passage of the boat."

"How fascinating, Begur Sir! I knew that Mark Twain was not his real name but I didn't know the story behind it."

Begur smiled. Instantly, Cylinder carried a small frown.

"What did you say after Samuel Clemens?"

Begur jogged back on his words.

"Oh! A. K. A."

"You use this occasionally but strangely, I have never given it a thought; never understood it. My mind has always focussed on the names, and this—aka—whatever it is, has always registered as an inconsequential sound in between.", said Cylinder.

"You don't say it as a word. You say the letters individually. A. K. A." Begur instantly corrected him.

"Oh!", said Cylinder reflecting on it.

In order to stress his point further, Begur reeled off a list of names.

"George Orwell a.k.a. Eric Arthur Blair.
Isaac Asimov a.k.a. Paul French.
Stephen King a.k.a. Richard Bachman.
Erle Stanley Gardener a.k.a. A.A. Fair.
Charles Dickens a.k.a. Boz.
Louis L'Amour a.k.a. Tex Burns."

By the third, Cylinder had joined Begur in uttering ` a.k.a.' He hit the side of his head chastising himself for ignoring it all these years. Now, his mind dived deep into it. He liked the sound and loved its purpose. Its sole reason for existence was to open up a box of stories behind a character. How many words were birthed to sit in such a coveted position? Plus, it was a palindrome though of the most elementary kind.

"What does it mean, Begur sir?" He asked hungrily.

"It stands for `Also Known As'. It is used for people with pseudonyms—pen names for writers, stage names for actors, fake names for criminals etc."

Cylinder listened intently before responding excitedly.

"Now, I understand. We have so many a.k.a.'s in Mogga. Ravi a.k.a. Percentage Ravi, Mansoor a.k.a. Readymade Mansoor, Nagaraj a.k.a. New News Nagaraj …"

Cylinder paused on his list as Begur shook his head.

"Cylinder, those are not pen names. Those are nicknames."

Cylinder was confused.

"What's the difference, Begur Sir?"

Now, Begur was confused.

"I haven't given it much thought. But I think a nickname describes a person by his characteristic … ummm … not really sure."

They sat in silence, Cylinder intrigued by a.k.a. and Begur, by the concept of nicknames.

Expectedly, he went on a mind trip mumbling through a conversation he began having with himself.

`Nicknames! An interesting phenomenon! Definitely, it has to be older than religion. What would have prompted the first person in history to think of a nickname? Ummm! Awe? Disdain? Ridicule? Or something else?'

With a faraway look (one that seemed to travel back thousands of years) and a curious smile, Begur pondered on.

`They are a world unto their own. From mild to severe, factual to frivolous, they exist in numerous shades, sentiments and significance.'

He recollected some oft-heard names that Cylinder would talk about.

`Nicknames have so many prompts, from the obvious to the absurd, that they can come from anywhere. An idiosyncrasy (ISV and Percentage Ravi), a skill (New News Nagaraj), a random spur-of-the-moment coinage (Jackie, the cow), one's livelihood (Tempo Tony), a mispronunciation (Herculees Pirate) …'

"Cylinder, tell me the stories behind some more nicknames in Mogga."

While it was academic for Begur, it was exciting for Cylinder. He knew so many characters in great detail, either in person or through conversations with Chikkanna and others. As they started discussing a random list of names, both found the back stories highly engrossing.

1. Readymade Mansoor: His family owned a store that sold readymade garments; a small store but it was a big deal. Technically,

Mansoor was in First Year B. Com but practically he was already into the family business. He spent most of the time at the store, and would occasionally land up in college to while away time, and show off the latest fabrics (stone wash, acid wash, monkey wash), cuts and designs. Most of the youth in Mogga admired and envied him because they bought cloth and got dresses stitched while he picked clothes. Since the age of twelve, Readymade Mansoor had never been to a tailor. The difference between the two, especially for young, impressionable minds was enormous.

2. TT Shyam: He wasn't eminent in table tennis by any yardstick. The town itself had players more promising than him. But he could play with either hand. Some days, he would decide to play with his regular hand and on some, with his left. He was a regular at the Mogga City Club.

3. Gym Krishna (or Protein Krishna): The son of a betel nut wholesaler, he had dropped out of college after six months. While meandering through his teenage years, he had developed one precious interest: fitness. Since he didn't read textbooks, he had a lot of spare time. He spent this, reading magazines on bodybuilding. Obviously, he read visuals more than words and was fascinated with Sandow, the man widely considered as the `father of modern bodybuilding'.
[Born Friedrich Wilhelm Muller in 1867, Sandow achieved worldwide fame for his sculpted body and acts of strength. Somewhere along the journey to stardom, he had adopted the stage name of Eugen Sandow. Such was his legend that even after his death in 1925, his name had lived on in the form of Sandow banians, the sleeveless vest that adorned the muscle mass of any self-respecting fitness fanatic.]
When he was twenty-three, Krishna arm-twisted his father quite effortlessly, took ten thousand rupees and set up the first modern gym in Mogga. He spent early mornings to late evenings there, training himself and the new breed of wide-eyed bodybuilding aspirants.
Armed with muscles and a muscular bike, the Rajdoot 350 cc, he was mostly seen around town in a Sandow banian. Some of his ex-classmates used to remark among themselves that he had bigger biceps

than brains. But truth be told, he had fared well for himself. He was all brawn but not a fight-monger. Within five years, Sandow's Gym had become a destination for the muscle-minded. Members had increased year on year. He had returned the initial investment to his father, employed three of the first ten members as additional trainers, and spent time with the most promising and driven. To these select few, he supplied precious protein powder at cost price, the ones he bought from his trips to Bangalore. Most of the town called him Gym Krishna while a select few called him Protein Krishna.

4. Mallige Mariamma: Outside the Shani temple sat a line of flower-sellers. Now in her 50s, Mariamma had been a constant for 17 years at this spot. And all through, she had been constant about one thing. Depending on the season and demand, every other vendor sold different varieties of flowers: hibiscus, lotus, champa, marigold, coral jasmine, chrysanthemum, and jasmine (called `mallige' locally). But Mariamma sold only `mallige' irrespective of the season or the opportunities to earn more. Her jasmine flowers weren't better than what others sold. Yet, while people bought flowers from different vendors, they always came to her for jasmine. They would haggle but end up buying from her even if she charged a few paise more than the others. No one understood her resolute business logic, or the lack of it. She was wedded to jasmine, that's all!

Over the years, she had been asked about this by her fellow vendors, some regular customers, her fruit-seller husband, and a few members of her family. In every instance, she had only smiled, shrugged and mumbled that jasmine was her flower. Only once, she had let out a little more to her 16-year-old daughter, though it was deep and cryptic.

"Everyone else is known as a flower-seller. I am known as a flower."

She had her logic if one could derive any meaning out of it.

Begur and Cylinder discussed more names—Googly Ramesh, Samantha Fox Harish, Blade Manja, Fish Tank Derrick.

"Cylinder, your question about a.k.a. opened up an interesting topic for us."

"So, now can I use a.k.a. with these names?", asked Cylinder hopefully.

Begur considered it.

"I am still not sure, Cylinder. Technically, it's for pseudonyms and not nicknames, I think. Anyway, I have a good alternative. Instead of a.k.a., use b.k.a."

Cylinder knitted his eyebrows trying to work it out.

"Better known as.", said Begur.

Cylinder muttered `b.k.a.' several times and didn't look excited. It didn't sit right on his tongue. It lacked the cadence that a.k.a. held. Begur could see that Cylinder was too sold on it, whether it was technically correct or not. His mind scrambled frantically to humour Cylinder.

"Cylinder, yes! You can use a.k.a."

Cylinder grinned like Kipling's Kim as Begur added, "In fact, let's make a.k.a. more imaginative and interesting."

Cylinder was all ears.

"Let's start with you. Cylinder a.k.a.?"

"Cylinder, also known as … ummm … bookseller?"

Begur clicked his tongue and shook his head, looking more animated than Cylinder. Then, with a smile of triumph crossing his face, he said, "Cylinder a.k.a., always known as."

Cylinder burst out with joy.

"Begur Sir, that's so true and beautiful!" He continued to smile reflecting on this wordplay.

Begur was itching to continue but paused for Cylinder to extract maximum happiness and settle down. Then, he let out the next.

"Readymade Mansoor a.k.a., aspirationally known as."

A second wave of excitement hit Cylinder, closely followed by the third as Begur said, "Percentage Ravi a.k.a., appropriately known as."

"What about the cow?", asked Cylinder trying in vain to make up his own.

"Jackie, the cow! Let me see …ummm … yes … Jackie a.k.a., accidentally known as."

As Cylinder's peals of laughter rang loudly, Begur presented the next one.

"Herculees Pirate a.k.a., ambitiously known as."

"Ha ha ha ha! Begur Sir, you are too good."

"And then there's ISV.", continued Begur.

The mention of ISV made both of them double up with laughter.

"So, what is a.k.a. for ISV?", asked Cylinder eagerly.

"It is a pseudonym which is also an acronym. ISV a.k.a., amusingly known as."

As they convulsed with laughter, Cylinder thought he saw a flash of light outside the window.

"Begur Sir, I think he's here."

They both jumped up and ran to the window. A taxi stood outside the main gate, its bright headlights cutting through the darkness of the night. Immediately, the porch light downstairs came on and Begur's parents walked out. Begur and Cylinder turned around and hurriedly headed towards the staircase.

"I am so excited, Begur Sir! But I don't know what to call him.", squealed Cylinder running down the steps.

Fifty-two hours, three flights and a six-hour taxi ride later, a knackered Y.B. wearily got out, hugged his mother, smiled at his father and waved at Begur and Cylinder who were striding up.

(IV)

THE NEW BEGUR

(36)

THE MAN WITH NO NAME

Decades earlier, a handful of years after Begur had graduated to shorts from diapers, his parents had decided to invite diapers into their lives again. They got blessed with another boy though they would have considered themselves more blessed if it had been a girl.

The boys, separated by five years, grew up with all things that all siblings grow up with—fondness, fights, shared interests, stark differences, silly taunts, knick-knacks, nicknames etc. They would run around the farm shrieking, roll together in the mud, throw pebbles at fruit trees, and at each other every now and then, pinch, punch, run up to The Airport with one chasing the other, and trundle down the staircase with roles reversed. They were fond of the same sweets and loathed the same vegetables.

A few years went by and with time, their core personalities began to take shape and size. Begur had now touched double digits and was drawn deeply into his expansive and endless world of new companions: books. He would hardly spend time outside on the farm, or with his brother. Sibling conversations, silly activities, adventures and squabbles reduced. They'd go to school and come back together, and Begur would eagerly make his way up to his pages waiting inside The Airport. In these formative years of what would become a life-long obsession, Begur was going through a phase of fascination with initials. The oddball-ness of this ten-year-old boy had begun to set in.

He would devour his comics and in between, walk around the room, look at books and memorise names of authors, including what their initials stood for. Some books carried the complete name of the author while some didn't. For those, he had a ready reckoner, one that he loved to open and look at. It was a handwritten notebook that his grandfather had maintained, in which, decades earlier, he had neatly penned down the complete names of several authors, for his own reference and delight. Though the two had been destined to spend very little time together, Begur loved the old man and felt supremely connected to him. Going by his handwriting, Begur carried a strong impression that his grandfather was a very handsome and elegant man, which indeed he had been. Each time he'd open this notebook, Begur would read odd bits of trivia about books, stare at the handwriting, smile, think fondly about his grandfather, and then turn and look up at the neatly framed picture of this striking man adorning one wall of The Airport.

He would set question papers for himself and answer them when he got back from school. Initially, his test papers were in alphabetical order; that somehow seemed to help him remember every part of the name. He had then graduated to mixing it up. Begur would put down his questions on the left and fill in his answers on the right, and he'd almost always get them right.

J.R.R. Tolkien	: John Ronald Reuel Tolkien
C.S. Lewis	: Clive Staples Lewis
J.D. Salinger	: Jerome David Salinger
A.A. Milne	: Alan Alexander Milne
Agatha M.C. Christie	: Agatha Mary Clarissa Christie
H.G. Wells	: Herbert George Wells
Ian L. Fleming	: Ian Lancaster Fleming
P.G. Wodehouse	: Pelham Grenville Wodehouse

Anton P. Chekov   : Anton Pavlovich Chekov
Ray D. Bradbury   : Ray Douglas Bradbury
Arthur I. Conan Doyle : Arthur Ignatius Conan Doyle

To him, a letter with a dot was mystifying and alluring. The dot always seemed to tell him, "Unlock me if you can." For a few months, he was intoxicated with this game of complete names.

One day, during his heady trip, in a moment of being annoyed by his little brother, he had turned around and instinctively yelled, "Y.B.! Stop troubling me!"

Even as the little boy had sneered, Begur had broken into a victorious smile as his mind raced around the initials. In a trice, irritation turned into exultation. He got up and kept yelling the initials in repeat mode.

That evening, at dinner, Begur had said excitedly, "Dad! Mom! I have a new, wonderful name for him. Y.B.! It's perfect. From today, we will all call him just that."

More casual than curious, his father had asked, "Why Y.B.?"

"Because he's my younger brother." Begur had retorted with a sharp smile.

Smiling while serving, his mother had countered.

"He's your younger brother. So, you call him that. We'll call him by his name. Why should we call him Y.B.?"

"Mom! Both of you should also call him Y.B. because ..." Begur had paused for dramatic effect.

His mother had held the ladle just above his plate and had repeated the last word of his sentence.

"Because?"

"Because he's the youngest Begur." Begur had delivered his checkmate response.

So delighted was he with his coinage that he had smiled through while chewing on a handful of one of his loathed vegetables. Between mouthfuls, Begur had reiterated.

"From today, we will all call him that. Okay? Done."

With a gentle raise of their eyebrows, the parents had marvelled and smiled.

Moving his little face around the table, from here to there to there, the little one had also smiled. He was big enough to understand that he was the subject of the conversation but not big enough to grasp the play of it. But it hadn't mattered. He had been happy just to see his elder brother delighted and his parents sporting an appreciative look.

The family had then eaten with soulful smiles, savouring the delightful taste of childhood inventiveness and innocence. Since that day, the family had called him `Y.B.'

(37)

ONLY CHIPS, NO TRIPS

Years came and went. Y.B. grew into his own. He too was a reader but not as avid as his brother. While Begur got high on the magic of words, Y.B. got fascinated with the logic of things. Whenever outside on the farm, he would spend packets of time looking at the tractor, staring at each part, and the whole. Inside the house, his two favourite companions were the torchlight and the transistor. He would dismantle them, look closely at each component, think deeply and put them back together again.

Y.B. turned out to be a sharp student, needing little effort in mathematics and physics, the double whammy for many students. By the time he was in his mid-teens, he was clear about the `What?' and `Where?' of his life:
Study electronics. In a prestigious university. In America. Join a legendary firm. Live the dream.
"My clarity. My reality." He would often say to his parents.

Soon after Begur had come back from England, Y.B. had left for America. After graduating with enviable grades, he had landed his dream job. What books were to Begur, chips and semiconductors were to him.

Stepping inside Intel on his first day, he had smiled to himself.

`This is one of those places that will pave the future course of mankind. This is the place where I can trade intelligence. Gain, as well as give.'

He had then proceeded to his desk, excited as a child.

At that very moment, back on the farm, Begur had opened a newly arrived parcel and pulled out a book, `The Lost Continent: Travels in Small-Town America.'

He had sat down, flipped the pages, and found a handwritten note inside. Putting the note aside on the table, he had inhaled the book, a few pages at random and exclaimed in his mind, `Aaaaah! The smell of a new voice! This is aphrodisiacal!'

He had then looked at the note.

Big Brother,

There's a lot of talk about this book here. And so, I read a book for pleasure after a long time. I found it unputdownable. This is insanely funny, inventive and insightful. I am pretty sure you'll find it equally delightful. So, while I live the big American dream, you live your little joys of fantastic writing, this one being about small-town America. I hope you enjoy this book as much as I did.

Take care. Walk around the farm every few hours. Don't sit glued at the desk.

I thought of signing off this little note with my real name but that would have muted your childhood thunder.

Y.B.

Begur had carried a smile in his heart while reading the note. He had then looked at the name of the author again and loudly uttered it.

"Bill Bryson."

This time, he had carried a smile on his face. Saying aloud the name, especially someone new to him always made Begur feel closer to the author.

In the heart of Silicon Valley, Y.B. had begun to expand his mind and live his heart's desire. He began to love his work so much that he had little time for anything else, including his family back home. He would make the customary call to his parents once every two weeks. As time progressed, naturally there was less and less to talk about, other than the perfunctory.

[An unyielding rule of life, a reality in the case of most people, with some exceptions here and there. As children grow up and develop their own interests, the interactions between them and their parents grow duller. The `conversation chasm' gets wider.]

Like any child, Y.B. was primarily interested in knowing if they were healthy, and they were essentially interested in knowing if he was healthy and happy. Beyond that, there was little in common between their `farm life' and his `valley life'.

At home, the telephone set was downstairs, and Begur was almost always upstairs. In addition, the brothers had little in common. Y.B. would speak to his parents, and after all routine matters were exchanged, enquire about Begur and what the big fella was up to.

"All good with him. He's happy.", used to be the standard response from his parents.

Y.B. would chuckle and say, "Dad! Mom! You both sound like an IVR." The first time he had used it, his parents had reacted, "IVR?"

"It means Interactive Voice Response. Pre-decided. Pre-recorded. It's still not widely used but in the future, IVR will be a big thing. So, does Begur help you out on the farm or is he stuck inside The Airport always?"

"He's there whenever we need him.", used to be his father's response to which his mother would add, "Unfortunately, we can't be there for you whenever you need us."

Their conversation would always end with Y.B. saying the same four things, in the very same order.

"I am doing fine, mother. I'll see you all soon. This year looks unlikely though. Say hi to The Airport inhabitant."

"Now, you sound like an IVR." His mom would say and chuckle.

It was always delivered in good humour, not as a touché.

Well, all this was the past, and presently, it wasn't the time to reflect upon it. Y.B. was finally home and his parents were smiling like two Malnad elephants whose baby had gone missing for several hours and was back. Big Sir entered the kitchen with a placid smile. His wife was immersed in making savouries and sweets of several kinds, with a soulful smile.

"One son who never leaves home, and the other who rarely comes home." He said, placing his hand on her shoulder.

He said it matter-of-factly, not as a barb. They smiled at each other. The scent of parental joy wafted around the kitchen, waltzing around the aroma of numerous tasty eats.

Beyond the kitchen, the excitement was much more. The chatter on the farm got punctuated with, "Y.B. Sir has come. Y.B. Sir has come." Some of the labourers had never seen him while a few (the new ones) didn't even know that he existed.

"Does Y.B. Sir look like Big Sir or Big Mother?", asked one farmhand.

"Fifty fifty.", said an older farmhand.

"Oh! Then he must be looking like Begur Sir.", commented the first.

"Same same height but thinner than Begur Sir. At least, when he was here years ago.", said the second.

But the most excited on the farm was Cylinder. He had been a little over three years when Y.B. had last visited. His memories were sketchy, to say the least. He would occasionally hear about him from Big Mother or Big Sir, just little packets of mundane information. The Begur universe had three distinct worlds: Big Sir & Big Mother, Begur & Cylinder, and Y.B.

All three existed in complete harmony but operated quite independent of each other.

Cylinder sauntered into the kitchen and saw Big Mother and Big Sir standing in front of the stove even as Big Mother was frying something.

`Something special for someone special.' He thought and smiled.

He then walked towards the second bedroom downstairs, paused outside the closed door, and stood thinking for a minute, unsurely. Feeling disabled by curiosity, he gently nudged the door and peered at the man fast asleep inside.

`Y.B. Sir! I cannot tell you how happy and curious I am to spend time

with you. You please rest and wake up. Then we will catch up. I want to listen to all of your stories and tell you all of mine. Shhhh!'
His mind uttered these words, not his lips.

(38)

THE MAN WHO SAW TOMORROW

"Begur Sir! Y.B. Sir is fast asleep.", whispered Cylinder to Begur upstairs even though Y.B. was conducting his `snore orchestra' in the bedroom downstairs.
Begur spoke in a normal tone.
"He will be, for a few more hours. He's crossed multiple time zones. His body clock will need time to recalibrate. I guess he will wake up around lunchtime. Even if he doesn't, mom will wake him up, feed him and only then allow him to go back to bed again."
"I am not going to work today, Begur Sir. Maybe not for a few days. I've informed all the regulars at the traffic signal that I want to spend time with Y.B. Sir. I don't know when I'll get the chance again. He lives so far away."
"That's right. He's the only person in our family who actually took off from The Airport and landed in the land of Asimov, Ursula Guin, Bradbury and Frank Herbert.", replied Begur without taking his eyes off the book that he was into.

Cylinder looked lost.

"I know of the others. Who's Frank Herbert? I haven't heard of him."

"What's common to these names?", asked Begur.

Cylinder thought. He ran up various combinations in his mind.

"Hmmm! Fantasy?"

"Not quite off the mark, Cylinder. You can say that. There are genres and sub-genres, and some of them do overlap. But I would say, science fiction."

Cylinder's curiosity was piqued.

"Sci-fi! Tell me about Frank Herbert."

Begur put his book down.

"He's the creator of the Duniverse."

"The ... universe?"

"The Duniverse." Begur corrected.

In all these years, Cylinder was usually all ears but this time even more so. He hadn't heard this name, seen his books across any of the shelves, and hadn't the faintest idea what Duniverse meant. Begur held back for a bit, waiting for Cylinder's mental questions to quell and curiosity to swell.

"He is the author of Dune, the best-selling sci-fi novel of all time. Several literary critics consider it to be the best sci-fi book ever written. And it won the inaugural Nebula Award."

The Law of Recency took over Cylinder's mind. The conversation had begun with Y.B. and now, it was about Nebula.

"What's Nebula Award, Begur Sir?"

"Oh! It's the award for the best sci-fi novel of the year. It was instituted in 1966 and in its inaugural year, Dune carried it home between its pages."

"Yessssss!" Cylinder pumped his fists. The victory of any book and its author always filled him with adrenaline. It made him hold onto the `ess' syllable for far longer than required.

"Yessssss!", said Begur measuring his hold precisely.

"Do you know what Arthur C. Clarke had to say about it?"

Cylinder wanted to shake his head but it remained transfixed on Begur.

"I know nothing comparable to it other than The Lord Of The Rings."

Begur parroted Sir Arthur's words.

So filled was Cylinder with awe and curiosity that his next set of words came out in a whisper.

"And Begur Sir, what did Tolkien Sir feel about it?"

"Hmmm! Well, Mr. Tolkien refused to review the book saying he disliked it intensely and therefore his comments would be unfair to Frank Herbert."

For several moments, there was pin-drop silence. Both were running their thoughts around the confusion in their conversation:

A great piece of work, lauded by one great, disliked vehemently by another. So, did that make it great or not?

Cylinder looked at Begur beseechingly for clarity.

"Let me tell you what Carl Sagan had to say about it." Begur offered.

"The stories are so tautly constructed, so rich in the accommodating details of an unfamiliar society that they sweep me along before I have even a chance to be critical."

Cylinder listened intently soaking in every word. He allowed himself to smile for a few moments before the next question topped his mind.

"So, what is Duniverse? No, no, no, no, Begur Sir! Don't tell me. I think I know. Duniverse is the fictional world that he created. Correct?"

Begur's smile carried the affirmation.

"Duniverse is an intricate, profound, expansive sci-fi world with a twist. Unlike the majority of sci-fi literature, it is set tens of thousands of years in the future …"

Cylinder cut in, with a faraway look in his eyes.

"What's the twist, Begur Sir?"

"Dune explores themes of human evolution, the long-term survival of our species, ecology, religion, politics, economics, power etc. But here's the twist, Cylinder. It's about a civilisation that has banned all thinking machines such as computers, robots and artificial intelligence. I struggle to think of any popular sci-fi work that is bereft of these three."

"Okay. I don't fully understand what computers, robots and artificial intelligence mean, but I do understand that sci-fi doesn't work without them. That's why it's so special. Correct, Begur Sir?"

Begur nodded absent-mindedly carrying a distant look in his eyes. He was either thinking back recollecting his reading of the book or thinking millennia ahead wondering about the future of our species.

Cylinder held back his next question till Begur returned to the present.

"Begur Sir, I know the position of every book in The Airport, and I am familiar with all the names. But I don't know about Frank Herbert and Dune, because he, it, is not on any of these shelves."

"Do you see that trunk in the corner? The Dune series is in it."

Cylinder turned and looked at the trunk, one that he had seen innumerable times since childhood but never spared a thought.

"Y.B. used to read while growing up. Not as much as me though. The Dune series used to be his favourite. All through high school and college, he'd finish his studies, read them and re-read them. When he left for America, he packed all his childhood memories in that trunk. I let him have it."

"Begur Sir, can I please open the trunk and have a look?"

"Of course."

Cylinder jumped up, walked to the trunk and lifted the lid with a smile. He saw an abacus slate, a few decades-old Nippo batteries, parts of an old transistor, a torch, a Camlin geometry box, a kaleidoscope and a few other old, meagre items. All of them lay upon two stacks of books underneath, which were wrapped in polythene.

"Begur Sir, can I take the books out?"

"Of course."

Pushing the assortment of items to one side, Cylinder looked at the stack. It carried a handwritten sticker that read: My Textbooks.

Pushing all the items in the other direction, Cylinder looked at the other stack. The sticker read: My Tech Books.

He looked confused as he could see a stack of novels through the polythene.

"Begur Sir, what are tech books?"

"Technology books, Cylinder. From a young age, Y.B. was always drawn to technology."

Cylinder lifted the stack of three books, unwrapped the polythene, and looked at each of them in wonderment—Dune, Dune Messiah, Children of Dune.

Begur was by his side. He took them from Cylinder, lifted each one to his nose, and smelled the Duniverse after years.

"Subsequently, there was God Emperor of Dune, Heretics of Dune, and Chapterhouse: Dune. Those three aren't here. Y.B. had moved on by then. I don't know if he's read them later on."

He handed the books back to Cylinder who felt, smelled, placed them back and closed the trunk.

"Tech books?" He muttered to himself. It sounded nice, simple yet exotic.

"Begur Sir, what does Y.B. Sir do in America?"

Begur thought awhile wondering what exactly to say.

"Y.B. works on things that will someday make science fiction a reality."

The circumference of Cylinder's eyeballs expanded to its maximum.

"Does he work on computers, robots and artificial intelligence?"

"I don't know, Cylinder. I suppose so. He works on things called chips, semiconductors and whatnot, the building blocks of intelligent machines. You can ask him when he wakes up. As far as I am concerned, the most intelligent tools are books."

"Let me see if Y.B. Sir has woken up."

Cylinder darted towards the staircase.

(39)

Y.B. VERSUS PARENTS

Begur and Cylinder sat inside The Airport immersed in their respective books. Lunchtime was still half a clock face away. Cylinder had repeatedly gone downstairs to check if Y.B. Sir had woken up and at some point, settled down with his book. Big Mother would surely call out to them when it happened.

At quarter past noon, Y.B. suddenly woke up. He staggered out of the room (half awake, half sleepy) and walked to the dining table. He saw his parents sitting there facing his room. As soon as he sat down, his mother gently pushed a bowl of boiled-and-salted groundnuts towards him. In the pecking order of things on the table, this was probably the lowliest. It was the poor man's poor snack, but it tasted oh-so divine. He helped himself to a few and instantly got transported to his childhood.

While growing up, Y.B. would yearn for it and pester her regularly. Having a bowl of this while disassembling the transistor would transport him to a blissful state.

"Mouth and mind. Both in bliss." He would say this to his mother and smile.

If Begur happened to be around, Begur would always counter it with, "I can think of a better combination. A great writer reading aloud a chapter from one of his books, to himself, to hear in his own voice what his mind has managed to cook up. Nothing can beat that."

Y.B. would then make a snarly face at him while she would place a bowl next to Begur, smile and walk away.

"There are Indian stores in America. I get our sweets and savouries though they are nowhere close to what yours taste like. But these groundnuts! Just a few of them and my jetlag is gone. Thanks mom."

Y.B. smiled at her like a grown-up child.

"Am I Kaikeyi?" She asked.

"Huh?", said Y.B.

"Did I get your father to banish you from home?" She asked without sounding acidic.

"Mom! You're being silly.", said Y.B. munching on more.

"Me or you? Does it take you a decade to come home? Don't the Americans have holidays?" She retorted, pushing a plate of coconut barfis (a childhood favourite of his) towards him.

"Of course, they do."

Y.B. picked up one and bit into it. He closed his mouth and with it, his eyes too. As delight spread over his face, he held his palm up signalling her to stop her inquisition. She smiled herself into silence and allowed him his moments.

As soon as his eyes opened, she opened her mouth.

"Then? Can't you make a trip every year? Or, at least once in two years? We will send you the ticket."

"Mom, it has nothing to do with holidays or money. It's just that I am working on a very advanced chip. It takes years to bear fruit. Like the tamarind tree." He threw in a farm analogy hoping to veer the topic.

"Whatever! I hope you've found someone to bear fruits with?" She veered it in another direction.

Y.B. responded with a coyish smile. The parents exchanged a barely noticeable smile and turned towards him.

His smile was a bloody ruse. It perfectly camouflaged what Y.B. had activated behind it: his IC. He was thinking of a quick and quirky response to the silly question he had been posed with.

[He preferred referring to his brain as an Integrated Circuit. A steadfast believer in the power of machine computing, he was sure that the day wasn't far when machines would take over most tasks of the world and do a far better job than humans. He would often sermonize the younger members in his team.

"Since the beginning of time, man has measured intelligence in the form of IQ. Its days are numbered. IC will be the new ruler. The better and faster ICs we build, the better and faster the world will be. ICs will run everything for us, more efficiently and quickly, unimaginably so."]

Several chips in his IC were working at full capacity and within seconds, they had served him several options to counter his mom. He picked one that he felt worked best for him.

"Uffff! Mom! How many times have I told you? I like being on my own. Like Newton."

"Who's Newton?"

"Isaac Newton, mom. Remember apple and gravity?"

"I know who Newton is. I thought you were talking about some American friend of yours."

Y.B. quickly said, "Dad, did you know this?"

Startling his father, he managed to wall off his mother, at least momentarily.

[Big Sir was a man with all the emotions of a father but with a mere fraction of the words of a regular being. He cared for everyone, took care of everything, without expressing much. He had always been this way, a complete contrast to his parents. Unlike Y.B.'s grandfather, his father was like a grandfather clock—always around, ticking away in the background, making sure everything in his little world stuck to its simple schedule.]

"Huh?", said his father.

"You know, mom?" Y.B. instantly switched his gaze towards her.

"Newton worked seven days a week, 13-16 hours a day. He never socialised. He had no relationships. He never married. He wanted no distractions. And see what all he achieved!"

"I am not interested in Newton." She countered. "You are already in your forties. Someday, you'll grow old. You'll be done with all your chips. Then? You'll need someone to be around with—to talk to, laugh with, argue about silly things, watch TV together, share a bowl of dessert with, and someone who can look after you."

"Relax, mom. By then, there will be robots. They'll be more efficient than any human."

"Sometimes, I wonder ... of the two of you, who's less sensible?"

In a jiffy, his IC served him the rightful sentence at the right time.

"Of the four of us, you are the most sensible. Dad, the most simple. My brother, the most solitary. And I, the most single-minded."

She felt disarmed and smiled. Her inquisition waned.

While Y.B. didn't think very highly of IQ, he was a man with a lot of EQ. This was the moment (a long pending one) when his deepest emotions rose to speak.

"Mom, I do think of this from time to time. I think about us and wonder if we all belong to the same family. It's quite natural that children turn out different from their parents, that siblings can be more dissimilar than strangers, but to this extent? We, the Begurs, are quite a case study. My brother has taken after our granddad, but I don't know whose personality I have inherited. By any chance, was our great grandfather a man of science?"

"He did study agricultural science.", said the father.

"Aaaah! See the connection, mom." He paused and thought about it. He wasn't play-acting.

"On a serious note, I need to tell you this. Thanks to our forefathers, and providence, we are a lucky lot. Yet, I cannot label the two of you as lucky parents, though with absolute conviction, I can say that the two of us are the luckiest children on this planet.

You've let us do whatever we wanted to, however out of the ordinary. You've placed no expectations on us for your own satisfaction, delight or need. Any other set of parents in your place would have lamented, openly or silently, and quite frequently, saying, `We are blessed in many ways, but we are also cursed in some ways.'

But I know this for sure that you and dad have never harboured these sentiments. The two of you are special children of the Almighty. He's poured in all the simplicity, divinity and contentment that He could muster up. I love you both though I don't say it often or see you often."

He got up and placed his hand on his father's shoulder who patted it gently. He then walked around to the other side of the table and hugged her, long and hard, till his teardrops wet her forehead. She wiped hers before wiping his.

(40)

Y.B. VERSUS CYLINDER

A week had passed since Y.B. had landed and Cylinder was still unsure about him. He had had so many questions to ask, so many conversations to have, so many things to share, but nothing had happened. Y.B. seemed very reticent. He carried a polite smile towards Cylinder most of the time, and Cylinder did try several times to strike meaningful conversations with him but to no avail.
`Perhaps he's tired from the journey.' He told himself initially.
As days passed and things didn't change, he told himself several other things.
`Perhaps he's like Begur Sir, an introvert.'
`Perhaps he thinks I belong to Begur Sir, and since the two of them hardly speak, he's treating me the same way.'
`Perhaps he thinks he's a big inventor, and I am a small child and that I have nothing important or interesting to tell him.'
`Perhaps he thinks he's far superior to everyone, including Begur Sir and his parents.'
Each of the thoughts felt right.

`Perhaps it is a combination of all the above.'

Whatever it was, Cylinder felt disappointed and hurt.

After a few days of being troubled, he told himself, `It's okay, Cylinder. Don't bother about him. He's here for a few more days and then he'll be gone for several years. Good riddance. I am quite sure his parents and Begur Sir must be thinking the same. It's sad really, but such is life.'

He then supplied himself a code of conduct.

`Ask nothing. Say nothing. Just smile politely and move on.'

He walked to the mirror and practised the smile several times till it looked authentic. He then strode into his routine with gusto.

    That evening, when he got back home from work, he saw Y.B. standing at the front door, sporting his usual smile.

"Cylinder, keep your bag, freshen up, eat something and come out. I want to talk to you."

He ran up to The Airport.

"Begur Sir, what does Y.B. Sir want to talk to me about?"

"I have no idea.", said Begur, immersed in his book.

Cylinder hurriedly washed his face, skipped his snack and walked out to the porch.

    Immediately, Y.B. started walking and Cylinder followed. He sauntered across to a tractor, patted it fondly, climbed up on it and signalled Cylinder to join him. Cylinder did as he was told. Y.B. gazed up at the sky and then swept his eyes across the farm. It was early evening. The bluish orange sky looked magnificent. Several flocks of birds were making their way home, from wherever, chattering animatedly about their day. Several labourers were winding up their chores. Y.B. took in all the sights with a smile even as Cylinder kept looking at Y.B. trying to read the situation.

`Begur Sir and his parents are so normal, but he is quite an eccentric fellow! Good that he stays on his own, far far away from home.' He thought to himself.

"So, what are you planning to do with your life, boy?" Y.B. interrupted his thoughts.

"Huh?", said Cylinder.

Grow up and be like my brother?", asked Y.B. in a gentle tone.

"I would love to be like him, Y.B. Sir.", said Cylinder earnestly.
"As in, do nothing? Waste your life?", said Y.B. emphatically.
Cylinder got riled, and in the very instant also realised that he ought to hold his tongue. He had no right whatsoever to talk back in the same tone. He took a deep breath, reminded himself of his code of conduct, remembered his rehearsals in front of the mirror and smiled politely.
"Begur Sir is my inspiration. He's unlike any other person. I love and respect Begur Sir a lot."
Y.B. looked up at another flock of chattery birds.
"Just being different, idle and wasted doesn't qualify for love, respect or inspiration ... at least in my book."
"Nobody has read more books than Begur Sir.", said Cylinder as emphatically as he could manage.
"Is that of any use?"
"Yes! He made me fall in love with books. And I will do the same for hundreds of others. In his own way, Begur Sir is spreading so much joy and wisdom. Is that a useless pursuit?"
"Huh! My brother is a good-for-nothing fella.", said Y.B. dismissively.
"Please don't say that! Every person has his or her own purpose. As long as it doesn't harm others, it's a good thing."
"And your purpose is to stand at the traffic signal and try and peddle books to people who are otherwise gainfully engaged in life's activities? Useless pursuit, boy!"
Cylinder wanted to counter but kept mum. He decided to disengage. He didn't want to continue this losing argument because it was with a loser. Several thoughts floated around in his mind.
`A highly intelligent man. A man who has grown up reading a decent number of books. Extremely well-educated. Living in America. Working in a big company. Begur's own brother. And yet, such stupid notions? Such brashness?'
"Useless! Your pursuit is useless. Drop it. Get back to school. Become a man, unlike my brother.", said Y.B. looking up at the sky.
`The less said the better.' Cylinder reigned himself with these words. He then looked up and tried to see beyond the sky.
`God! I don't know if you exist. Begur Sir surely thinks you don't and I will go with his judgement. But, for now, I need to tell you this. If you

do exist, please listen carefully to every word that I am saying.
Y.B. Sir is among the most intelligent and educated people on earth. And he chose to follow his pursuit which no one in his family understands. Yet, in all these years, I have never once heard Big Sir, Big Mother or Begur Sir say one negative thing about him, or his path of pleasure. Without ever knowing him, I always thought of him as a superhero. But now I know. If people like him don't understand passion and purpose beyond one's own, then the world that you've created is doomed. He's super zero! Please don't create more people like him.'

Y.B. was looking at him piercingly. His eyes lorded over Cylinder's small frame with authority — of age, intellect and quasi-guardianship.
"Hmmm! I can see that you've stopped arguing and started thinking. Good boy! And, good that I came down. Someone had to fill some sense into you."
Cylinder sniggered without being obvious.
"Everything has a shelf-life, Cylinder. For centuries, books have been occupying our shelves. Now, if I have to talk like Shakespeare, their time is nigh!"
Cylinder locked his eyes with Y.B.
"Okay, let me offer you more clarity. Before my brother dies and long before you die, books will be dead!"
The last part jolted Cylinder. His bile rose. Along with it, his defiance and his entire self.
"I am sorry, Y.B. Sir. I am going."
"Sit down, Cylinder. Don't run away from reality. Both of you have done it for years already. I've given up on my brother, but my conscience is pushing me to salvage you."
Cylinder sat down, partly curious, mostly confused.
"We are now in the 80s. Another 20 years, maybe 25-30, tops ... they will be a thing of the past. No one will be reading books, thankfully. And the world will be a better place. No more of chopping millions of trees. No more of wasting precious real estate for bookstores, printing presses, circulating libraries. No more ink, no more weight, no more volume, no more idiotic manual labour. Oh! The sheer wastage of mankind! It'll all come to an end."

Cylinder was numbed into silence. It was a lot for him to process.

"I've gotta go now." Y.B. got up.

"Please sit down, Y.B. Sir. I need to ask you something."

"Shoot, Cylinder."

"You know more. You have seen more of the world. You are a lot older than me, but younger than Begur Sir. I have no idea about any of the things you said, but from what Begur Sir has always told me, how can there be a world without books? Without stories? Without emotions? Without characters? Without imagination? Without words? If ever there is a death-day for books, Begur Sir will die happily before that, and so will I."

"Good point, Cylinder. I said books will die, not stories."

Cylinder looked confused.

"In the future, not too far ahead, the world will only watch and hear, not read. Books can go to hell or sit here on earth till they all die of boredom."

"Y.B. Sir, you are talking about cinema, not books. You mean to say that the world will be going to cinema theatres every day?"

Y.B. smiled, not his shallow, polite smile but a deeply victorious one.

"My brother told me about a dialogue of yours, and he called it legendary.

`If people don't come to the books, the books will go to the people.'

Similarly, stories will go to the people, not merely words. Stories on screens, with music and voice, straight into their palms. You will be able to savour any story, whenever and wherever, twenty-four seven. All day long, all night long. You can watch it while sitting, shitting, lying down, walking, talking, working, travelling, eating ... even while bathing! Now, can you bathe with a book? The world doesn't know it yet, and you have no idea. But, by the time you sprout a manly moustache, the world would have switched from books to a scintillating stories-on-screen experience called `mobile phones'. I, and hundreds of technologists like me, are working on the building blocks to make books obsolete."

Cylinder shook his head, the insides of which were in disarray.

"Mobile phones." He muttered this alien word, unable to make any sense of the first part of it. The sound of it seemed harmless, genial even. But Y.B. Sir's explanation of what it would do to people, and books, agitated him. The more he thought about it, the more troubled he felt. He dug deep trying to think of something to counter this argument, or future reality or fiction, but he was woefully short of anything sensible.

Silence was his only partner.

Y.B. allowed him the companionship for a minute before breaking them up.

"So, Cylinder, it's only a matter of time before The Airport gets shut down. Books won't fly. You have two choices. Get back to school, study and pursue whatever you find worthy. But, if you love standing all day long at the traffic signal, switch from books to fruits. Sell berries, mangoes, jackfruit, papaya, chickoos … anything, depending on the season. From our own farm. So many genres of fruits. Better than books any day. Health and happiness for the buyer, success and satisfaction for you."

Y.B. locked his eyes with Cylinder.

"Thank you, Y.B. Sir, for sharing the future. I could have never imagined."

Y.B. smiled.

"So, A or plan B?"

Cylinder looked away but his words were angled towards Y.B.

"Before the world becomes a stupid place, I will make sure as many people read as many books as is possible. I cannot change the inevitable, but I have enough time to change a few hundred people. And when the world does finally change, I'll have the rich company of them. We'll talk about the good, old, golden days of mankind. We'll get together, read and reminisce, discuss and be delirious. That's a wonderful way to spend the latter part of my life. Just like Begur Sir."

He got up.

"Are we done, Y.B. Sir? I'll head to The Airport."

He jumped off the tractor and strode towards the house. At one point, he paused, bent down, picked up a small pebble, muttered `mobile phone', and with the effervescence of a child, chucked it as far as he could and smiled.

A little later, an hour before dinnertime, Cylinder, who would usually be in The Airport, was sitting downstairs with a book. Y.B. was upstairs and Cylinder had had enough of him for the day.

"What a pleasant surprise to see you here. Is everything all right?", asked Big Sir looking up from his ledger.

"All good, Big Sir. Y.B. Sir is sitting with Begur Sir. They are probably discussing mobile phones and that doesn't interest me at all."

"What's a mobile phone?"

"That's the future. It will destroy books, and many other things that we like and enjoy. That's what Y.B. Sir tells me. Maybe, it'll be a good thing for you, Big Sir.", said Cylinder.

"Why do you say that, my Small Sir?", he asked with mild curiosity laced with mild humour as he pored over his ledger. He didn't get much banter time with the youngest oddball at home, and he was quite liking it.

"You don't have the habit of reading. With a mobile phone, you don't need to. You can simply watch stories, like cinema. Thankfully, this will take some more years. So, I have ample time to sell books and save up money. I will buy you a mobile phone, Big Sir. You and Big Mother can sit together and watch. I personally dislike it but for the two of you, I think it'll be a good thing."

Big Sir smiled at the little boy.

"God has been kind to us, Cylinder. You know what Big Mother and I tell each other every now and then?"

Cylinder looked at him eagerly.

"We are not blessed with minds big enough to understand the minds of the three of you, but thankfully, God has blessed us with hearts big enough to let the three of you follow your hearts."

Big Sir looked upwards with his palms lightly pressed together. He held his gaze for a few moments and went back to his ledger.

(41)

Y.B. VERSUS BEGUR

Y.B. opened the bottle of Chivas Regal, one that he had carried for a special evening with his brother and fixed two drinks.
"Cheers to your chips and computers.", toasted Begur.
"Cheers to your books and your boy.", toasted Y.B.
They took a sip each. Followed by a few more.
"That boy is loco, as the Latinos in America would say. Loco in a good way. He's just the most intelligent, passionate, clear and sensitive kid I've come across." Y.B. said.
Begur smiled.
"If I had it my way, I'd happily take him off the signal, off the farm and make him a part of my team."
Begur chuckled.
"I have been testing him since I landed. Today, I pushed him really hard, but that little fella didn't budge an inch. I love him. He's special. I am so glad he happened to the family. C'mon, drink up. We need to celebrate Cylinder with another."
Y.B. fixed another round.

"May Cylinder live his dream. May his dream flourish even after mobile phones take over the planet."
"Dreams! That's what adds life to life.", said Begur.
Y.B. concurred.
"They do. And don't they come in all shapes and sizes? We don't need to look beyond our own family, the little fella included. For mom and dad, the dream is to sustain the contentment of their reality. Sometimes, I wonder if that's indeed a dream, but I suppose so. Yours, is to feast on words. Cylinder's, is to feed the world with it."
"And yours is to make science-fiction a reality.", said Begur sipping and smiling.
Y.B. beamed feeling the joy of his own chosen dream.
"Ha ha ha ha. Aren't we quite a bunch? A blessed bunch though, for we allow each other to pursue one's own."
"Not just allow but we wallow in it too though it's mostly tacit.", said Begur.
The brothers smiled into themselves and sipped on their drink which was as smooth as their mood.
"One more before mom calls us for dinner?", asked Y.B.
"Why not? This helps. I am so not used to making conversations, other than with Cylinder and about books."
[The brothers liked their tipple. Both were regular, moderate drinkers. Every day, they got high on their pursuits, and once or twice a week enjoyed a glass or two. Just like their grandfather. This was the other thing that had made a comeback in the Begur lineage after skipping a generation.]

This evening, both felt the need for more, the lubrication for conversation. Fixing the third, Y.B. started off.
"I know we hardly speak but from here on, we'll be in regular touch. We need to do this for the sake of the boy. I will keep you abreast of advancements in technology. The age of computers, the internet, mobiles, isn't too far off. It'll still take a while but when it does happen, the world will change rapidly and dramatically.
Now, sitting here in Mogga and living the lives that the four of you do, I am sure it'll blindside you all. It won't affect your life or that of mom and dad. But Cylinder's dream, his traffic signal enterprise, will come

crashing. He will be crushed. When that happens, Begur Farms will be home to three generations, four souls, all living-dead. How can I live with the thought of that?"
Begur pursed his lips, deep in thought.
"Oh! I've never thought that far ahead, and that deeply."
"Naturally. You are the `Here-and-now' chappie. I've always been the `What's next?' laddie.", said Y.B.
"Hey! On your third drink and you've suddenly turned Scottish. I hope you aren't peloothered."
"What the hell is peloothered?", asked Y.B.
"Since you suddenly turned Scottish, I decided to turn Irish. Peloothered is what the great Irishman James Joyce, said in 1914, in Dubliners. Oh! He was the master of coining words, to delight himself, and surprise his readers. The kink of a writer! Peloothered means to be drunk. To be hammered, plastered. There used to be a word in usage called bloothered. I suppose he twisted it."
Y.B. reflected on it momentarily and smiled. It was indeed a kink, a trip almost aphrodisiacal to someone as obsessive as his brother.
"Do you know his most lunatic and fantastic coinage?", asked Begur, eyes aglow with whisky and James.
Y.B. shook his head while Begur took a few moments to recollect the exact sequence of letters, unintelligible and almost interminable.
"Bababadalgharaghtakamminarronnkonnbronntonnerronntuonn-thunntrovarrhounawnskawntoohoohoordenenthurnuk."
"What on earth is that?"
Begur had the silly smile of a child delighted by inanity.
"That's the word for the sound of thunderclap that accompanied the fall of Adam and Eve. It appears on the very first page of Finnegans Wake. Oh! The joys of reading Joyce."
Y.B. broke into a smile too, amused by the foolishness of both, the writer and the ardent reader.
"How peloothered was Joyce when he thought of this? I am quite certain no person in a normal state of mind can conceive such randomness, and more importantly, stick with it."
"True. Joyce has not only admitted to his drinking habits but has also claimed that drinking made for an excellent writing aid. He is believed

to have said that liquor heightened feelings, and that he would be unable to write as well as he did without it.", clarified Begur.

Y.B. gulped down and stood up.

"One more? Let's raise a toast to Joyce."

"Do the honours, dearthair beag. It means `little brother' in Irish.", said Begur, in a happy state.

"Cheers to two astounding men of words.", declared Y.B. with drunken vibrancy.

"C'mon Y.B., don't belittle that great man. He, the creator, and me, merely a consumer of his concoctions."

"How can mere words make you so heady? Even now, I wonder about it from time to time.", said Y.B.

"So do I. How can mere transistors or chips or whatever you obsess about keep you so driven?", retorted Begur.

Y.B. smiled, a foolishly joyful smile. In his mind, Begur imagined it as the smile of a drunk meerkat and giggled like a child.

[The relationship between the two had always been binary: zero and one. Though, never once had either felt that he was one, and the other, zero. They had always been two alternate characters, side by side. They liked and respected each other to the extent that they unhindered each other from sibling expectations. Since childhood, they lived such separate interests that they hardly made any conversation. Even in adulthood, separated by time and continents, when they would meet after a few years, they would hardly have anything to bond over.

What will (or would) or can (or could) you call them? Friends? No! Strangers? No! Two people from the same womb? Inarguably, the safest definition.]

But for once, the Begur brothers were having their most bountiful conversation. It hadn't ever happened. This evening, restraint had retraced. Lubricated by Chivas or Cylinder, or both, quart-this-part-that, they conversed heartily. Both felt much lighter, and quite light-headed too. They looked at each other wondering how and why they had never explored each other's delightful company in over half a lifetime. Glasses empty. Hearts full.

Y.B. spoke, stressing on random syllables, effected by the bottle that stood three-fourths empty.

"Brother! Between usss, let's make sure Cylinder moves with the world. Someday, books will be orderred on compyooters, not bought in stores or at traffic signals. They will be bought and read on compyooters, or mobile phones even.

My duty is to keep you updated about where the world is headed, and how quickly. And yourrs? To keep the boy uppp-to-date, equip him. When we are all gone, his dream needs to live on. In whatever form the world is in."

Downstairs, Cylinder was getting impatient and inexorably inquisitive.

`What are the two of them discussing for so long? Y.B. Sir must be complaining to Begur Sir about me! That's fine. He has the right. I am sure he's doing all the talking and Begur Sir is silently listening. I am also sure that right at the end, Begur Sir will say just one or two lines that will make Y.B. Sir realise that he's wrong about me.'

His thoughts were broken by Big Mother's voice.

"Boys! Dinner will be ready soon. Come down whenever you are ready."

Cylinder burst into peals of laughter. He found it cute and funny — Big Mother calling such big men, boys. Momentarily, he fantasised about addressing them similarly.

"Begur Sir, you are a good boy. Y.B. Sir, you are a bad boy!"

Whispering these words into his cupped palms, he tittered.

A minute later, the two walked down the staircase. Y.B. held a big box and behind him, Begur carried a big smile. His hands were on Y.B.'s shoulders, holding them gently. Cylinder looked at Begur whose expression and demeanour suggested that he was holding something precious. Begur looked at Cylinder and patted Y.B.'s shoulders as if to mean that he meant the world to him. In that instant, although ignorant of what had transpired upstairs, Cylinder had a complete change of heart towards Y.B. If Begur Sir felt such endearment for his brother, it meant that he was a good man. Begur Sir wasn't one to suffer a fool, even if it was family.

Y.B. descended the last stair.

"Cylinder, my boy! Come to the dining table."

As Cylinder joined the two brothers at the table, so did Big Sir and Big

Mother.

Y.B. hugged Cylinder with the warmth of the morning sun.

"I've got something special for a very special boy."

Placing the box on the table, he opened it and pulled out a spanking new Sony camcorder, one that he had already charged earlier.

"My present to you. A present, which at any time in the future, will show you your past."

As the other four smiled, Cylinder stood agape taken in by the gadget, but more so by what Y.B. had just uttered.

`Present, future, past? This is as good a line as any, in any of the books.' He thought to himself in wonderment.

"This is a camcorder. You can record videos and play them back. We can capture this very moment and watch it anytime, even fifty years later. A hundred years ago, this would have been in the realm of science fiction but here it is now, a reality. Let me show you. Ready to be shot?"

"Shoot, Y.B. Sir! Shoot us all!", squealed Cylinder in delight.

Balancing it at shoulder height, he moved a few paces back, framing and focussing. The three members of the family smiled while Cylinder beamed. Waves upon waves of fondness and admiration swelled up in his heart and gently lashed against the insides of his mouth, pushing his lips wider.

`How wrong I was about Y.B. Sir! He is so intelligent and knowledgeable. He is so different from Begur Sir yet similar in some ways! How blessed are they to have Big Mother and Big Sir! And really, Cylinder, how blessed are you!'

He smiled even wider upon realising that he was addressing himself in third person. Existential thoughts usually made him step out of himself.

"Are we done, son?", asked Big Sir.

"No! Don't move.", said Y.B.

"Dad, this is not a camera. This is a video recorder. I cannot have you all standing wooden, like cacti in Nevada. There has to be movement and sound, not just silly static smiles. Okay, here's the idea. Cylinder, I will ask you something and you answer. And the three of you, knowing how expressive you are, can react to Cylinder with your best possible smiles. Okay?"

He lifted the camcorder and focussed, while the four braced themselves.

"Ready?", asked Y.B.

He saw four nods, three reticent and one, robust.

"Who are you?", yelled Y.B.

"I am Cylinder, the bookseller of Mogga!" He yelled robustly.

Instinctively, the other three repeated in unison.

"The bookseller of Mogga!"

All five broke into warm smiles.

"Mom, my heart is full. Now, stomach time. Should I lay the table?", said Y.B. lowering the camcorder.

"I will do it. All of you boys, relax."

She walked into the kitchen, a very happy woman. Clasping her fingers at her navel, she looked up and smiled at the unseen Lord.

"Thank you for keeping him a Begur despite him being far away from us."

Y.B. placed the camcorder on the sofa, walked up to the table and enveloped his father and brother in his arms. As adults, this was the first time the three had embraced each other. A display of affection was not in vogue among the Begur men. Verbally? No. Physically? Never! After the initial awkward moments, the three men hugged tightly.

Y.B. put out his left arm and pulled Cylinder into the huddle. For several moments thereafter, the four of them felt one with the universe. Each of theirs was in harmony, and complete.

(42)

FAREWELL TO THE MASTER

A sci-fi short story by Harry Bates, `Farewell to the Master' was first published in the 1940 October issue of Astounding Science Fiction, a copy of which lay in The Airport. It belonged to Begur's grandfather. He had the habit of picking up things on his travels; anything that carried stories—books, magazines, newspaper cuttings, maps, museum brochures etc. `Farewell to the Master' was read and relished by a select populace when it had first appeared. There wasn't anything more to it.

Some years later, Robert Wise chanced upon a copy of the magazine, happened to read the story and it stuck with him, like a mole. A director, producer, and editor, Robert Wise went on to create masterpieces on screen such as West Side Story and The Sound of Music. But long before that, in 1951, he turned this short story into one of the finest sci-fi movies of the times, capturing the imagination of the public at large as well as garnering great acclaim. Released as `The Day The Earth Stood Still', it became a landmark film.

Presently, it was a big day in the little town of Mogga. Big banners had sprung up everywhere. Large groups of policemen stood vigil at various points, from one edge of the town to the other.

Cylinder decided to carry double the number of books. He had been a bookseller for over three years and had done decently well. He had got the readers of the town to read more and had also converted some of the others into readers. Of course, he had a lot more ground to cover. The reading culture was yet to seep in. Most townsfolk still looked at books as avidly as the north pole of a magnet looked at the south pole. To Cylinder, this meant only one thing — the scope was immense. It reminded him of a story that people in the region often spoke about.

[Several years earlier, one of the popular hoteliers from the region had gone to north India to look for business opportunities. After a week of travelling around, he had realised that the taste of delicious south Indian dishes was a distant thing; no one was even remotely familiar with the names. He had summarily dismissed the idea, come home and shared his observations with family, friends and employees. Upon hearing him, everyone had scoffed at the north Indians while a lowly waiter in his hotel had seen a goldmine. He had resigned, rolled up his holdall and reached north India. Within three years, he had a chain of south Indian restaurants across four cities in the north. Every year, he was earning more than what his wealthy ex-employer had made in ten years.]

Cylinder always saw himself as the waiter, waiting patiently at the signal each day to serve delicacies to the mind.
"Begur Sir, it's only been a week but I am already missing him. When do you think Y.B. Sir will come next?", asked Cylinder getting ready for work.
Hearing no response, he looked up at Begur who was lost between the pages of a magazine. Between finishing a book and starting a new one, Begur would sometimes pull out an old magazine and read parts of it.
"Begur Sir, I know we have spoken about this earlier, but I am yet to understand magazines. I don't find them as filling as books."
"Treat them as snacks that you have between meals.", said Begur.
"I prefer to snack on comics. If they were called books, I might have read them. Maybe. But why are they called magazines?"

"It comes from an Arabic word, makhazin, meaning a storehouse."
"Hmmm! Interesting." Cylinder smiled hoisting his bags.
"I will see you in the evening, Begur Sir. Good day."
"To you too."
Muttering "Makhazin! Makhazin!", he traipsed down the staircase.
"Why are you carrying two bags of books?", asked Begur's mother seeing the child overloaded.
"Just like a writer has his good days and bad days, so does a bookseller. Today, more than half of Mogga will be on the streets. I'd rather be ready than repentant." Cylinder said.
"But people will be lining the streets to see the ministers.", added Begur's father.
"You know ministers and motorcades. They plan it to the minute and invariably it gets delayed by hours. It is always a test of patience for the public. Who knows? Out of boredom, someone might buy a book and that might set off a chain reaction." Cylinder said with optimism.

Given the hullabaloo around town, it seemed as if the Premier of the Soviet Union was visiting. It wasn't so. It wasn't even the Prime Minister or so much as the Chief Minister who was passing through Mogga. It was some minister, either the Minister of Power or Irrigation or Fisheries. Different people said different things.

Now, a minister passing through wasn't a big deal. It became bigger since he was to be accompanied by his counterparts from the neighbouring states of Tamil Nadu, Andhra Pradesh and Kerala. Metaphorically, this became the equivalent of an anthology: The Best Short Stories From Some of the Best Short Story Writers.

The general public wasn't clear what the trip was all about. Apparently, the ministers were heading to Jog Falls, the highest single-drop waterfall in India situated about a hundred kilometres from Mogga. Part of the Sahyadri Hills range, this was abundant in forests, fisheries and fertile land. The Mahatma Gandhi hydroelectric project had been operational here since 1948, the same year that George Orwell had finished 1984, and Begur's grandparents had completed The Airport. At that time, it was one of the largest hydroelectric stations in India.

The word on the street was that the other ministers wanted to study this marvel and implement similar projects in their own states. This wasn't the reason for the frenzy in town. It was because word had spread that there would be a motorcade of forty Ambassador cars ferrying the ministers, their aides, support staff, the press et al. In addition, with an equal number of jeeps and cars with security personnel, a couple of ambulances, and a fire engine, the motorcade in its entirety would be twice as long as the longest train that passed through Mogga. Now, this was a spectacle that most people would have never seen or imagined; a once-in-a-lifetime sight-and-sound show.

More than eighty vehicles, with red and orange beacons twirling to the tune of their masters, their electronic sirens blaring sounds of stature and significance, wailing or yelping (the two standard settings that most electronic sirens came fitted with—wail being a gradual increase and decrease in pitch, and yelp, more rapid) would pass through the town creating an impression that any great writer could describe in his or her own way but would never do justice. To the people of the town, and the thousands sprinkled across villages around, it was a pageantry not worth missing.

And so, armed with water bottles and snacks, thousands had lined up the streets of Mogga. The pavements held as many as they could and threw the rest up on the trees. The entire police force, assisted by dozens of volunteers belonging to grassroot divisions of various political parties, maintained protocol. Walkie-talkies crackled intermittently creating ripples of excitement among those assembled. The motorcade was supposed to pass through around noon.

Laden with two heavy bags, Cylinder stood at the junction surrounded by some of the regulars in his life. Chikkanna, despite heavy odds of getting posted elsewhere had managed to be at the junction. Percentage Ravi and Tempo Tony were present. Dharmaraj, the super cop was moving through different sections of the crowd keeping a keen eye for pocket pickers. ISV stood next to Cylinder, unflustered. He was there only because he was retired and had nothing much to do.

"It's a small thing but it's a big thing. Huh!" He said pulling out a line from his unfinished book.

"I didn't realise this was such a big thing. I made a mistake. I shouldn't have carried any books at all." Cylinder said.

No one was remotely interested in books. Moreover, because of the surging crowd, Cylinder could not even put his bags down. He stood in discomfort carrying both on his shoulders.

It was past 1 o'clock and there was no sign of the motorcade. People kept checking with Chikkanna who was as clueless as them.

As everyone stood waiting endlessly, Cylinder told ISV excitedly.

"I am looking forward to seeing the fire engine. I find it fascinating. Long back, Begur Sir had told me that a few months after I was born, a fire engine had come to the farm."

Instantly, a pained and pitiful expression enveloped ISV's face, and he was about to click his tongue to express his anguish but somehow managed to hold it back. His mind raced to find a jovial reference to the fire engine. He suddenly broke into a smile.

"So, why is a fire engine red in colour?"

Cylinder laughed. Over time, ISV had learnt a lot of trivia from him. He had also shared his repository of quotes, amusing anecdotes and interesting riddles. The fire engine riddle was one of the things that ISV had told Cylinder more than a year earlier. Cylinder had loved it and true to his nature, memorised it. As he started to answer the riddle, ISV joined along.

Because it has six wheels
And it is operated by six people
Six plus six is equal to twelve
Twelve inches make a foot
A foot is also a ruler
Queen Elizabeth was a great ruler
She ruled over the seven seas
The seas had fishes
The fishes had fins
The Finns fought against the Russians
The Russians won the war
The colour of the Russian flag is red
Hence the fire engine is red

As they laughed, they heard the wail of sirens at a distance. The police lining the streets stood alert. The first white Ambassador came into sight, and then a seemingly endless line of cars with windows rolled up, sirens blaring, interspersed with jeeps with blaring sirens, zoomed past the deactivated traffic signal. Some screamed, some whistled, some clapped, some counted, some tried reading the registration numbers and some stood gobsmacked. Chikkanna stood erect, hand raised in salute. An ambulance passed followed by more cars, jeeps, and another ambulance. The motion picture played out without interval. Cylinder kept looking towards the rear end of the line waiting for the fire engine. After what seemed like a long time, the final car, a Press Vehicle went past the signal. Much to Cylinder's dismay, there was no fire engine.

All of a sudden, several youngsters and kids spilled onto the street feeling jubilant, regarding what one knew not. The police immediately got into action trying to disperse them. Chikkanna jumped into action yelling that there were more vehicles. Hearing this, Cylinder went in to help, pushing people off the streets. The wail of a siren was heard, and the fire engine was trundling down the road. The police managed to clear everyone except for a five-year old boy in the middle of the junction. Cylinder shoved the boy towards the pavement and began to run after him. The fire engine driver saw this but kept driving with the instinct that the boys would clear out in time. Laden with two bags of books, Cylinder lost his centre of gravity and tumbled over.

There was a wild screech as the driver braked with all his might. The six wheels of the fire engine held onto the road as resolutely as they could. The monster slowed down considerably, inches before the tumbling boy but the momentum pushed it forward. The fender hit Cylinder's head, and then his head hit the road. Several books tumbled out of the bags and lay strewn.

For many moments, the earth stood still, in Mogga. There was no sound, not even a gasp from the thousands who had gathered. Only the siren continued to wail. A pool of blood trickled from the side of Cylinder's head, oozed between the pages of a book and flowed towards another.

(V)

THE STATUE

(43)

THE LAST WALK

Begur had finished lunch and it was his siesta time. As he was into the last few pages of `Midnight's Children', he had decided to finish it before resting. Suddenly, he heard the wail of a siren, looked up from his book, saw an ambulance and a police jeep surrounded by a big crowd of wailing people, approaching the farm gate. He stood up, staggered awkwardly and held the table tightly. He knew.

He saw his parents rushing out shrieking. He saw the farm labourers yelling sounds of lamentation and running towards the gate. He couldn't move. For a man who had rarely wept, other than at times in his childhood which he had no clear memories of, he began to sob uncontrollably. Tears, big drops of them, heavy enough to make a sound as they fell on the book, flowed relentlessly. He wailed and whimpered in the silence of The Airport.

The front area of the farm held over a hundred people facing Begur's parents and the labourers. Cylinder's body lay between the two grieving groups, each owning the boy as much as the other.

Minutes went by. Not a word was spoken. Begur's parents asked nothing of anybody regarding what had transpired. It didn't matter. A gathering so massive did not produce a single sound. There wasn't even a sniffle. Every person stood in silence, not merely distraught but totally destroyed.

And then, the sound of heavy steps was heard. The large crowd saw a heavyset man shuffle slowly out of the main door, moving towards them. Everyone knew this was Begur Sir though several had never seen him. He looked significantly older than what they had imagined, based on Cylinder's description. As he walked up to the body, his parents saw their son who just an hour earlier at lunch had looked at least ten years younger.

Chikkanna, ISV, Percentage Ravi, Tempo Tony, Herculees Pirate, and a few others were right in front. They tried to catch his eye but Begur's glance was downward, looking at Cylinder. His eyes held no tears, only emptiness. He stood there for minutes staring at the boy (or the body?) without a sound; not even a faint sniffle.

Then, he bent down, lifted the body, and shuffled towards the house. He slowly clambered up the stairs and entered The Airport. With his left palm, he held up Cylinder's head as much as he could and began to walk, inch by inch, along the perimeter. He knew Cylinder's eyes were shut but that didn't stop him from showing the boy all the books he had grown up with.

Suddenly, words from nearly fifteen years earlier sprang up in his head.

`Child! This is The Airport. From here, you can go anywhere. Go beyond Mogga. Go around the earth. Go above it or underneath it. Go ahead of time ...'

Sobbing, he turned the corner of the second wall, walked three steps alongside the third wall and stopped in front of the mirror. After gazing at Cylinder's reflection for a long time, he kissed him on his forehead, turned around and walked towards the staircase.

As he re-emerged from the house, every pair of eyes which had been staring at the upper storey, lowered themselves towards him. Begur walked up slowly, lay down Cylinder's body and looked up at the people. ISV and Chikkanna held out a bag of books each. Begur took them and nodded, lost in thought. They tried to utter something ... anything ... but nothing came forth.

They slowly turned around. Seeing them, the entire crowd shuffled around and began to walk out of the farm gate. Some of them hesitatingly looked back briefly and carried on. Begur's parents, Begur, and the labourers stood rooted staring vacantly at the backs of grieving strangers. Fifteen minutes later, the last of them went out of sight.

Begur put his arms around his parents who sagged into them. With help from the labourers, the three of them sat down in front of the body. The others sat down too forming a circle around Cylinder. Then, in nearly half an hour, the first word was spoken.

"Let's start the preparations for cremation." Begur's father said, barely audible.

Begur shook his head slowly.

"Dad, let's not cremate Cylinder. Let's bury him on the farm."

"But son, how can we do that? The child was a Hindu.", said his mother between sobs.

Begur put his arm around her.

"Mom! Does it matter? Cylinder didn't believe in God. His religion was books."

There was silence. It was a hard call but faced with the calamity that lay in front of their eyes, it was insignificant. They agreed without fuss. The labourers were made up of mostly Hindus, a few Muslims, two Christians, all of whom carried hardened beliefs. Strangely, everyone felt extreme consolation.

In the original site of the outhouse stood two beautiful gulmohar trees. From his desk, Begur had a clear view of them. They were almost as old as Cylinder; a few months younger, to be precise. Pointing to a spot between the two trees, Begur, for the first time in his life, picked up a pickaxe and began to dig. Some of the men joined him, wetting the earth with teardrops.

(44)

STATUE OF CYLINDER

The next morning, a tormented and teary-eyed town woke up to the two newspapers, Kannada Kesari and Malnad News. Both carried extensive coverage of the event—where the ministers had stopped for lunch, how many dishes had been prepared for dinner, what had been the discussions etc. Both newspapers also carried a little column about an unfortunate accident that had occurred.

News had reached New News Nagaraj late in the day. He had been a part of the motorcade heading towards Jog Falls to cover the jamboree. He had spent a large part of his day jostling with senior, reputed journalists working for prominent publications across the four states, trying to get something a little extra or unique. After filing his story, when the news had finally got into his bones, he was a shattered man.

The second day of the Ministers' Meet became as insignificant as a mite, and he had rushed back to Mogga. The only thing he wanted to do was pay a fitting tribute to Cylinder, his friend, and the most unusual and unfortunate soul. He sat up for hours wondering what to write, and how to.

On the second morning, readers of Malnad News woke up to a lengthy story. The headline carried the unmistakable stamp of New News Nagaraj:

New Cylinder. Working Cylinder. Empty Cylinder.

It spoke about Cylinder's parents, his birth, misfortune, providence in the form of Begurs, fascination for books, school life, dropping out of school, life at the signal, and losing life at the signal. It spoke of his undying love for books, intelligence, wit, knowledge, kindheartedness and passion. It was a biography of sorts. The article ended with statements by a cross-section of people, the ones who knew him intimately and those who used to see him regularly.

`Every day, I drive past the signal many times. Sometimes, the signal is working, sometimes it is not. But that boy was always working.' – City Bus Driver

`I have seen many curious cases in my life but none more curious than that boy with books at the signal.' – District Magistrate

`Aiyo! That little boy used to stand with so many books every day. I had seriously thought that when I make enough money, I will buy another cart and give it to that boy.' – Roadside Vendor

`I am mostly fixing streetlights and so I have always seen that boy from above. And even in broad daylight, I could see a light around his head. Something special about that boy.' – PWD Electrician

`Most people live up to 70-80 years but just exist. But Cylinder existed to make others live.' – ISV

`I was lucky to spend a good percentage of my time with him. The biggest thing I learnt from him is this. You go out to people with what you love, and slowly, people will come to you for that. And don't worry about how slowly, slowly.'
– Percentage Ravi

'For me, every day used to be duty, and beauty. My traffic signal was duty, and my Cylinder was beauty.' – Chikkanna

'Every day, he used to carry so much weight.' – Gym Krishna

'I had read his palm once and it told me that one day, he will stand head and shoulders above everyone else in Mogga. I am usually not wrong.' - Shastriji

Days passed but the town found it difficult to shake off the shock. He belonged to no one, yet to everyone. Wherever one went—shops, places of worship, police station, street corners, classrooms, tailor shops, roadside carts, bus stand, courthouse, banks, ration shops, gas agencies—the conversations centred only around Cylinder.

The symbolic thirteenth day went by but the collective consciousness of Mogga refused to tide over the incident, becoming even more resolute about the matter. Various groups of people had started discussing ideas for a memorial. New News Nagaraj continued to write about them. Word had reached other towns in the region as also the local administrators and politicians, and the bigwigs in Bangalore. Everyone felt equally aggrieved. It wasn't a case of *The People of Mogga Vs. The Administration*. Within a month, to everyone's relief, sanity and solace, it was decided that the traffic junction would hold a statue of Cylinder.

A committee was set up comprising some of his friends and some prominent people of the town. Though it was to be funded by the local administration, some sums of money came in from the other three states. The residents of Mogga voluntarily decided that they would contribute whatever they felt like. There wasn't a single exception, not even the beggars outside Raghavendra Swamy Mutt, the mosque, or elsewhere. From one rupee to five, ten to a few tens, and a few hundreds, money came in, in all denominations, and from all directions. Everyone wanted a small piece of oneself in the statue. The only ones whom the town forbade from making any donation were the Begurs.

Some of the most reputed sculptors in the state offered their services free of cost. The committee decided that one of their own should sculpt the statue for one of their own. Mogga had one of the most sought-after idol makers in the region: Statue Shankar.

[His father had been a reputed maker of Ganpati idols and Shankar had grown up watching him. By the time he was in his twenties, he had become as good as his father, and thereafter even better earning the prefix, Statue. During the Ganpati festival, Statue Shankar would make the idol for the oldest and the biggest pandal in town. This had been going on for years, and every year the idols had become bigger, towering over every other idol in any part of the state. The previous year, the 34-ft idol had set a new record. While he was a craftsman of clay, Statue Shankar was equally comfortable with stone.]

Nine months later, on May 5th, 1985, the Statue of Cylinder was inaugurated. The traffic junction had been converted into a circular island. A lush carpet of grass held varieties of ferns and flowery plants (seasonal and perennial) all of which had come from Begur Farms. The committee members had decided that this would be the only thing they would ask of the Begurs.

In the centre of the island, the statue had been installed. The base was a large 6-ft square block, six feet high. Atop this stood the 24-ft statue of a boy with a smile, a stack of books held between his hands, body leaning slightly forward, left foot ahead, as if he was eagerly walking towards a prospective book buyer. The main face of the base block faced the side of the traffic lights where Cylinder used to stand. It carried his timeline followed by a line.

CYLINDER
(May 5, 1972 – August 6, 1985)

"If people don't come to the books,
the books will go to the people."

A long list of names, in no particular sequence, were distributed across the other three faces.

Enid Blyton, Franklin W. Dixon, Agatha Christie,
Rudyard Kipling, Oscar Wilde, Arthur Conan Doyle,
H.G. Wells, Jules Verne, Salman Rushdie, Carl Sagan,
Louis L'Amour, Jeffrey Archer, Harold Robbins,
Sidney Sheldon, Frederick Forsyth, Charles Dickens,
Leo Tolstoy, James Joyce, Ernest Hemingway ...

George Orwell, Jane Austen, Vladimir Nabokov,
J.R.R. Tolkien, Franz Kafka, Gustave Flaubert,
Virginia Woolf, Miguel de Cervantes, Herman Melville,
Gabriel Garcia Marquez, Albert Camus, J.D. Salinger,
Edgar Allan Poe, Anton Chekov, C.S. Lewis, Harper Lee,
Victor Hugo, Roald Dahl, Joseph Conrad, Aldous Huxley ...

Ayn Rand, John Steinbeck, Henry James, Emily Bronte,
Lewis Carrol, Ray Bradbury, Hans Christian Andersen,
Stephen King, Isaac Asimov, Fyodor Dostoyevsky,
Alexandre Dumas, Nikolai Gogol, Douglas Adams,
V.S. Naipaul, Mark Twain, Erle Stanley Gardner,
William Faulkner, Arthur C. Clarke, Robert Ludlum ...

Thousands had turned up. Several stray donkeys, pigs, dogs and cows stood in and around this massive gathering, their animal instinct telling them that something momentous was taking place. It seemed as if `Animal Farm' stood alongside human form. Jackie was there too, lazily chewing on cud.

Begur was present along with his parents. They had been asked in advance whether they wished to speak at the beginning or at the end. Despite some insistence, all three had refused saying that the boy had left with all their words. After the last of the committee members had spoken, Begur and his parents got up, shook hands with each of them, walked around the island with pressed palms, acknowledging the crowd. Then, they kissed all four sides of the base of the statue, touched his feet with their foreheads and left.

(45)

CYLINDER CIRCLE

The Statue of Cylinder calmed the troubled conscience of the town. Life slowly limped back to normal. Everyday conversations and transactions resumed. People began to smile again. They walked, rode or drove past looking upwards. Quite often, the signal would turn green and the motorists in front would be lost in it, inviting honks from those behind.

Chikkanna didn't feel the bereavement as much. He would have imaginary conversations with his late signal-mate. ISV, Tempo Tony, Percentage Ravi and the others regularly stopped at the signal as they used to do earlier. They would stand with Chikkanna, reminisce about the good old days and share some of the moments with the statue. Since it faced them, they felt that Cylinder was listening and smiling at their conversations.

Cylinder Circle became a landmark, the pride of Mogga. People came visiting from other towns and cities. The locals at the circle would eagerly take the visitors through the legend of Cylinder. More often than not, it was Chikkanna who doubled up as traffic guide-cum-tourist guide.

Several cart vendors cropped up around the circle serving a variety of tasty eats: dal vada, masala mandakki, pani puri, masala nippatu, aloo bonda, menasinkayi bhajji, deluxe goli soda, badami haalu, cotton candy, chocobar, kulfi etc.

Entry into the island was allowed only for PWD cleaners and horticulturists who would often get requested for flowers, seeds and saplings. People held the belief that any house which had a plant from here would be blessed with intelligent children.

Students of Fine Arts from colleges in Bangalore, Mysore and other places began to visit regularly. They would be seen sitting on the pavement, sketching the statue. Some of them would also try and get an appointment with Statue Shankar if he happened to be in town.

All of this was expected but it threw up a surprise as well. Despite Cylinder's efforts, the town hadn't developed a reading culture. The day after the inauguration, Malnad News had carried photographs of the statue, including close-ups of the four sides of the base. People read the names, most of which were unfamiliar to most. But it made a lot of them curious. Some cut out these clippings and saved them. And out of the blue, several people across the town (young and old) developed an interest in books.

A few months later, ISV started a book club and got a decent number of members. They would meet at the circle on Sunday mornings—reading, listening, narrating, discovering, exchanging stories and books.

By the end of the year, some of the stores around the circle turned into book shops—Cylinder's Bookstore, Cylinders Bookstore, Statue of Cylinder Book Depot, Cylinder Circulating Library—selling novels as well as stationery. All of them did decent business.

It was quite a common sight to see people walking around with books, or even sitting on parked mopeds and reading, especially in winters. There were stray cases of books left behind unintentionally in the inter-city buses.

Some of the brute-looking pigs in different areas of the town were named as Napolean.

When people recounted the brilliance and the horrifying impact of the movie Jaws, which was a regular occurrence even a decade after its release, there were now a few who after singing glorious praises of Steven Spielberg would also mention the book. In this regard, Chikkanna without having read a single page of any book had become a hardliner.

"Without Steven Spielberg, there would be no Jaws. And without Peter Benchley, there would be no Steven Spielberg." He would say with absolute conviction and literary authority.

The town now had fan clubs and worthy discussions, at times even heated arguments, such as:

"Herculees Pirate is good but he's not Sherlock Holmes. If we had Sherlock Holmes, the SBI bank robbery case would have been solved within a week. Nobody still has any clue even after so many months. Huh!"

"Hey! You first read about Herculees Pirate, okay? Then we'll talk. Simply talking without reading. Huh!"

"I am not wasting my precious time reading about a detective who's named after a bicycle. Huh!"

All in all, it was a beautiful phase in the timeline of Mogga.

Begur and his parents rarely stepped out of the farm. It wasn't any different from what it had always been. They lived within their island just like Cylinder stood within his. Chennamma Begur Primary School had added more classes and students, extending up to Class VII. Rangappa now had two assistants. Partha Sarathy Sir had become the principal. There were three additional teachers.

Begur had stopped conducting his special classes, but they had become a part of the school curriculum. He had taken a long time to get back to his rapacious reading self. As usual, he would sit at his desk with a book and for every five lines he read, spend several minutes staring blankly at the spot between the gulmohar trees.

His trips outside the farm had been reduced to, two a year. One of these had been reserved for August 6th when he would mount his moped, ride up to the statue, ride around it a few times before heading back.

The other was on May 5th when he would drive his parents to the statue early in the morning, park the car where Cylinder used to stand, and wait till his mother would ask him to turn around. On these trips, he had begun to notice more bookstores, book clubs and people with books.

Years went by.

(VI)

THE BEGINNING

(46)

MOBILE CIRCLE

Then, the world leapt in a way very few had anticipated or imagined. It was a manic leap in the timeline of mankind, as significant as the invention of the wheel, perhaps infinitely more so. A marvel of technology, nothing short of a miracle, burst forth promising a far superior way of life. In the big cities of the world, this phenomenon had already spread faster than the news of The Spring Shoes Gang had spread in Mogga years earlier. Such was its might and magic.
This was palpable from the headline in the paper one morning, a line that carried the unmistakable stamp of none other than New News Nagaraj.
God's Greatest Invention: Man.
Man's Greatest Invention: Mobile Phone.

In the spring of 1998, a crowd of hundreds had gathered close to Cylinder Circle. Huchche Gowda, the big businessman of Mogga with the big, white Contessa car stood with his family, friends and figures of authority. A slew of other luxury cars—a Maruti 1000, a Cielo, two

Ford Escorts, an Opel Astra—all belonging to him were parked next to each other. He had bought Cylinder's Bookstore and the shop next to it and converted them into one. A big board carried two words in big, bold letters: MOGGA MOBILES.

He had hired three people from Bangalore who had the experience to unravel the mysteries and magic of this new species.

No other invention in history had captured the imagination of people quite like this. Soon enough, the rich, the poor, and everyone sandwiched in between fell prey to its allure. It hijacked fingers by the thousands, many of which had begun to hold books and turn pages. Within eight months, Cylinder Circle got effortlessly overwritten. This landmark now became popularly known as Mobile Circle. The towering Statue of Cylinder with its stack of books stood mutely as the town chatted incessantly in high-pitched tones, all through the day and with increasing frequency, during odd hours of the night.

On May 5th, 2000, Begur parked the car and sat with his parents who kept gazing at the statue, filling themselves with their annual dose of his memories. Begur looked around and saw people unusually excited, hands stuck to their ears, speaking animatedly to near-and-dear ones. He didn't see anyone with a book.

Twenty minutes later, he turned the car around the island to head back home. His parents sat in silence looking into themselves. As he cast a glance at the rearview mirror and saw the Statue of Cylinder diminish in size, a line from years earlier rang in his head: `Time is a sweeper.'

ACKNOWLEDGEMENTS

This book has reached its destination the way it was destined to, and that wouldn't have been possible without the involvement of several people, each of whom have played a part in their own way. My sincere thanks to them.

To Vishak Acharya for lending me `Five on Finnston Farm' by Enid Blyton, my first novel when we were in Class IV, and several more subsequently.

To Deepak Shetty for being one of my accomplices during our daring book heists from the Shimoga Central Library.

To Phalgun Tiruvasu and Aditi Chaudhuri for tasting the `khichuri' while it was being cooked and smacking their lips.

To Adarsh NC for being my ready reckoner on the most random things that I had figure out for the book.

To Balki for his valuable time and precious gut without which this story would have turned out less enjoyable, like a north Indian idli.

To Rachna Kalra, Shweta Sharma and Teesha Cherian for going out of their way to find a way forward for the book.

To Harpal Singh, my partner and closest friend, for designing the book as well as large parts of my work-life.

To Rohan Tandon, my partner, for always pushing me to pursue my passion.

To Archana Nagpal for always believing in me and being with me.

To Larry Page and Sergey Brin. If they hadn't created what they did, I wouldn't have been able to create what I did.

LEGAL DISCLAIMER
There has been no wilful intention or attempt to infringe on the copyrights of any of the literary masters referred to or quoted in this work. Every reference that is used is to merely demonstrate the lasting impact of the words of these literary figures on the minds of their readers and fans.

ABOUT THE AUTHOR

Anand Suspi published his debut novel in 2016 titled `Half Pants Full Pants', his childhood autobiography. The book was adapted into a web series and released on Prime Video in 2022. This is his second novel.

In his spare time, he dives deep into the world of hip hop to understand and appreciate what he considers as the most masterful form of storytelling and wordsmithing.

A TEDx speaker, he also conducts corporate talks across a range of topics that interest him.

You can reach him at
asuspi@gmail.com

www.ingramcontent.com/pod-product-compliance
Lightning Source LLC
LaVergne TN
LVHW041911070526
838199LV00051BA/2590